Pumpkin To Talk About

A Welcome to Amoresville Book

Brandy Ayers

Contents

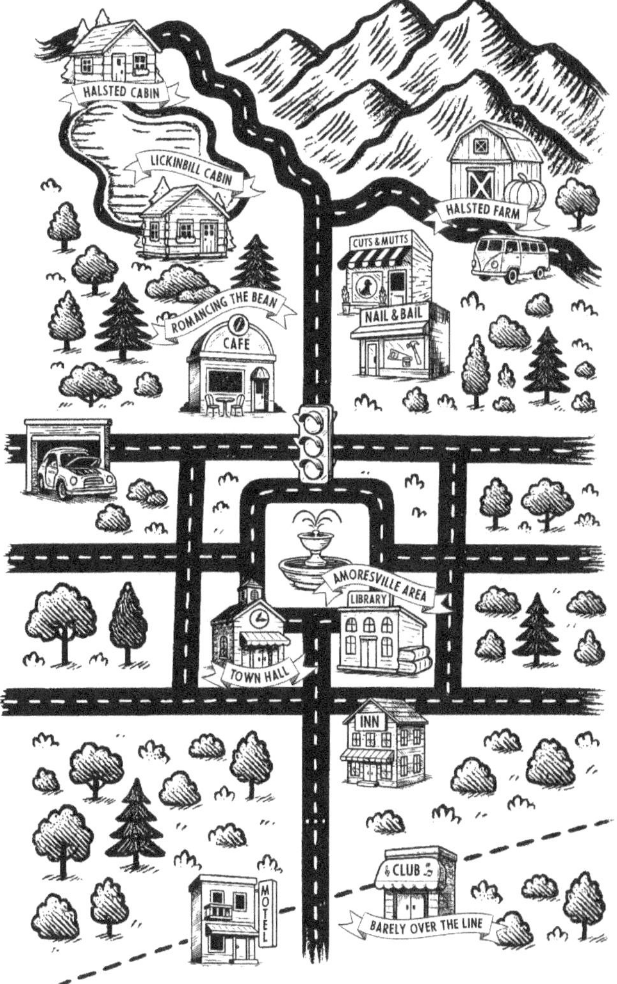

WELCOME TO
Amoresville
HALSTED CABIN
LICKINBILL CABIN
HALSTED FARM
CUTS & MUTTS
ROMANCING THE BEAN
CAFE
NAIL & BAIL
AMORESVILLE AREA
LIBRARY
TOWN HALL
INN
CLUB
MOTEL
BARELY OVER THE LINE

Chapter 1

June

No matter how many backroads I drive down, the expansive views of each new place I explore never cease to take my breath away. I should be keeping my eyes on the road, but a field full of wildflowers between swelling mountains is just too tempting.

Thankfully, this road is so far in the boondocks I haven't seen another car in hours. In truth, I had no intention of coming this far north in Pennsylvania. But at a conference for travel writers last week, I met someone who couldn't stop gushing about the tiny, quirky town in the state's smallest county where she grew up. With no press trips lined up for the next few weeks, my adventurous spirit kicked into high gear. I ended up pointing my powder-blue VW van, lovingly known as Daisy, toward the mountains.

A new adventure is my favorite way to outrun my responsibilities.

The previous night was spent googling the small town of Amoresville and ignoring my mother's phone calls. Honestly, my searches didn't bring much in the way of results. No official website for the town. No business websites that I could find. The whole county only has a population of roughly fifty thousand people. The county seat holds over half that population. Amoresville is *not* the county seat, so I don't expect there to be much in the way of things for me to do. Hell, I'm fairly sure there are more deer in the thick woods surrounding me than people in the town I'm heading toward.

I'll stop in Amoresville tonight, find a spot to safely park the van while I sleep, then spend the day tomorrow exploring. One day should be more than enough, then I'll make my way even farther north to camp at Pennsylvania's version of the Grand Canyon, Pine Creek Gorge.

After that, who knows?

I've been trading emails with a PR rep for a hotel at Niagara Falls. Maybe I'll make my way up there? Or possibly south to some place a little warmer now that the Northeast is heading into the colder months.

The peace inside my beautifully decked out van-slash-home is cut short by the sharp, far-too-loud ring of a call coming through the Bluetooth. Is it weird that I have my own mother listed in my contacts by her first and last name? Meredith Ammer, former CEO of the nation's largest mortgage company. For a mother who couldn't bother with me for most of my childhood, she sure is making up for lost time with non-stop phone calls and texts lately.

I go to press the ignore button on my phone mounted to the dashboard, but a squirrel runs out in the road ahead of me, and my sudden swerve has the bonus of accidentally swiping my finger across the screen, connecting the call.

"Hello? Junie?"

"Shit." I hazard a glance behind me to make sure I didn't hit the furry little rodent and see him happily scampering across the other lane, no idea the trouble he just caused.

"Junie, are you okay?" My mom sounds panicked, so I take a deep breath and accept that I am just going to have to talk to her for a little while.

"Yes, Mom. I'm fine. Just a squirrel in the road, no big deal."

A relieved sigh crackles across the phone. "I really don't like the idea of you driving all by yourself in the middle of nowhere. You could get in an accident, and no one would know where you are. Or killed by a serial killer. You know not to pick up hitchhikers, right?"

I roll my eyes, annoyed that the woman who once went an entire week without knowing where I was at the age of thirteen is now so concerned about my safety. "Mom, I've been traveling like this for years. It is literally my job. Trust me, I know how to keep myself safe."

"You wouldn't have to work at all if you would just take care of that business with the lawyer—"

I cut her off, not wanting to go down this road with her once again. "Mom, I really can't talk right now. I need my GPS to find the town I'm heading to."

"Right." I ignore the tone of disappointment and hurt. I have nothing to feel guilty about. A couple years of trying does not make up for a lifetime of ignoring me. "Where are you going this time?"

"A little town called Amoresville. Apparently, it is very charming."

Truthfully, this is one of the most beautiful drives I've ever been on, let alone in my home state of Pennsylvania. Between the fall leaves just starting to change and the sun shining between them without any clouds in the sky, the views are incredible.

I used to travel to some of the most exotic places on earth. I've drunk cocktails on the beaches of Morocco, hiked miles to Machu Picchu, ate at the most expensive restaurants in France. Hell, I even went to a clothes-optional resort in the Caribbean. Not only did I travel to those places, I got paid for it. Never once did I get a phone call from Mom worried about my safety in all those years.

But the events of 2020 brought that all to a screeching halt. After being stranded in Italy for weeks at the start of the pandemic, I finally made it home with nowhere to go since I never bothered to get myself an apartment, choosing to stay on the road as much as I could and opting for short-term leases on the rare occasion I had downtime between assignments.

When the world shut down, I had no choice but to move in with my mother for the first time since I was a teenager. She worked from home for a while, and we pretty much ignored each other. But then her company forced her out, and she opted to take the early retirement plan rather than start over at a new company. Suddenly, we couldn't escape each other. Self-help books appeared on her bookshelves. She took online cooking classes and wanted me to eat with her every night. She wanted to reconnect.

I had other ideas.

I escaped to her garage and fixed up the old VW van that had been my grandpa's back in the sixties. After he passed away, the van sat in that garage waiting for my mother to figure out what to do with it. I hated to see it sit there, untouched, after my grandpa had spent so many years in his retirement tinkering away to keep it in pristine condition. One short, awkward conversation and Mom officially gave it to me.

I got to work immediately. Thanks to YouTube, no-contact delivery from the hardware store, and a lot of cursing, I not only got the old van running again, I updated it to have solar panels on the roof, a small apartment in the back, and a few modern amenities like Bluetooth and running water. Plus, she is the prettiest van you'll ever see with the wispy daisies I painted down her sides.

The minute restrictions started easing up, I hit the road.

"Since you're close, any chance you could swing by Philadelphia? I could go over some of the paperwork with you. Make a plan."

"I don't think I'll have time, Mom." No matter where I end up next, it will not be in the same city as her.

The road curves in front of me, and I take it a little faster than is probably necessary. But just talking with the woman who supposedly birthed me has me itching to escape.

She tries to respond, but the reception in the mountains must finally start to crap out because her words become garbled.

"Mom, you're breaking up."

Another curve in the road puts the sun directly into my eyes, and I squint, turning my head just as a huge, dirty pickup truck hauling something behind it pulls out of nowhere.

I turn the wheel hard, slamming on the brakes. Burned rubber and squeals fill the air inside the van. "*Fuckfuckfuckfuck.*"

Everything is a blur of sunlight, metal, and trees as I completely lose control of Daisy and go careening into the muddy ditch beside the road. There's a loud thud and what sounds like hail all around me. All my stuff that had been carefully stowed in cabinets just seconds ago rains down behind me, something smacking me in the back of the head for good measure.

Suddenly, the van rocks forward hard and comes to a stop askew, half on the road, half in the ditch.

Air refuses to fill my lungs. The van may have stopped, but my head still feels like it's spinning.

What the hell just happened?

Slowly, I peel my eyes open, only to be met with a riot of orange covering my windshield and smoke seeping out from somewhere. Shit, the van is on fire. My home is on fucking fire!

My lungs open back up, but instead of sucking in the air, they let out a horrific scream.

Chapter 2

Knox

"Motherfucker."

My truck comes to a standstill across both lanes of the country road that runs the length of the back end of my property. Thankfully, it doesn't seem like the truck was actually hit by anything.

Doesn't mean I'm not going to give hell to whatever asshole was driving too damn fast down these winding roads. Couldn't be anyone local. No one around here would be dumb enough to drive like that during prime deer season. Not even stupid teenagers would be that reckless. Around these parts, you're more likely to hit a deer than another car. Just my fucking luck. I got swiped by some idiot leaf peeper, probably lost and looking for the state park.

Flinging the door open, I step out of my truck, only to be greeted by a high-pitched scream. *"Help! Fire! Fire!"*

What the hell? No fire is coming from the oddly painted van sitting cattywampus in the ditch. The carnage around me is hard to ignore, but I can't look just yet. It's too fucking depressing. All that hard work in the literal fucking ditch.

Instead, I stomp past the pieces of my future and wrench open the dented door of the van. A blur of blue, brown, and pink lunges out from the van in the shape of a woman.

Still screaming, she falls directly into my arms. "Get back. It's on fire!"

"Lady, calm the hell down. There is no fire." She tries to push me back farther from the scene of the accident, which is goddamn hilarious, considering I have about five inches on her. "Lady, it's not a fire. There's just pumpkin guts all over your car."

The fight seeps out of her, and she turns to face the wreckage. It's an impressive sight, I gotta say. The van is an older model Volkswagen Microbus. The top half is painted creamy-white, while the bottom half is a robin's-egg blue. There are daisies painted all over the blue part, and bright yellow curtains hang in every rear window. There are even what look like solar panels dangling haphazardly from the roof.

That isn't the crazy part of the scene, though. Nope, that would be the huge chucks of pumpkin littering the road and the front half of her vehicle.

The woman stands gaping at what I'm guessing is her unique vehicle. "What... How..."

There's a pretty decent dent in the driver's side door, some smaller dings from the chunks of projectile pumpkin, but otherwise, it really doesn't look too bad. Needs to be cleaned up, obviously, but it should still drive fine after what remains of my once-prized giant pumpkin is cleaned off it.

"You killed Gertie," I say. "That's what happened. How? Well, I'm guessing you were driving too damn fast down these roads."

She rounds on me, curiosity and anger at equal war on her face.

Her face. This is the first real look I've gotten at the troublemaker speeding down our roads. The breath rushes from my lungs, and something tightens low in my belly. She's gorgeous. Dark brown hair with streaks of blue strategically placed in the front. Blue eyes almost as bright as that unnatural hair color. Long lashes, plump lips, and a quick scan of her body looking for injuries tells me that's not the only thing plump on her. She's curvy, just as curvy as these roads, and probably just as dangerous.

"Excuse me, but *you* are the one that pulled out from nowhere. There isn't even another road out here that I can see." She does a scan of the area where I pulled out and confirms there is nothing but a couple of dirt grooves in the ground where my truck was.

I take her momentary distraction to get a better look at her. She's wearing black leggings that cling to every inch of her legs, a hot pink top so short it shows a little strip of belly above her pants and a big cream cardigan sweater over it all.

Fuck, I need to stop checking this woman out. I'm pissed. She destroyed one of the best pumpkins I've grown in years. "I was pulling out of my field onto a road I've driven hundreds of times. Trust me, I checked my surroundings before pulling out. You, however, were driving like something was chasin' ya."

That comment seems to piss her off even more. "What are you doing carrying so many fucking pumpkins, anyway?"

"Just one."

"What?"

"Gertie is, well was, just one pumpkin. One giant pumpkin."

She turns back to the devastation behind her. "Holy shit." Her eyes land on a particularly huge chunk laying in the ditch. "*Holy shit!*"

I'm gonna have to try and collect as many of the seeds as I can salvage. They won't go for quite as much since I didn't get the chance to officially weigh Gertie. But I can't afford to let them rot on the side of the road when I could still get some money for them.

"Should we call the police? Exchange insurance information?"

Seems the lady has gotten some of her senses back, but her question confirms she isn't a local.

"No police around here. State Police cover this territory, but God knows when they would get around to coming out here."

"Oh. Um, well, let me get my insurance."

"Don't bother. They won't cover eviscerated pumpkin, and my truck isn't damaged." I shove my hands in my pockets, not sure what else to do with them at the moment. "Listen, there's no way you can drive that thing right now. I'll radio Simone to come tow it into town. In the meantime, I'll give you a ride and drop you off at the garage."

Why is the thought of her beside me in the front seat of my truck sending a shock of anticipation through me?

I push the thought aside. It must be the adrenaline seeping out of my body. I make my way to disconnect the trailer, which is also covered in pumpkin guts, from the truck hitch.

"I can't get in a car with you. You're a stranger. You could be a serial killer."

The laugh slips out before I can stop it. "Lady, I would be one talented serial killer to plan all this."

"June."

I turn to her, confused. Maybe she hit her head because it sure as hell isn't June. We're almost done with September. "What?"

"My name. I'm June. You can stop calling me lady."

June. It fits her. Soft, pretty, full of sunshine.

"Knox."

"Nice to meet you, Knox. I guess we're not strangers now, so might as well let you give me that ride."

I nod and get back to work unhitching the trailer while June starts grabbing some stuff from her van. It takes some maneuvering, but I finally get the mangled trailer off the road enough that it won't cause a problem. The van is still sticking half on the blacktop, so I text Simone real quick and ask her to put the word out for others to avoid this area for now.

June has disappeared around to the back of her van, and I follow to see if she needs any help. The sight of her bent over to reach for something through the backdoor has me damn near swallowing my own tongue. The huge sweater has ridden up to reveal what just might be the world's most perfect ass. Round, plump, incredible.

It takes effort, but I tear my eyes away from her butt just long enough to see she is pulling clothes out from a drawer under what looks like a platform bed and stuffing them in a duffel. Why the hell does she have a bed in her van? I look past the askew mattress and see the interior of the VW has a small kitchen area with cabinets painted a bright pink and a tiny sink. The ceiling is covered in that shiplap stuff I hear so much about when Mom is watching HGTV. Truthfully, the inside of the van looks better than some of the places I've lived.

"Wait, do you live in your van?"

June turns around and smiles. "Yup, just me and Daisy on the road."

She named her fucking van. True, I name my pumpkins, but that's different. The thought of this bright, beautiful woman living in the back of a van makes me irrationally angry. "Why the hell are you living in your van?"

"Because I like it." She turns and places two heavy bags in my arms then turns back for more. "I get to go wherever I want, whenever I want." She grabs a handful of underwear and shoves them in another bag, followed by a bunch of flimsy lace things that I can't place but would very much like to see on her.

Once again, I have to shake myself out of the lust stupor this woman is putting me under. Sure, she is hot as sin. But she killed Gertie. She was speeding on roads she knew nothing about, and she was probably doing something stupid like reading some social media app or something while she was driving. And apparently, she's a transient.

Contempt firmly back in place, I lug her heavy bags to the truck and sling them in the back.

"Hey, be careful with those. There is like three thousand dollars' worth of camera equipment in there." The slap of her flip-flops against her feet echoes through the quiet around us, setting my teeth on edge.

"Yeah, well, you destroyed about twenty thousand dollars' worth of pumpkin." I take the new load of bags and place them next to the other ones.

"Bullshit. Who would pay twenty grand for a pumpkin?"

Her things safely stowed, I turn and glower at her but don't bother to answer, opting to yank open the driver side door of the truck and climb in. The racket those flip-flops make penetrates the steel frame of the truck as she jogs around to the passenger side.

Quickly, I brush stray hay and goat hair from the truck seat and throw some empty coffee mugs into the space behind my seat. Just 'cause I'm pissed at the lady doesn't mean she should have to sit on the mess my truck holds on a daily basis.

She opens the door and hops up into the seat with a look of absolute curiosity on her expressive face. "Seriously? Twenty thousand dollars for a pumpkin? I mean, how many pies could the thing really make?"

"Giant pumpkin would make a horrible pie. Big suckers are watery as hell. I take the big ones to state fairs and other competitions. Between prize money and selling the seeds after the official weigh-ins, I can usually make about that much off one pumpkin." I don't bother to tell her that the optimum level of money is completely dependent on placing first in the competition.

"I'm so sorry." She really does look upset that she cost me so much money.

"A little too late for that now."

Fuck, I'm an asshole.

Chapter 3

June

What an asshole.

Okay, I cost him a lot of money with our little accident. But it's not like I was on some mission to sabotage his giant pumpkin championship chances. I'm not some giant pumpkin community spy.

No point in talking to the dickwad even if the silence inside the truck cab is incredibly awkward.

From the corner of my eye, I see his sharp jaw flex as he grinds his teeth together. Not only is he a stupid asshole, but he is stupidly handsome too. He has red hair streaked with sun-bleached blond, a bushy, unkempt beard that is a slightly brighter shade of orange-red, and green eyes that make me think of thick pine forests. He's tall and broad with huge arms barely contained in a stretched-tight flannel shirt and thighs encased in dirt-covered jeans.

But being devastatingly handsome in a dirty kind of way does not make up for being a complete asshole, so I sit in silence with my arms crossed and stare out the window.

How long does it really take to get into town? I try to remember how much time was left on my GPS before Mom's unexpected call, but the excitement has completely scrambled my brain. Maybe that's why I can't stop thinking about those thick arms wrapped around me in a bear hug when I leaped from the van earlier.

After what seems like hours of stony, fraught silence, but is probably only about fifteen minutes, we turn onto a slightly bigger road. I start to see signs of civilization outside the dirty window. At first, it's just a few cars driving out of town, each person giving Knox a wave, which he returns with a slight nod. Not even a smile, just that stern incline of his head.

Soon, some squat ranch-style houses pop up sporadically along the road between the trees. Each home is separated by huge swaths of green lawns. Even as a kid, I never had much of a yard. Cities like Philly and Pittsburgh aren't known for their big lots. But out here, there is no shortage of land.

The closer we get to town, the closer together the houses are. Another turn and a big sign proclaims, "Welcome to Amoresville!" in faded gold paint on a navy blue background. The main street is dotted with big Victorian-style houses, small businesses in brick buildings, and even more lush green lawns. I can't help but smile a little at the small church to one side of the road with a sign declaring, "*Prevent truth decay, brush up on your Bible.*" I love a good pun.

About a block away, I see an almost painfully hot-pink sign poking out from the surrounding neighborhood.

Romancing the Bean Cafe. The sign out front is the most aggressive shade of pink I've ever seen, the lettering a plum purple. The logo is an open book lying flat with a coffee bean in the middle. It almost kind of looks like a vagina in the middle of spread legs. I must be reading too much smut at night because there is no way that's what they were going for.

The cafe is housed in an old Queen Anne style house with a huge wraparound porch and turrets everywhere. The siding is a pale pink, with all the trim from windows to railings the same hot pink as the sign.

The truck slows, coming to a stop just in front of the building. The moment the truck rocks to a halt, Knox slams it into park and jumps out like it's on fire.

I climb out as well, glancing around at my surroundings. People walk the sidewalks, waving and stopping to have conversations. Everyone seems to know each other. Pumpkins and hay bales are piled on porches even though Halloween is still nearly a month away.

Okay, I see what the lady who told me about this place meant. Amoresville is just so damn cute! The familiar itch of curiosity spreads through me, urging my feet to get to work exploring a new place.

A heavy boot thumping on a wood stair pulls my attention. Knox stomps up the stairs to the cafe's porch with all four of my bags in his hands. "Hey, what are you doing with my stuff?"

He ignores me and pushes his way through the front door as I chase after him. As soon as I cross the threshold, I'm surrounded by the smell of strong coffee and sweet treats. The front door drops me right into a large foyer with beautifully restored wood floors. A huge staircase looms in front of me, splitting the first floor in half.

To the left is a large room with pocket doors wide open. There are small café tables dotted around the space, a few with customers sipping at drinks. The walls are painted in black chalkboard paint with a riot of colorful drawings on almost every inch. Some are the scribbles of children, and some are the work of true artists. Between the drawings, there are coffee puns written in swooping scripts. I lean in to get a better look and notice a set of French doors leading into what looks like a library.

The hint of colorful book spines has me taking a few steps in that direction when a cheerful voice calls my attention to the opposite side of the house.

"Knox? What are you doing here, honey?"

A middle-aged woman with incredibly long gray hair twisted into an intricate braid leans over a worn, live-edge wooden coffee bar that runs the length of the room to the right of the staircase. As she rounds the end of the counter, I get to see the full effect of who I am assuming is the café owner. She's wearing a loose turquoise peasant top with the neckline pulled down to expose her shoulders and a flowing maxi skirt in a colorful paisley design. Her face has a kind, concerned expression as she approaches Knox. "I thought you were pulling Gertie out of the field today."

"Hi, Ma." Knox dumps my bags to the side of the bar and goes around back to give the woman, apparently his mom, a kiss on her cheek. "Ran into a little trouble." His eyes dart in my direction as I hover in the foyer, and hers follow. I must be trouble.

"Well, hello there." The woman smiles warmly, and I shuffle up to where they stand in front of the counter.

There is a huge espresso machine behind the counter with shelves of different flavorings beside it. An old mail sorting rack holds coffee cups in various sizes and designs, none of which match. Along the walls are more café tables and a few baking racks that hold jewelry, stationary, and other knick knacks that appear to be for sale.

"I'm Roxy." Bracelets jangle around her wrist as Roxy holds out her hand for me to shake.

"June. Nice to meet you."

Roxy's eyes shift between her son and me as an awkward silence descends around the three of us.

"Well, you are pretty enough to be classified as trouble." Roxy's wide smile and a wink in my direction let me know she doesn't mean anything by the comment, but Knox's sneer sets my annoyance back on edge. "What seems to be the problem?"

"His pumpkin exploded all over my van."

A low growl seeps out from his throat, and Knox glares at me. "That's an interesting way to put it. June ran me off the road and smashed Gertie with her van would be the correct version."

"I did not run you off the road. The sun was in my eyes, and I might have been driving slightly over the speed limit."

"Slightly?" Knox scoffs and turns to his mother. "If they let minivans into the Indie 500, this girl could give them a run for their money."

The sharp gasp that escapes my mouth has everyone in the café turning in my direction. "Daisy is not a minivan. She is a 1967 Volkswagen Type 2 that I spent months restoring."

"Same thing."

"Take that back!"

Somehow Knox and I have been inching toward each other until we are toe-to-toe, glaring at each other, both of us breathing like we just *ran* the damn Indie 500.

"Oh my." Roxy comes around from her spot behind the counter, fanning herself. "The heat coming off you two could power the whole block."

We both hop away, avoiding each other's gaze.

"Dear, are you okay? That sounds like quite the ordeal." Knox turns to answer his mother, but she breezes past him, puts her arm around my shoulder, and herds me to one of the small round tables nearby. "Would you like something to drink?"

The concern in her eyes brings the emotions of the day dangerously close to the surface as I fight to hold back tears. "Actually, a drink would be nice. Just water would be great."

"Nonsense, let me make you a nice, calming chamomile honey latte. It will soothe your nerves."

I give Roxy a watery smile, and she hurries off behind the counter to whip up my drink.

"Seriously, you have more concern about a stranger than your own son, Ma?"

"You look just fine, Knox," she retorts with her back to us. Roxy places a couple spoonfuls of tea into a mug of steaming water and pours some milk into a metal pitcher. "I'm sorry to hear about Gertie, though. Are you going to take one of the others to the fair this weekend?"

I glare at Knox once again. "There are others?"

"Of course." Roxy starts steaming the milk as she shouts over the hissing of the machine. "Knox has four contenders this year."

The high-pitched whistling cuts out, and Roxy's last words fill the room.

"So, you could still make twenty thousand dollars this weekend?"

Knox looks everywhere but at me. "Technically, Gertie was never going to bring in that money this weekend."

"Oh, son, she wasn't going to come even close. I would have been surprised if she made it in the top three."

I quirk one eyebrow as Knox finally makes eye contact with me again. "Huh, interesting."

Roxy places a mug on the table before me. It has a layer of white foam with a cinnamon-dusted heart in the middle. As I take the first sip, the drink warms me with its sweet floral notes. Placing the mug back down, I notice the tabletop for the first time. It is decoupaged in old romance book covers. Couples are depicted in various states of dress, clutching each other with windswept hair.

Looking around, it seems the romance theme has been pulled through to the names of the drinks on the menu board as well. The drink Roxy made for me is actually called the *Sweet Romance Latte*. There is also a drink called the *Enemies to Lovers,* which seems to be a dark and white chocolate latte, and a *Spicy Read,* which is a hot chocolate with cayenne.

I desperately want to take pictures of this place for my Instagram, but there are more important things to deal with at the moment. Like the fact that both my mode of transportation and my home are unavailable to me.

Roxy settles into the chair across from me and props her chin on her palm. "So, June, what are you doing in town? We don't get a ton of visitors around here."

"Actually, I was headed here when I had my little run-in with Knox." I glance over at the man himself and notice him trying not to listen to our conversation as he pours himself a cup of coffee from one of the carafes at the side of the bar. "I'm a travel writer, and I was coming here to check out the area for my blog."

Roxy perks up, her eyes brightening. "Well, isn't that something! I'm surprised I didn't hear anything about your visit. Usually, word travels pretty fast around here. Are you staying at the B&B? It sure is going to be busy over there."

"Actually, I didn't book a room. Though, I might need to now." I take another sip of my drink and savor the sweetness as it washes over my tongue. "My van is also my home, so I usually just get a spot in the nearest state park or find a camping ground someplace nearby. If all else fails, a Target parking lot is usually pretty safe."

A crack from across the room catches our attention. Knox has somehow dropped the mug he was holding and is glaring at me like it is *my* fault.

Chapter 4

Knox

A Target parking lot is safe to sleep in? Really?

I shouldn't be this pissed off at the idea of a near stranger and where she sleeps. But I am, dammit. I'm so pissed I dropped the fucking mug I'd been sipping coffee out of.

"Knox, grab a towel and get that cleaned up." Mom turns back to her new friend with a look I know all too well. She's found a new story she wants to dig into. Only this time, it isn't a new book she's discovered. It's a real live woman. "That's so exciting. You must have been to some wonderful places."

"Yup. I used to do more international travel. But since I've been making road trips with Daisy, my following has really taken off. Now I try to find little towns that no one has heard of but have a lot to offer visitors." June has fallen into my mother's trap, and I have no doubt the two will be exchanging phone numbers soon enough. "The plus side of staying in the van is

I never have to worry about hotel reservations. Until now, that is. I'm hoping that the B&B you mentioned might have a room available."

"Actually, that's why I'm so surprised. Lou Ann Reed is getting married this weekend, and the B&B is filled up with family from out of town. At first, I thought you might be with them, but you have all your teeth, so I knew that couldn't be the case."

I'd totally forgotten about the wedding this weekend. That's what happens when I only make the trip into town a couple of times a month. The town news tends to just sweep by me.

June slumps down in her chair. Not that I'm watching her. "Damn. Is there a hotel nearby?"

I sweep the last of the bits of the mug into my hand and grab a rag. "There's a motel about fifteen miles down the road, but it's a nasty place. You don't want to stay there."

"He's right, honey. That place has more bed bugs than it does clean sheets."

June bites her bottom lip seeming to think over her options. "Well, I guess I could just stay in the van. You said it was going to be towed someplace, right? I can just sleep there while it gets fixed up."

The fuck she can. She might be stubborn and drive like shit, but I am not letting this woman sleep in the parking lot at Simone's garage. "What about the upstairs apartment, Ma? You haven't rented it out yet, have you?"

Mom's eyes dart back and forth between us a few times before answering. "Actually, Ruth has booted Chuck out on his ass for looking at porn on their computer. Again. He's staying until she cools down."

"Really, I can stay in my van. Trust me, I've slept in weirder places than a mechanic's parking lot."

Before I can shoot that shit down again, the bell above the door rings, and as if on cue, Simone stomps in the door. She's a very tall, very muscular woman with dark brown skin, long hair dyed every color of the rainbow and pulled back into a ponytail, makeup to match, wearing bright lime green coveralls with the logo for her garage across the pocket. She's a lot to take in at once, and I notice June's eyes widen slightly.

"Knox, I got that van you called in about." She lets out a low whistle. "That thing is messed up."

June jumps to her feet, her face going pale. "What's wrong with Daisy?"

"That your van?"

June nods, her fingers twisting together as she waits to hear the verdict on what is obviously an important part of her life. I have the strange desire to pull her into my arms and tell her everything will be okay. Apparently, I'm developing a brand-new white knight complex.

"Well, you know she's a mess on the outside. But some of the gooier parts of Gertie got down into the air ducts, between the brake pads, all over the solar panels you installed on the roof, which are now hanging off the roof, and one tire blew, too." Simone lets out a breath and tugs at her ponytail. A telling sign I've seen her give a hundred times when she's about to lay some bad news on a patron. "The clean-up won't be a big deal; it'll take a couple of days at most. The air ducts and brakes will be another story. And honestly, I'm not sure I'll be able to find a tire that fits that model in the state."

The more Simone talks, the paler June gets, and I'm a little afraid she's going to pass out. "I know a guy that can get you the tire," June mumbles. "He was a friend of my grandpa's and helped me get the ones that are on Daisy now."

"That will speed things along." Simone shoves her hands into the pockets of her coveralls. "But you're still looking at a couple days at least before she'll be road-worthy. And it won't be cheap either."

Mom stands up and slings her arm around June's shoulders. Is it weird to be mildly jealous of your mother? "Don't worry, June, Simone is really fair. Doesn't do any of the price gauging crap you hear about at other garages."

"Aw, thanks, Mrs. Halsted." Simone actually blushes. That is the power of my mother.

"June, it sounds like Daisy is in no state for you to be spending the night in." Mom turns the stranger-turned-friend to face her. "I have the perfect solution. You'll just have to stay on the farm."

I gape. "Excuse me?"

She could not be suggesting this woman who killed my pumpkin and has been nothing but a pain in my ass in the short time I have known her stay on my farm.

"Knox, you have all those bedrooms with no one but yourself rattling around in that big old house. It just makes sense." Mom gives me an admonishing look that normally would have me biting my tongue, but this is too much. June can't stay with me.

"Oh no, Roxy, I couldn't possibly." June tries to back away from my mother. "I'm sure the motel isn't that bad. A night or two won't kill me."

Simone, Mom, and I all cringe in unison, and June looks around at us in fear.

"It's really that bad?"

"I towed a car from there a few weeks ago. Belonged to a guy that died in one of the rooms." Simone cringes, seeming to turn a little green. The owners didn't notice for a week."

June turns around, her fingers still working at each other as she considers the problem. "What about a cabin at one of the state parks? I could hang out there for a few days."

"During leaf-peeping season?" Mom looks at June with a soft expression, trying not to make her feel dumb. "Honey, those have been booked for months."

"What about Orion's cabin?" I ask.

My brother lives on our family's fifty acres up on the mountain. It's rough terrain and takes almost forty-five minutes to get there, thanks to what he laughably calls a road, but it's better than having her haunting my house with her smell and her curves.

"Don't be silly. How is June going to see our town from way up there and no transportation?" Mom brushes me off with barely a glance. "Besides, I highly doubt she wants to see your brother on his daily morning skinny dip in the pond."

Fuck, I hadn't thought about that. The idea of June up there all alone with my brother, who is two abs away from a twelve-pack thanks to his years in the military and the habit he picked up of working out five hours a day, does not sit well.

I glance over at June just in time to catch a look of interest on her face at my mother's comment. So, "no" to the cabin.

"Really, other than the grumpy roommate—" Mom points her thumb at me.

"—Hey!" I'm not grumpy. Or at least not to the people I know. Right?

" — the old farmhouse is great. It was built by my late husband's great-great-great-grandfather. One of the first homesteads in this area. The only building older is the one you are standing in right now. Built by the original settlers of this town, my ancestors."

Mom leans in closer to June and whispers, "Remind me to tell you about the years it was a brothel." She straightens back up, her spine just a little taller after mentioning this side of the family's illustrious history. June's eyes widen and glow with curiosity. "Anyway, he's got hot water, a full fridge, and nice soft beds. It will be a nice break from sleeping in the back of a van, I'm sure."

June seems to be considering the offer, a longing glimmer in her eyes at the mention of hot water.

I'm honestly not sure why I'm not fighting this idea more. I should be insisting she can't stay at the house. Shutting down this insanity. Putting my foot down. The house is my sanctuary, the place I feel more myself than anywhere else on the planet. I grew up in that house. The only time I haven't lived there were the years I spent getting my degree in Agricultural Business at Penn State.

The only other person to live there since Mom moved out was my college girlfriend. She loved the idea of living on a small-town farm right up until it came to actually working on the farm. When she got bored with collecting eggs and baking sourdough and figured out how much it took to run the place well, she took off faster than June driving the backroads. Ever since, it's just been me in the house.

I should not want some out-of-town interloper invading my space, even for one night. So why am I just standing here like an idiot? Why did my heart rate speed up at the thought of this infuriating woman sleeping next to me? In the room next to me, that is.

"Well, it would be nice." June turns to me with an uneasy look on her face. Is she scared of me? I don't much like that idea. "I haven't showered anywhere other than gyms and truck stops in way too long."

Fuck. I really don't like the idea of her having to go to a truck stop to shower. That can't be safe.

She looks at me hopefully, and I know I'm fucking done for. "I could pay you. Maybe the same rate as the B&B?"

"I don't need your fucking money."

Mom and Simone are both kind enough not to contradict that statement. Everyone in town knows the farm has had some real lean years recently. But I refuse to take this woman's money.

"It's no trouble. I mean, I did destroy your pumpkin. Plus, if I stay at your house, I should pay for the inconvenience."

"I said no!" The words come out louder than I intended. I run my hands through my hair in frustration and take a deep breath. It isn't this woman's fault that my financial situation embarrasses the living shit out of me. "Just don't come near any of the other pumpkins, and we'll call it even."

June nods, looking a little more nervous now than before.

That settled, Mom turns away from us to head back behind the counter. I don't miss the smirk of satisfaction she's unable to quash. She got what she wanted, and she loves nothing more than getting her way. I just don't know why she was pushing it so hard.

"Oh, don't forget it's family dinner night," she adds. "We'll all be there right after closing."

Just what I fucking need.

* * *

"So, your family has been in this town for a long time, huh?" The ride from the café to home has been blissfully silent. But June had to go and ruin the tentative peace with questions.

"You could say that." There's no reason for chit-chat. She's staying one night, and then we'll figure something else out tomorrow. We certainly don't need to get to know each other.

"Did the café really used to be a brothel?" She tilts her whole body toward me, the curiosity beating off her in waves.

"Yeah." Back in the 1920s, before the decency laws made their way to our little corner of the world. It wasn't very successful to begin with. Turns out there wasn't a huge market for prostitutes in the middle of the mountains where hardly anyone lived. "Ask Mom about it at dinner tonight. She'll give you all the dirty details."

The only thing Mom likes talking about more than the brothel is the love story that started the town. I'm sure they'll get around to that if June is here more than a few days.

"I'll ask her." From the corner of my eye, I see June's fingers once again weaving themselves together, twisting, fidgeting. She just can't stay still. "Your mom is quite the character."

A sardonic laugh slips out before I can stop it. "You could say that."

"And you have a brother? Older or younger?"

"Sister, too. Both younger."

"You really have a way with words. Has anyone ever told you that before?"

"People talk too much and say nothing. I don't really see the point." The beauty of the farm is I can go days, weeks without talking to anyone. I went a whole month this past winter without saying one word to another human, thanks to a blizzard cutting off the roads and the phone lines and making our monthly family dinner impossible.

It was amazing.

"I don't know." I glance over to find June gazing out the window at the trees as we pass by. "You learn a lot about a person when they think they aren't saying anything."

An awkward silence hangs between us since I don't know how to follow that up. Or if I should. I turn into the long gravel road that leads to the farm, relieved that my forced proximity to this woman will come to an end soon.

June gasps and leans as far forward in her seat as the seatbelt will allow as the trees fall away and the fields come into view.

I try to see things as she does. As someone who didn't spend their entire childhood running these fields with his siblings and tracking mud through the kitchen.

My property sits on a soft hill nestled among higher mountains that rise up behind in the distance. The front pasture is split by the driveway, and both sides are bursting this time of year with goldenrod and purple clover. I don't believe in wasting good land on dull green lawns, so I keep almost every inch of the property covered in either food crops or cover crops that attract pollinators.

To the left is the huge redbrick barn where I keep my machinery and the few animals that have come to call this place home. To the right are half a dozen greenhouses where I grow some of the hardier produce over the winter. Right in the center of it all is the farmhouse. White with a wrap-around porch, it's simple yet undeniably beautiful.

Pride swells in my chest, and my lungs and heart tighten with an emotion I haven't let myself feel since inheriting the farm from Pop. Pride. My family built this. Struggles aside, I'm keeping it going for at least one more season. If I have anything to say about it, one more generation.

June is taking it all in, her gaze sweeping from left to right and back over and over. "Knox, this is amazing."

The five goats and two sheep that have found their way to my farm come scurrying up to the fence behind the barn, undoubtedly hoping I brought something for them to nibble. A few chickens have wandered away from their coop and strut around, pecking at the ground.

A joyful giggle bubbles up from beside me, and I wish I could capture that sound. Maybe there are more sounds than just irritated sighs I could inspire in this woman.

I banish the thought from my head. She's my guest, and I will not make her feel uncomfortable. I may not like this arrangement, but Mom taught me how to be a good host and, more importantly, a good man. Letting her down is no more an option than letting my Pop down by allowing the farm to fail.

The moment I shift the truck into park, June is out and wandering over to where the animals are making a racket, trying to get her attention. She hunches down to pet one of the younger goats through the gaps in the fence and is immediately surrounded. Some stick their noses through the chicken wire and try to nip at her clothes and hair. Instead of being freaked out as some newcomers to farm life might be, she laughs more and tries to pet them all in turn.

June turns to me, her face lit up with delight, and my damn chest squeezes so tight I'm unsure how to breathe anymore. Her brow furrows, and she cocks her head to one side. "Huh, you don't look like quite so much of an asshole when you smile."

Okay, nice feelings are gone. I honestly hadn't even realized I'd been smiling at her. "Come on, Speed Racer, I'll give you the tour and set you up with a room."

Hefting her bags once again, I clomp up the stairs to the front porch and shove the door open.

She follows behind me after a few minutes, and I show her around. The downstairs is pretty open thanks to a renovation to modern the place up a little before Pop died. Walking in the front door, you can see damn near everything. The huge open kitchen to the left comes in handy during canning season. The center of the space is taken up by a worn wooden dining table big enough to seat twenty. But the place I eat most nights, the couch in front of a TV tuned to the weather channel, is on the right side of the door. Unseen on the back end of the house are a huge pantry, guest bedroom, bathroom, and sunroom that gets next to no use.

In silence, I lead her upstairs, my palms mysteriously sweaty as I invite the first woman into my space since my college girlfriend left me.

I tell the overeager prick in my pants to calm down. Nothing is going to happen.

"Right here is the bathroom." I nod to one of the two bathrooms upstairs. The other is off my room.

She pokes her head into the bathroom, gaping at the claw-foot tub that has been in this house since it was built. "Oh my god, that tub is huge!"

It was honestly too big a pain to get rid of during the renovation, so we worked around it. Now I'm happy it is still here.

I lead her down the hall and dump the bags in the last bedroom on the right. The one with the big king bed and view of the mountains.

The one right beside my own.

Chapter 5

June

After showing me to my room, Knox practically sprints outside, I assume to do farmer-like things. Even knowing I'm alone in the house, I'm too scared to wander around. I've made a career of being in unfamiliar places, but the only place I ever truly feel at home is inside Daisy. Even as a kid, I never felt like I had a real home. My parents' houses were just places I stayed, not homes. Just like then, I make a point to stick to my space so as not to bother anyone. Even when I'm at an inn or a hotel, unless there is a scheduled activity that I'm contractually obligated to participate in, you'll find me curled up in my own room with a book or editing my next post.

Speaking of which, I really need to get something on The Gram about the accident and why I haven't posted yet today. But as soon as I pull up the app on my phone, I get a notification there is no reception or internet available. *Well, shit*, I forgot to ask Knox about the Wi-Fi when we got here.

That plan shot, instead, I putter around the room I'll be staying in until Daisy gets fixed or Knox gets sick of his space being invaded and kicks me out to the supposedly unacceptable motel.

The room is so cozy it almost makes me want to cry. And not cozy in the way realtors use the word as a stand-in for "small." But warm, relaxing, like the room equivalent of a hug. The bed is a huge king with a headboard made from what looks like old doors. They are painted white but scuffed up in that shabby-chic way that everyone loves but few manage to pull off. Crisp white sheets cover the bed, with a patchwork quilt folded at the foot. Stroking that soft cotton, I realize this isn't some mass-produced quilt bought in a store and meant to look handmade.

It is actually handmade. Something about the stitching and the haphazard way the fabrics are pieced together let me know this blanket has meaning. It was made and used with love.

I smooth the quilt back into place, suddenly afraid that I might ruin it.

The floors are wide wooden planks that I would not be at all shocked to learn are original to the house, but they gleam between the area rugs placed sporadically around the room.

There isn't much furniture in the rest of the room. Two small nightstands on either side of the bed. A dresser against one wall, a chair next to that. The walls are painted white, but it's not stark or cold. Can white be warm? The art hanging on every wall is a wide range of photography prints and paintings. No two match in style or color scheme, but somehow, it all works in this perfectly bohemian farmhouse way. I wouldn't be able to decorate a room like this if I studied every décor magazine on the planet.

Did Knox put this all together? His mom or sister? Or did another woman use to live here with the grumpy farmer?

I find I don't like the thought of another woman putting her touch on this place. The strange day must be wearing on me, because it would be utterly insane of me to be even mildly jealous of a woman who isn't even here. Who might not even exist? Especially when I've only known the man for two hours.

I can't take the stillness in the house, especially without the escape of my phone or computer to occupy my mind. Every creak of the floorboard under my feet has my nerves on edge. I'm not used to being in such a huge place. My tiny van has become my safe place, but an actual house? Freaking terrifying.

With a deep breath, I turn, put on some music I have downloaded on my phone while it charges, and go about checking over all my camera equipment to make sure it wasn't damaged in the crash. Next to Daisy, this equipment is the most valuable thing I own. Losing it would be a major dent in my ability to do my job.

By the time I've inspected each lens, camera, and even the mini drone I use for ariels, it is dark outside the window. That doesn't mean much this time of year, though. It could still be anywhere from five to eight in the evening.

My stomach rumbles, reminding me it has been hours since the delicious drink at the cafe and even longer since the granola bar I shoved down my throat while driving this morning. Would Knox mind if I grabbed something from the kitchen real quick? Roxy did say his fridge was stocked.

The calming effect of my task slowly ebbs away as I realize I'm going to have to leave my room and face the impossible hotness of my host, in both temper and attractiveness, to get some nourishment. But there's no avoiding it, so better to just rip the Band-Aid off than let my nerves compound on themselves while stalling.

The floors creak with every step I take, reminding me that no matter how updated, this house is hundreds of years old. I can't imagine being a teenager and trying to sneak out in the middle of the night to meet friends.

When my foot lands on the top step, the most delicious smell wafts up from the first floor. Something herby and creamy. My stomach rumbles in response.

As delicious as the smells coming from the kitchen are, the sight is even more delicious. Knox stands at the stove, his back to me, jeans hugging his ass and thighs in a way that I know he doesn't mean them to but looks so damn good I can't help but stare. I can't picture this man trying on jeans and looking at them from every angle to make sure they play up his very best assets. Pun intended. No, he probably picks the first thing in his size and buys it without a single trip to the dressing room. But damn, he fills them out so incredibly well.

On top, he wears a black and white plaid flannel shirt and an apron that looks like it would be better suited for manning a very large grill than a gas stove. The fabric is obviously thick and sturdy, with leather straps tied behind his neck and around his waist. His hair is freshly washed and still a little damp. But I don't remember ever hearing him go down the hall to his room. And yeah, I was absolutely listening for him.

"Are you just going to stand there, or do you want something?" Knox asks without turning around.

Aaaaaaand the moment is ruined.

"Sorry, just didn't think I'd find you cooking." God knows my father never cooked. My childhood meals were all prepared by chefs, nearby restaurants, or me when my parents forgot I required food.

"There's a reason the family comes here for dinner." Knox bends over to check something in the oven, and I avert my eyes quickly before I land into another ass-induced stupor. "My siblings can't cook for shit. Mom claims she's cooked enough meals for this family and town that she's done. So that just leaves me."

"I totally forgot your family was coming over for dinner. There was a lot going on." Finally remembering how feet work, I take a few steps closer, not yet ready to breach the invisible line between the open common area and the kitchen. "Do you mind if I grab a sandwich or something, and then I'll head back upstairs."

Knox chuckles, one deep rumble, and finally turns to me. Goddamn, he is even more handsome than I remembered. "If you think there is any chance in hell my mom is going to let you stay in your room while she's here, then your first impression of her was way off. She'll drag you out of that room and down to the table the minute she gets here. Trust me. It was a near-daily occurrence when my sister was in her sullen teenager phase."

What must that be like to have a mother who won't let you eat alone in your room? That insists you come down and spend time with the rest of the family. "Well, if I'm going to be part of the family dinner, can I at least help prepare it? What are you making?"

"Chicken herb lasagna. If you could stir this sauce while I get the salad together, that would be good." Knox stands to the side, holding the handle of the spoon out to me from the pot. "Just keep it moving, or the cream will scald."

Should I mention that my cooking experience is pretty much limited to packaged ramen, salads, and sandwiches? It's stirring. I can't possibly mess that up, right?

As I take the spoon, our hands brush, and I have to suppress a gasp because I swear that slight friction of skin against skin has my blood rushing to my cheeks in a deep blush that travels down to the apex of my thighs. I've never understood the whole one-touch-and-I'm-hot-for-you trope. I always figured that part of romance novels was the equivalent to aliens in sci-fi books: wishful fiction.

Until now.

Knox could lay me out on the floor and have his way with me, and I would be all too willing after just that slight touch.

But it all must be in my head because Knox turns away and goes about his business as if nothing happened. Which I guess nothing did, just my overactive imagination and libido going crazy. Even with his indifference, I can't help but be aware of every move he makes behind me, shifting from the island to the fridge to the pantry, gathering ingredients.

"Keep stirring. I can smell the sauce starting to go too far." I look down and am dismayed to find the milky substance bubbling away rapidly in the pot.

"Um, oh, shit." The bubbles rise higher in the pot, and I'm pretty sure they are going to pour over the sides onto the stove. A sizzle fills the air as my fears come true.

Knox rushes over and takes the spoon from me. He reduces the heat and picks up the pot, stirring as he goes. "Never mind, why don't you take over chopping the salad?"

"Yeah, that might be for the best."

I move to the cutting board while Knox takes my spot. I also refuse to notice how amazing he smells as we cross paths. Laid out around the island are a head of romaine lettuce, some peppers, cherry tomatoes, and a red onion. I can do this. Salads are easy, right? Granted, usually, my salads consist of just lettuce, croutons, and ranch. Sometimes, I don't bother ripping up the lettuce and just dump the dressing on top and bite into it like an apple.

With the knife in hand, I start on the onion. This knife must be really sharp because it slides through the middle of the onion with ease. I can totally do this. I flip the two halves, so they are cut side down and get to work breaking them down into neat wedges like I see in restaurants. With each slice through the firm flesh, the pungent odor stings at my eyes, tears forming against my will. Tilting my head back to look at the ceiling seems to help keep the waterworks at bay.

"Ouch, fuck, goddamn it." The knife clatters to the floor, and I jump back, clutching my finger to my chest as blood seeps out from a thin slice to my fingertip.

Knox is at my side in a second, grabbing me by the wrist and dragging me over to the sink, where he turns on the water and lets it run over the cut.

I groan. "I guess looking at the thing you are cutting is probably better than looking at the ceiling."

Knox doesn't respond, and when I glance from the blood-tinged water to his face, it becomes more than obvious he is pissed as hell at my complete ineptitude in the kitchen. "Sorry. I hope I didn't get any blood in the salad."

"Should have known I needed to keep you away from sharp objects and moving vehicles."

Before I can respond to that insane sentence, the front door swings open with a bang, followed just a few seconds later by Roxy gliding into the kitchen. She pauses when she takes in the scene: Knox in his apron, holding my hand under the water while I try to hold back tears.

"Knox Charles Halsted, what did you do to this poor child?" She plunks a canvas bag down on the island and marches over to the sink.

"Nothing. She did this by just existing near sharp objects."

He pulls my hand from the stream of cool water and holds it up so Roxy can see as the blood begins to seep out in a red rivulet down my finger all the way to my wrist.

Roxy's eyes widen, and she turns on her heel. "I'll get the first aid kit."

She hasn't taken more than two steps when the front door once again bangs open. "Dorkus Maximus, what is this I hear about you taking in a homeless drifter?" A woman who could only be his little sister practically skips into the room. She has strawberry blond hair woven into two braids with strands artfully framing her face. She's wearing a pink velour sweatsuit and is much shorter than I would have expected given both Knox and Roxy's heights. Her eyes dart from my bloody finger, still held above the sink, to the knife on the floor. "Holy shit, are you becoming a serial killer in your old age?"

Roxy returns from the back of the house with a tackle box that looks like it is more suited for fishing than first aid. "Delia, leave your brother alone and try to be of some use. Clean up the counter and finish up the salad." Next, she steps between Knox and me, pushing him back toward the stove. "You promised me your famous lasagna, so get back to it, and I will take care of June."

He hesitates, almost taking a step back toward me, but then stops and turns away, facing the stove.

Roxy leads me to the long dining room table. "Now you just come right over here, sweetie, and we'll get you fixed right as rain."

"Honestly, it's not a big deal."

Roxy practically body slams me into a chair while she holds a towel to my hand.

"I probably just need a Band-Aid."

"I'll be the judge of that." Roxy sits next to me and rifles through the tackle box. Gauze, bottles of iodine, various ointments, and tubes of unknown substances get piled onto the table as she looks for some elusive cure for my finger. "With my three children, I had to be prepared for anything. The nearest hospital is almost an hour away, and those hellions were known for getting hurt the minute I turned my back."

"More like Delia was known for trying to murder us." A deep voice fills the room, and I look up to see a slightly taller and much leaner version of Knox walk through the door. His hair is obviously very long, but pulled back into a messy bun at the back of his head. It is more on the brown side of the spectrum than Knox's, but still firmly in the ginger realm. His facial hair is more five o'clock shadow than beard, but there is no mistaking these two are brothers. Big, sexy, ginger brothers. Something about the man seems incredibly familiar, but I chalk it up to the family resemblance. "You must be the hooker Knox picked up on the side of the road and brought home."

"Excuse me?"

"Do not call her a hooker!" Knox exclaims.

"Orion James Halsted!" his mom adds.

"I never tried to murder you," Delia grumbles.

The four of us all shout at the same time, but rather than look chastised, Orion's stern face breaks into the slightest of grins. "I'm just repeating what I heard Frank say when I stopped by the post office to check my box."

"This town is fucking crazy." Knox moves pots and pans around the stove with a little more vigor than is probably necessary.

I shrug. "Okay, so I'm a homeless drifter and lady of the night, according to the people of Amoresville. Good to know I've made a lasting first impression."

I could go weeks in my hometown of Philadelphia without a single person even noticing my presence, but a few hours in this little town, and I have everyone buzzing.

"Don't pay any attention to them, dear." Roxy places a small tube on the table along with a bandage specifically meant for use on fingertips. "Our family has had more rumors spread about us than I can keep track of."

"My favorite was that we were a bunch of Satanists that held séances naked in the fields at night." Delia chuckles as she finishes chopping the veggies that were supposed to be my job. Only, unlike me, *she* doesn't nearly stab herself while doing it.

"Mmmm, or when they insisted I was an assassin in the Marines." Orion plops down onto a chair across from his mother and me. "I was a mechanic, and I never saw a single bit of action."

Roxy nods, laughing lightly as she spreads what I think and hope is antiseptic on my finger. "I was always fond of the talk about me being a bisexual swinger who forced my husband into my wanton lifestyle."

"Dad would have killed a man before he let them touch you." Orion shakes his head, gripping the bill of his hat—a gesture that stirs the nagging feeling that I've seen him somewhere before.

"And our father was very much a pacifist."

"What about you, Knox?" I ask. "What rumors did the town spread about you?"

Through all his family's banter, he has stood silently by the stove, assembling the lasagna to go into the oven.

"I don't listen to any of that shit."

"Oh, I'll tell you my favorite!" Delia dumps the last of the veggies into a giant wooden bowl and gives it a good toss with some tongs. "It's a tie between the one where he fertilizes his pumpkins with blood from virgins, and that's why they grow so big. Or that Lesley ran off because she couldn't take the screaming from the women he kept chained in the cellar."

Everyone at the table laughs, but Knox keeps quiet by the stove.

"Who's Lesley?" I ask between my own chuckles.

It must have been the wrong question, because gradually, the laughter dies away, and in its place, an awkward silence swells.

Chapter 6

Knox

Goddamn it. I love my family. I truly do. But sometimes, I also wish I could just shut them all up.

I very much took after our father. Keep my head down, get the work done, and don't bother with town drama.

Delia, however, takes after our mom. She loves to be in all the town antics and gossip. Hell, most of the time, she's starting it. I think at one point, she had dreams of getting out of our town and making her own way in the world. But when they found a tumor in Dad's brain, that all kind of went away, and she never talked about it again. Instead, she put on a happy face and got to work taking care of Pops and Mom.

Orion, on the other hand, is a weird mix of Mom and Dad. He prefers living in his own little corner of the world, cutting down trees and building furniture in the shop next to his cabin. When he does come into town, you can always find him leaning up against the counter at the hardware store, chatting with the owner, or down at the barbershop listening to the old-timers' stories. But then he disappears again up into the wooded mountains, and we don't hear from him for weeks. I don't know if his penchant for disappearing has something to do with his time in the military, which he rarely talks about, or if that is just who he is.

Thanks to my little sister's inability to keep her mouth shut, there is now an awkward silence hanging around the kitchen and dining room.

I slide the lasagna into the oven and snap the door shut. With a deep sigh, I stand again to find my guests all staring at me. I shoot my sister a look that I hope says, *You are a pain in my ass, and if we were younger, I would go find your favorite stuffed animal and threaten to rip its head off.* She shrugs in response and mouths, *I'm sorry,* before joining Mom and June at the huge dining room table.

It will be another fucking hour before the lasagna is ready and we can eat, and more importantly, when I can get everyone the fuck out of my house. That's what I get for spending too much time out in the fields and not enough time here getting things prepped.

"Lesley was my college girlfriend," I grumble. "She moved here with me after we graduated but only stuck around for about six months," I say the words as matter-of-factly as possible, ignoring the slight sting I still feel at the way things ended.

Nothing near as painful as it was when I came back in from working on the farm to find an empty house and a note on the counter explaining she couldn't take farm life and was moving back to her parents' place in Harrisburg. I tried calling and texting, but she blocked my number, and I never heard from her again.

Delia smiles sheepishly. "I promise it had nothing to do with the women screaming in the basement."

It's been five years, and even though I no longer miss Lesley, I do miss the presence of another person in the house and the ability to lean on a partner when things are rough. Or good, for that matter. I always imagined I would have the same kind of relationship my parents had. Not just madly in love but also deeply engaged in each other's dreams and goals.

At thirty, I'm five years older than they were when they had me. I know I'm still young, but it's hard not to compare myself and my life to them when I spend each day in the house where they raised us, working the farm my father made thrive.

"Well, I know the screams from the cellar haven't bothered me in the least," June pipes up with a mock-serious face. "Granted, I've only been here a few hours, but they just blend right in with the sounds of the chickens and goats."

The tense atmosphere loosens at once, almost like the house is taking a sigh of relief, and we all laugh along with June.

Done with her nursing of June, Ma stands from the table with a pat on my temporary roommate's shoulder. "I'm going to see what Knox has to snack on while dinner cooks." She breezes past me, mumbling just loud enough for us all to hear, "Dinner is always at six, and yet it is never actually ready on time," then disappears into my pantry.

As is tradition for family dinners since I took them over two years ago, I shout after her, "How quickly you forget the rules of farm life. Animals and crops get fed before family."

My brother and sister, now both sitting at the table, snicker and roll their eyes.

Delia leans across the table, obviously fascinated with the stranger to our little town. "So, June, if you aren't a hooker or a homeless criminal, what exactly are you doing in Amoresville?"

"I'm a travel writer. I have a blog and a decent following on YouTube, but I'm most popular on Instagram and TikTok."

"Oh wow, that is so cool!" Delia gets up from her chair and moves to the one vacated by our mom. "You can actually make a living doing that?"

On reflex, I glance over to my brother, who is sitting a few spots away from the two girls. We exchange the same look we have for as long as my sister has been able to walk and talk: *Here we go*. Delia is famous both in our family and around town for constantly starting new projects. She's had at least seven business ventures since graduating high school. Only one of them has seen any real success, but I don't like to talk about that.

"I mean, I'm not getting rich any time soon from it. But yeah, I make a half-decent living. Most of the money comes from brand deals or sponsored posts. A little bit comes from my followers' sending badges when I go live. YouTube pays out a fair amount, but I'm still trying to build up my long-form video library to really have that be an impact." June shifts in her seat so she's facing Delia more face-on. It's like the two have locked into just their conversation and totally forgotten the rest of us. "It also helps that since I live in my van, my living expenses are stupid low. The van belonged to my grandpa, and he left it to my mom, then I bought it from her. He kept it in perfect condition, so really, all I had to do was normal maintenance stuff, convert it for living, add the electrical system, solar panels, and batteries."

"And you did all that yourself?" Delia asks.

I can practically see my sister forming plans in her head. I'm not sure if it is the social media monetization aspect or the living in a van part that she is latching onto, though. With any luck, she'll forget whatever idea it is before she wakes up in the morning.

"Mostly. My grandpa had friends in the vintage car circuit who helped me with some of it, mostly sourcing parts and advice. But yeah, YouTube and lots of literal sweat and blood can work miracles."

"Are you ever scared of living in a van?"

Delia's question has me frozen in place, ignoring the cleaning I had been doing. The idea of June being scared in that van does not sit well.

"In the beginning, sure. The first night I slept in Daisy that I wasn't parked in my mom's garage, I don't think I got more than four hours of actual sleep." June pushes one strand of hair behind her ear, leaning in closer to my sister. "But that was almost five years ago. I've learned how to keep myself safe and how to listen to my instincts."

Delia nods sagely. "Women's intuition is so important."

I fight hard not to roll my eyes again.

"Exactly. I used to try and ignore that little voice telling me something wasn't right."

Why can I not look away from June? It's like the woman has a tractor beam that forces me to watch every move she makes. I swear, I even felt it out in the fields.

"But then I had this one really awful night." June leans her elbow on the table and begins twisting a strand of hair around her finger as she speaks. "I was staying in this parking lot of a huge strip mall. And something inside me kept nagging at me to leave. But I just kept telling myself I was being paranoid. Then a bunch of cars showed up and were doing donuts and racing and causing a bunch of noise. They were throwing bottles out their windows, the whole deal. I turned all the lights off in the van, made sure my shades were drawn as tight as I could get them, and just sat on the floor of the van with my phone in my hand in case I needed to call 911."

Jesus Christ, I do not like that visual at all. A scared June hiding in her van from a bunch of hillbillies raising hell in a parking lot in the middle of the night? It makes me want to do irrational things, like break another fucking mug.

Delia gasps and sits back in her seat. "What happened?"

June shrugs as if this story isn't fucking insane. "They noticed my van and came over, trying to look in the windows and shaking it back and forth. At one point I was convinced they would flip it on its side just from rocking it. Right as I was about to call the cops, some security guards showed up and chased them off. The whole thing didn't even last more than like fifteen minutes. Once they were gone, I got out of there and found a motel to stay in for the night."

I am so intent on listening to June's story that I jump when my mother clears her throat beside me. "Son, has that spoon done something to personally offend you?"

Finally, my gaze moves from June, who continues to chat with Delia, down to the wooden mixing spoon in my hands. I'm gripping it so tightly that the thing is bent in the middle and about ready to snap. Slowly, I release the pressure and place it back on the counter.

Mom pats me on the back and gives me a knowing look, which I ignore.

"Orion, right?" June asks.

My gaze swings back over to the table the minute June starts talking to my brother.

"Yup, that's me. Middle-and-best-looking child." He laces his fingers behind his head and tilts his chair back.

"I swear, you look so familiar." June turns to face him straight on, tilting her head as if trying to figure out how she knows him.

I don't like it.

Orion nearly falls backward on his chair but stops himself by gripping the edge of the table and pulling himself forward until all four legs of his chair plunk down hard on the floor. "Huh, weird. I think I'd remember you if we had met before."

He winks at her, and when my hands move back to grip the spoon, Mom reaches over and snatches it away.

"I don't know what it is," she muses. "I just feel like I've seen you somewhere before."

A red blush starts creeping up Orion's neck, a telltale sign he's hiding something. It's why he can never win at poker and refuses to play in any game.

He gives her another wink. "You spend much time in Jacksonville? I was stationed nearby in the Marines. Spent a lot of time in bars in town."

June seems to think that over, inspecting my brother the whole time. "Maybe. I have been on a few press trips there."

"Alright, kids, I found some salsa and chips we can snack on until dinner is ready." Mom heads to the table with a bowl of tortilla chips and a jar of salsa. "June, Knox makes this salsa himself. Cans it and sells it at our stand at the farmer's market. I use it at the café too."

For the rest of the night, conversation flies between my family and June as if she's part of the group instead of a stranger who crashed into me just a few hours ago. I let the four of them carry the conversation, my own thoughts stuck on the image of June huddled in her van, terrified, and the weird exchange between her and my brother.

The dinner flies by faster than usual, with my siblings and Mom sticking around far later than they normally would. I practically have to chase them out so I can head to bed in preparation for another long day in the fields.

But once I finally manage to get them to leave, I do something I haven't done in years.

I lock the door behind them.

Chapter 7

June

A strange noise has me springing up to a sitting position in what has to be the most comfortable bed I have ever slept on in my entire life. Soft, golden sunlight streams through the gauzy curtains covering the windows.

I have no idea what time I fell asleep, but the journal I had been jotting notes in for blog posts about yesterday's fiasco lays sprawled open next to me on the bed.

The sound that woke me trills through the air again. A rooster. How freaking cool. I'm being woken up on an honest-to-god farm by a real live rooster. Agritourism isn't something I've dipped my toe into before, but I can see the appeal.

"Roger shut the hell up, or so help me, I will strangle you." A gruff voice that I have somehow gotten to know very well in the past twenty-four hours snaps at what I'm guessing is Roger the Rooster. I'd thrown both windows open last night, delighting in the sweet scent of mountain air and a cool breeze. "You wake her up, and I will send you to the butcher."

I cover my mouth with both hands, trying not to let out the laugh I feel bubbling in my chest. He talks to his animals. Knox is definitely an enigma.

Gingerly, I creep out of bed and tiptoe to the window. The enigma himself is already hard at work when the sun has just barely peaked over the horizon. Emphasis on the word hard. A pair of worn jeans cover his muscular legs, and a white T-shirt clings to his biceps, slight belly, and broad chest. He's ripping some rather crispy-looking plants from the garden and throwing them into a big wheelbarrow. Sweat is just beginning to drip down his temples, and he pulls out a handkerchief from his back pocket to wipe at his brow.

It's such a manly fucking move. Something I've seen in old black-and-white movies. The thought has probably never occurred to him that something as simple as wiping away his sweat would be sexy, but holy shit, it really is.

A needy moan slips past my lips, and Knox's head whips around to look directly at my window. I drop to the ground, plastering my body against the worn hardwood floors. *Fuck.* He totally saw me. He totally heard me.

Humiliation streaming through my body, I army crawl across the room to where my bags still sit from the night before. After the long drive and the crazy events of the day, and family dinner, I'd been so tired I only had the energy to shuck off the pants I'd been wearing and crawl into bed in a T-shirt and undies. I gather up some clean clothes and make a beeline for the bathroom, safe in the knowledge Knox is still outside working.

The tub calls to me, but I ignore it and get the water going in the decent-sized shower in the corner. The water pressure is blissfully strong, and the water heats up so fast that I almost let out another moan. What was supposed to be a quick shower turns into an indulgent soak under the beating stream of water. I swear I haven't had a shower this good since leaving Mom's house in Philly.

Once the water finally turns cold, I hop out, feeling refreshed and starving. Maybe Knox will let me take the truck into town to get some breakfast from his mom's cafe. I swear I saw books on shelves in one of the side rooms and desperately want to explore the titles.

I throw on some clothes and twist my hair up into a messy bun, not bothering to dry it.

The scent of fresh coffee leads me down the stairs and into the envy-worthy kitchen. This house looks like it was pulled straight from my Pinterest boards. Everything is bright and airy. There isn't much in the way of decor, and what there is, I have a feeling, is Roxy's doing, not Knox's. I ignore the passing thought those feminine touches could be from the ex-girlfriend Delia slipped into conversation last night.

Sitting on the counter is a big pot of coffee with a pink pastry box sitting beside it. A scribbled note sits in front. *Help yourself.* After opening and closing a bunch of cabinets, I finally uncover some utilitarian white mugs that are most definitely not the purchase of the former matriarch of this homestead.

My search of the fridge doesn't prove as fruitful, with no milk or creamer in sight. It is mostly full of fruit and veggies and some Tupperware containers filled with what looks like carefully planned meals for the week. They even have little sticky notes with what day and meal to eat on each one. Figures. Not only does Knox take his coffee black, but he also has meal plans. How very regimented of him.

Thankfully, I did come across sugar in my search for mugs, so I pour way too much into the bottom of the mug and fill the rest up with coffee. The pastry box is overflowing with buttery croissants, so I grab one and make my way outside.

Too late, I realize I left my shoes upstairs, but I spot a pair of rubber boots on the side of the door. With a shrug, I slip my feet into the entirely too-big boots and clomp my way off the porch while taking a bite of the croissant. It is utter heaven. The coffee is a little strong for my taste, but at least the sugar has taken away most of the bitterness.

I find Knox around back, still pulling out dead plants from neat rows and throwing them into the now nearly full wheelbarrow. Some of the dirt has stuck to his shirt and skin, and the sweat has made the thin cotton of his basic shirt nearly see-through. He looks like some kind of modern-day Marlboro Man, only without the gross breath and health implications.

"Morning, cowboy."

He stops his work to regard me, and I honestly can't tell what the man thinks. "You see any cows around? I'm a farmer, not a cowboy."

The eye roll I give him is so well deserved I don't even feel guilty about it. "Excuse me. Morning, farmer. Whatcha doing?"

"Working."

Well, apparently, someone is not a morning person. "Can I help?"

I don't miss the slight quirk at the corner of his mouth, as if he finds the idea of me doing manual labor funny. "I think I got it covered."

"Oh, come on, there has to be something I can do. Feed animals. Collect eggs from chickens. Water flowers. Something." I take another bite of my pastry and give him my most winning smile. "Give me the full farm experience."

"This isn't a tourist trap, June. It's an actual working farm." Knox pulls two more plants from the earth as if it takes no effort.

"I know that." I shove the rest of the pastry into my mouth and wash it down with a gulp of quickly cooling coffee. "I'll just pull some of the plants with you. Gardening always looked fun."

"Yup, gardening's real fun." That low voice of his is dripping with sarcasm, and I roll my eyes once more in response.

I grab one of the plants down by the base with one hand like I saw Knox do just moments ago and tug. Nothing happens. No problem. Placing my coffee mug on the ground, I wrap both hands around the stem and pull harder, leaning back with what seems like all my might until the stubborn thing finally breaks free, and I go reeling back onto my ass, dead leaves in my hand.

"Ha! See, I told you I could do it." I wave the dead plant around to prove my prowess in the garden.

"Sure, if by doing it you mean ruining my garlic." Knox stomps across the dirt and shoves his hand down into the soil where I just pulled the plant. He comes back up with a giant, dirty head of garlic gripped in his massive fist. "Looks like this one is going to my kitchen instead of the farmers' market."

"You're pulling up garlic?"

"Harvesting. I'm harvesting garlic." He places the ruined garlic on top of the full wheelbarrow and then stands between the handles, hefting it up. The muscles in his forearms bunch and strain, my eyes following the veins and sinew up to where his impressive biceps disappear into the sleeves of his T-shirt. "I'd appreciate it if you stopped trying to help before you ruin the rest of my crop."

I huff in annoyance. How was I supposed to know this was garlic and not just dead weeds or something? I climb to my feet, brushing the dirt off my butt from my fall. "Can I get a tour of the farm, then? I'm honestly really curious." Truly, I am. This land is so spectacular. How one man keeps it all running seems impossible.

With an exasperated sigh, Knox starts pushing the heavy wheelbarrow in the direction of the barn, and I hustle up to walk beside him. "All right. The least I can do is show you the areas to steer clear of."

"How very kind of you." I fight the urge to roll my eyes once again. At this rate, I'll give myself a migraine.

We start in the barn, where Knox shows me how he hangs the garlic from a rack suspended from the rafters.

"I dry the garlic out for a few weeks then my sister and Mom will come over to braid them into bunches that I'll sell. Don't mess with the ropes, or they could fall on your head and, more importantly, ruin the process."

Once he has all the garlic bulbs suspended from the rack, he hoists the whole thing back up so the leaves won't dangle down and get in the way. "I'll take most of what I harvest to nearby farmer's markets. A couple of the teenagers in town run the stand on the weekends when I need to be at an event for the pumpkins."

He wipes his hands off on the back of his pants and turns to me. "Most of the food I grow gets sold there. But what doesn't get sold either provides seeds for next year, gets canned for my own stores, or is donated to the local food bank. Stuff that isn't good enough for human consumption either gets composted or fed to the animals."

Next, he walks me through the neatly laid out plots of vegetables. It's obvious things are winding down for the season because most of the plants are turning brown and no longer hold much in the way of produce. There are varieties of veggies that I've never even heard of. Who knew there were so many varieties of squash?

We walk along a huge area that's crawling with green vines almost up to my knees that are apparently sweet potatoes due to be harvested in the next few weeks. "A bunch of kids from the town will come out and help with pulling up the tubers in exchange for some money and enough potatoes to get their moms through the winter. I supply a few grocery stores with root vegetables, and of course, the farm stand gets the rest. I'll save a few hundred of the small ones to make slips for next year's crop."

We cut across a field full of beautiful yellow flowers that are apparently cover crops to reinject nutrients into the soil between growing seasons. At the very back of the property, so far back in fact that we can barely see the house, are sprawling plants with leaves so large they remind me a little of the ones I saw in the tropics.

"Holy shit." Rising up like a giant chubby phoenix on the other side of the greenery is the biggest pumpkin I have ever seen. The top of it comes up to Knox's waist, and I don't think the two of us together could wrap our arms around it and touch hands. "Is this bigger than the one that exploded?"

"You mean the one you ran over?"

I won't dignify that with an answer and instead walk closer to the giant gourd.

"Yes, Lucy here is bigger than Gertie *was*." I don't miss the emphasis he places on that past tense verb. "Gertie was probably somewhere around fourteen hundred pounds. Right now, Lucy is closer to eighteen hundred. She's not my biggest this year, though. That would be Smashley on the other side of the property. You'll forgive me if I don't let you anywhere near her. I want to try and keep one of my girls safe from you, trouble-maker."

"What's with the names?" Honestly, he talks about these pumpkins like they are his children.

Knox blushes slightly under his thick beard and leans down to pick a weed near Lucy. "I pick an actress every year and name all the pumpkins after my favorite characters they've played. This year, it's Drew Barrymore."

"Why actresses?"

"All pumpkins, all squash varieties, in fact, are female. Same with melons. They have male flowers and female flowers on the same plant. But only the female flowers will turn into fruit."

Huh, who knew? "Smashley? What movie is that from?"

"*Whip It*. Smashley Simpson." Knox turns away and starts walking back in the direction of the house. I get the distinct feeling he's embarrassed about the naming conventions of his pumpkins. But I like it; it's cute.

It takes a little bit of jogging to catch up with his long strides, but I pull up even with him to traverse the fields once again. "Do you think I could take your truck into town? I'd like to start exploring so I can at least get some posts up while I'm stuck here. That reminds me, can I get your Wi-Fi password?"

"Don't have Wi-Fi."

I stop dead in my tracks. "Excuse me? How can you not have Wi-Fi?"

Knox turns to face me, a smile on his face. "Have you not noticed that I'm in the middle of nowhere? The major companies don't come out this far. And I didn't need a connection so much that I looked into it any further than that. Cell service doesn't reach out this way either. We have a landline phone for the house and barn. When I need to do business online, I head into town and use either the library or the cafe. Suits my needs."

"No wonder I wasn't getting notifications from Instagram or TikTok. I thought the accident messed up my SIM card or something." I'd been trying to post a pic of Daisy covered in pumpkin goo since I got here and just kept getting error messages. Honestly, I've been to some remote places, but I never thought of some place in my own state as being so far away that they don't even get internet. "Well, I am definitely going to need the truck then. My socials must be going insane with a crap-ton of messages and comments that need responses. I can't remember the last time I went more than twenty-four hours without posting."

"You forget I've seen you drive. There is no way I'm letting you behind the steering wheel of my truck." Knox starts our trek back to the house as I race to catch up with a low, simmering rage bubbling in my belly. "I'm sure your *socials* will survive."

"You'd be surprised. Social media algorithms are hungry beasts that need to be fed constantly, or they will leave you in the dust." Honestly, would he ever let the whole running into his pumpkin thing go? "And for your information, I have literally driven to every corner of the continental United States and have never gotten so much as a speeding ticket." Parking tickets are another thing altogether. "I am an excellent driver. My literal livelihood depends on it. I'm sure I can handle your little truck for the five miles to town."

Knox stops in his tracks so quickly that I run into his back and almost fall on my ass once again. But his strong hands wrap around my upper arms, keeping me upright.

"You can't even walk without almost causing yourself bodily harm. There is no way I'm letting you drive the *little* truck that *my* livelihood depends on."

"Has anyone ever told you what an absolutely stubborn jackass you are?" It takes everything in my body to keep myself from stomping my foot in frustration.

"Yeah, it's been mentioned a time or two."

"You don't even want me here. I'd think you'd be looking for any reason to get me out of your hair."

Our eyes lock, both of us huffing as if we'd just run a marathon as opposed to the verbal sparring match. Slowly, the warmth of Knox's hands still gripping my arms registers, his body alarmingly close to mine. My gaze flicks down to his lips, smashed together in a frustrated, thin line. By the time my eyes return to his, there is heat lying behind his irises that I don't expect. It's *not* the heat of anger.

Knox seems to realize his hands are still on me and releases me as if I'm a hot pan he took from the oven without a potholder.

He takes one giant step back while taking a deep breath into his lungs. "I need to pick up my order from the feed store. I suppose I can take you into town for a couple hours."

Without waiting for a response from me, Knox turns on his heel and heads inside—I hope with the intention to rinse off and change clothes. At a loss for what to do, I wander over to the barn to say hello to the baby goats. They are so stinking cute with their little faces and nubby horns. During the tour, Knox explained that all the animals on his property, except the chickens, are rescues and don't actually serve a purpose. The chickens provide eggs for him to use and sell.

I wish I had brought something for the little guys to eat because as soon as they realize I have nothing for them, they go back to hopping around in the enclosure, butting heads, and climbing on the various rocks.

During one of my hosted trips, the local visitor's bureau set me up with baby goat yoga, and I've loved the strange little creatures ever since. I honestly thought about smuggling one in my purse after the class. But he probably wouldn't have done well living in a van, so it was for the best that he didn't fit.

Once I get my fill of watching the goats play, I wander toward the barn doors to see what other animals he has inside. The barn mostly holds dusty equipment in the empty stalls, but there is one with a donkey that I instantly fall in love with and make a mental note to ask Knox about.

A loud noise that I've only ever heard from a distance rips through the air at the opposite side of the barn. Some weird combination of a honk and a screech. Silhouetted against the bright sun streaming in through the doors is a big duck with a long black neck and tan feathers along its back.

"Hey, buddy, how ya doing?" I bend down and hold my hand out to see if he or she will come closer.

It takes two steps toward me, making a sound I can only describe as hissing. That's my first hint this duck, which I am fairly certain now is not actually a duck, might not exactly be the friendly kind. Before I can make an exit, the thing spreads its wings wide and charges at me like a bull who's seen red. Its webbed feet slap against the dusty floor of the barn, and it continues making the most godawful sound I have ever heard.

"*Oh shit*!"

I turn tail and run, my heart slamming in my chest as I am literally chased from the barn by the biggest fucking bird I have ever seen in my life. I had no idea birds were so fucking fast when they ran.

I break free of the doors just as Knox comes running from the house. "Goddamn it, Cugo."

With Satan-on-wings gaining ground fast, I fling myself into Knox's arms, and he swings me around just as a flurry of feathers comes at us from what seems like every angle. Knox carries me to the truck, wrestles the door open without letting me slip, then tosses me into the front seat and climbs in. He pushes the feathered monster back with his foot, then slams the door of the truck closed.

Chapter 8

Knox

The second the door closes with my foot barely inside the truck, I slam the locks down. True, birds can't open car doors, but I would not put anything past the evil incarnate that is Cugo the Canadian Goose.

"Holy shit, why do you have a murderous duck on your farm?" June demands.

She is panting heavily, still clinging to me, half sitting in my lap, half sprawled across the center console next to me. I can literally feel the adrenaline leave her body as she starts shivering against my chest.

"Goose. Not a duck. Cugo is a Canadian Goose."

My own heart rate starts to return to normal as well, and as the panic leaves my body, my senses come back to life. Because, yeah, I'm absolutely still holding the far-too-sexy woman that I am trying my goddamn best to continue hating. She's making it damn hard, though, with her curious questions. And that isn't the only thing threatening to get hard.

"Okay, why do you have a fucking murderous *goose* on your farm?" To prove her point, Cugo comes flapping at the window, his beak pecking at the glass. The sharp taps make June flinch each time. "I thought Canadians were supposed to be nice!"

How do I explain Cugo? "About three years ago, some idiot kids were shooting rocks at birds with a slingshot. They hit Cugo, and he came down in my field. I found him flapping about, squawking in pain. I managed to get him wrapped in a blanket and to the animal doctor. He had a broken wing. It was so bad he could never fly quite right again. The doc thought the bird was pretty advanced in years, so I figured he could stay here with the rest of my misfit animals until he kicked the bucket."

What a fucking mistake that was.

"Obviously, he's still going strong, but he can't get his wings going enough to make it more than a few feet off the ground. Most the time, we stay out of each other's way. I leave out feed for him, and he chases off foxes from the chickens. Somehow, he became my equivalent of a livestock guardian dog. The problem is, he doesn't like strangers."

"Gee, you don't say." June shifts in my lap, the movement against my cock nearly making me groan, but I manage to choke it down. "A warning would have been nice."

Her voice has gone breathy, and I look up to discover she is also looking at my lips. Again.

How have we ended up in this position for the second time in an hour?

"I mean, you told me what crops not to go near because it would hurt your bottom line but not the fact that you have a guard goose loose on the property?"

"Sorry." I swallow hard, not sure exactly what's happening here. Her eyes slide down to track the movement of my Adam's apple. "Haven't seen him in a few weeks. Thought he finally met his maker in the woods or something."

The truck is off, yet the heat in the cab seems to be climbing higher. The air is thick with something I hadn't experienced in a long time. Too long. And never at this intensity. Desire. Need. It wraps around me like a humid day in the field, pressing in on my skin in an almost oppressive surge.

My heart rams against my ribcage, and I'm not sure if it's the pure need coursing through me or the edge of fear. Not from Cugo. He would never hurt me. But women are a different story altogether. Memories I try to avoid return with a jolt, shifting just at the edge of my lust-fogged brain. Memories of pain when they inevitably leave. My long stretch of self-imposed celibacy makes it difficult to ignore the throbbing desire in my body and regain my sense of logic.

I'm not sure if June is moving closer or if I am, but the distance between us seems to be slowly disappearing.

Thwack!

Cugo flings himself against the door in one final attempt to get to his victim, startling us both out of the lust cloud and returning sense to both of us. June skitters away, climbing over the center console and into the driver's seat.

With one glance out the window, I see the black and gray butt of Cugo waddling away. "I should have killed that bird ages ago. Bleeding heart be damned."

I finally turn to face June. It's a mistake. Her face is flushed, and I can't stop the hope that her reaction is from whatever was about to happen between us and not her near-death experience with Satan's goose.

"Huh, you really are like an onion," June says.

"Must not have showered all that well if I smell that bad."

"No, you have layers. Like Shrek." June holds out her hand. "Keys?"

My head isn't that mixed up. But a very uncharacteristic chuckle bubbles up from my belly. "Nice try, Trouble. I'm driving."

"Okay, but I'm not getting out of this truck until I see this town's version of civilization."

Shaking my head and chuckling even more, I climb out the door we just both dove through and walk around the front of the truck while June crawls back over the center console to the passenger seat.

And yes, I one hundred percent check out her ass through the window.

*　*　*

Five minutes into the silent ride into town, June's phone trills with an old-timey ringtone. "Holy shit, I actually got a signal."

But as soon as she looks at the screen, she groans and slumps back in her seat.

"Not someone you want to talk to?"

She stares down at the screen like she'll be able to determine what they want if she mind-melds with her phone. "Not particularly. But I guess I have to." She stabs the green button and swipes it across the screen, accepting the call. "Hi, Mom."

Her mom? I'm pretty sure my mom would slap me upside the head if I ever answered one of her calls like that. But not everyone has a mom like mine.

"Yeah, I'm fine. Sorry I didn't get your calls; this town has the worst reception." From across the truck, I can hear her mother's concerned voice, though I can't make out the words. "Yes, I got in a little fender bender, no big deal. I'm sorry. I should have realized you heard the accident and would be worried." June leans her head back on the headrest and stares at the ceiling of my truck. "Daisy needs a little work, but she'll be fine." More muffled concern from her mother, and June rolls her eyes. "Yes, I found a place to stay. A nice little farm run by a local family."

I snort because no one in my family helps with the farm all that much.

"Mom, I'm sure they aren't serial killers. There have been plenty of opportunities for them to kill me in the past twenty-four hours, and I'm still here."

I try my best not to eavesdrop on the conversation, but she's sitting two feet away, so there isn't much I can do about it.

"I don't need money, Mom. I promise." There's a long pause, and the tone of the conversation seems to shift from a little overbearing to tense. "No, I haven't called the lawyer yet. I will when I'm ready. You don't have to worry. It really isn't your business anymore."

I flinch at the comment, not even knowing the context, but that sounded harsh.

A few stilted goodbyes, and June hangs up with her mother. "Sorry about that."

"Don't be. I'm under contractual obligation to answer every single one of my mother's phone calls."

June doesn't smile, and for some reason, I don't like that.

"I don't think our mothers are much alike," she says.

I want to ask her more about the conversation, but I've never been one to pry into people's business, and I frankly wouldn't know how to start now.

With a deep sigh and a slight shake of her head, June turns back to the scenery around us. "So, what is there to do in town? Anything I absolutely can't miss?"

"Well, you got to see the gossip center yesterday. That would be the cafe."

"Mmmhmm, which I am planning to stop at first for more fuel."

I've lived in this town my entire life and know just about everyone by name, but I can't think of a damn thing this woman who has been all over the world would find interesting. The town has trouble holding on to the people who have lived here all their lives, many deciding to flee to bigger cities with more opportunities. A phenomenon I have become intimately aware of. There is no way my hometown could hold the interest of this woman for more than a few minutes.

"The Mutts and Cuts, maybe?" I think aloud. "It's a salon and pet groomer. People can get matching haircuts with their dogs."

I glance over quickly to gauge June's reaction.

She bows her head over her phone and rapidly types something in with both thumbs. "No way, that's hilarious. I love it!"

"You'll have to ask Mom about the fountain. There's this whole lore about the couple who settled here, but no one tells the story like her."

All the high school couples go to that damn fountain for their first kiss and throw in a coin. It's supposed to be some good luck thing to make your love last forever. I wouldn't know; I had planned on performing the ritual after proposing to Lesley, but we never made it that far.

Mostly, the town just fishes out the coins to pay for pothole repairs every spring.

"There are some shops in town," I continue. "A decent little distillery just outside the town limits."

June is furiously taking notes on her phone but looks up at the mention of the distillery. "Not downtown? I would think the main street would be great for a distillery."

"Nope. We've got some pretty out-there decency laws still on the books and a mayor who loves to enforce them. No alcohol, cigarettes, or porn can be sold within town limits."

"Wait until your mayor finds out porn is on the internet for free."

"Oh, trust me, he tried to figure out a way to block anyone's ability to access porn sites while in the town. Not as easy as he'd hoped."

"Wow."

"You should have seen him when Club Barely Over the Line, the local strip club, opened literally five feet from the town line."

"I love this place."

I can hear the smile on June's face, but I force myself not to look. Her smile is too much. It loosens something deep within me that needs to stay firmly locked down. Instead, I pull to the curb right outside the cafe and park in my usual spot. The spot that everyone in town knows is mine and leaves for my truck. That's just how predictable this place is.

Before either of us can get out of the truck, June's door swings open, and none other than Mayor Burt Lickinbill himself stands there with his trademark cheesy grin. June almost spills out of the truck but catches herself before taking a nose-dive.

"Here she is, the writer I've heard so much about!" Burt offers June his hand and helps her the rest of the way from the truck.

The pang of jealousy that zaps through me is both mildly painful and completely irrational. I have no reason to be jealous where June is concerned. Plus, Burt is a stick-thin man creeping up on his seventies with greasy, dirty-blond hair that I know for a fact he dyes with Just For Men. He has perpetual onion breath, and his entire identity revolves around being the latest in a long line of Lickinbill mayors.

"Um, yes, that would be me. And you are?" June allows herself to be pulled up onto the sidewalk while Burt continues to grip her hand and pumps it up and down in his trademark aggressive handshake.

I hop out of the truck and hustle around so I can help June disentangle herself from our ridiculous mayor.

"I am the mayor of this fine hamlet." He sweeps his hand out to indicate the quiet street. "Word made its way to me that there was a famous writer in our midst, looking to do some articles promoting our town, and I knew I just had to come to make your acquaintance."

June looks positively shell-shocked at this ambush. "Oh, well, I don't know about famous, but I have a pretty decent following on Instagram and TikTok."

Burt finally lets her hand go and instead starts wagging his finger at her in what I think is supposed to be a playful manner. "Now don't you be coy with me, Miss Best US Travel Destination Article of the Year winner. I did my research, and I am honored that a writer of your caliber would grace us with a visit."

Seeming to pull herself together, June plasters on a smile that doesn't come close to reaching her beautiful brown eyes, not that Burt notices. "Well, what I've seen of the town so far is wonderful. And the people here are very welcoming."

Bullshit. Burt knows it, too. He throws me a disdainful look. He's not a fan of our family since we've been in the town longer than his. But also, because we don't give a shit what he says.

"Would you like to join me for a cup of coffee before I start exploring?" June says with a sugar-sweet voice that she certainly hasn't directed my way up to this point. *Why on Earth is she humoring this asshat?*

Our illustrious mayor sneers at my mother's coffee shop, weighing his options. He has never once stepped foot inside Romancing the Bean. Even if he did, Mom would probably chase him right back out.

"Well, maybe for just a moment," he replies reluctantly.

Burt takes a few tentative steps toward the entrance of the cafe, and I pull June back by the elbow. "What are you doing? You really don't have to suck up to this guy."

"I've dealt with his kind before," June whispers under her breath. "You let them talk until they are blue in the face, and then they'll leave you alone for the rest of the trip. Trust me. I know how to manage men who think a little too much of themselves."

She gives me a pointed look, and I glare back.

"Absolutely not!" My mother's shout echoes through the open door of the cafe. "Turn your prudish, flat ass right around and get out of my place of business!"

A ceramic mug goes zinging past our heads and shatters against the truck. Goddamn it, not again!

Chapter 9

June

"Shit." Knox sprints for the cafe, leaping over the porch railing, and lands just in time to grab the mayor before he goes tumbling to the ground.

A very pissed Roxy stands in the doorway, her gray hair pulled back into an intricate braid, an apron covering her purple tie-dyed maxi dress, and a glass bottle filled with a fascinating fuchsia liquid in her hand. "So, help me, if you step one foot in this building again, I will beat you over the head with this candy cane syrup and not lose a wink of sleep over your resulting concussion."

Burt's face is pale, and his eyes round; there is no mistaking the blatant fear Roxy has struck into his heart.

"Mom, calm down. He was just going to have a cup of coffee with June. Tell her about the town." Knox gets Burt steady on his feet and slides between his mom and the shaken mayor. "She had some questions about the area."

Roxy glances at where I still stand, watching the scene go down by the truck. "Hey, June." Her face brightens, and she gives me a warm smile. "Sleep okay?"

"Um, yeah, great." I honestly have no idea what is going on here.

"That's wonderful." Her smile falls as she looks back at the two men before her. "Burt, I will not let you give this delightful young woman your bullshit revisionist history of my town. If she has questions, I will be happy to answer them. So why don't you scamper on back to your office and pretend like your title means something for the rest of the day."

Seeming to remember I'm there, Burt straightens his spine and smooths out the bland brown sweater covering his khakis. "Now Roxy, my title does mean something, and it is my duty to show our visitor the *decent* side of Amoresville."

"Yeah, *your* idea of decent."

"Okay, Mom, enough. Get back inside."

Roxy flips Burt the most aggressive middle finger I've ever seen, which is saying something considering I've spent most my life in Philadelphia. But eventually she does as her son says. With her safely out of reach of their mayor, Knox turns to Burt, the smile on his face barely hidden. "Mayor Burt, why don't you have a seat at one of the cafe tables out here, and I'll make sure you get a drink."

The mayor huffs his displeasure but takes Knox's suggestion.

With the rivals in their respective corners for the moment, the referee makes his way back down to me, keeping his eye on the door.

"What on Earth was that all about?"

Honestly, this town is fascinating. Forget the local attractions. I could write articles on just the few people I've met so far. Killer goose included. Forget articles. I could write whole books about these living characters. A familiar tug of longing echoes in the pit of my stomach at the thought of writing more than my typical thousand-word blog post or one-hundred-word social media post.

Knox rubs his hand over his face, and I have the strangest urge to give him a hug. "Let's just say our families have never exactly gotten along." He grips the back of his neck, his forearm flexing and relaxing as he massages the muscles there. "Plus, he shut down Mom's side hustle."

"Side hustle? What, was she dealing pot to the other grannies on the block?"

Knox looks up at me from beneath his unfairly long eyelashes. "Worse."

"Meth?"

"Vibrators."

Okay, I was not expecting that. A full-throttled belly laugh bursts from my mouth, and I clap both my hands over my lips to try and quiet it. "Roxy ran a sex toy shop?"

"Nothing quite so out in the open. Remember those decency laws? Well, they include a ban on selling adult toys. So anytime a customer would come in and buy a spicy romance book, Mom would pull out this box of toys and suggest which one would go best with that particular book. She was like a fucking underground sommelier for sex toys."

"That is amazing." Maybe if she still has some of those toys lying around, I could get one.

The lapse of judgment in the truck left me tingling between the legs and my panties uncomfortably wet. I didn't think to grab any of my own toys from the van after the accident, so I'm left with my fingers to ease the pain when we get back to the house tonight. "Just so you know, I might be a little bit in love with your mom."

"She's something."

Silence stretches between us. For a second, I think he might bring up our moment in the truck earlier, but instead, he shoves his hands in his pockets and looks back at the mayor who is perched on a wrought iron chair as if ready to run for his life if needed.

"Well, you should probably get this over with so you can get on with your exploring." He doesn't even wait for me to respond. Just turns and marches back onto the porch and into the cafe.

I wait for a beat, willing my body to stop reacting to the ornery farmer I have somehow become dependent on over the last day. When it becomes obvious that my lady bits will continue rebelling, I give up and follow him.

Roxy still has a good head of steam going, and the moment I walk up to the counter, she declares, "I will not make that man a drink. You get one coffee, and it is for you only." She slaps a chipped ceramic mug onto the worn wood between us. "A candy cane triple mocha for the road."

"Thanks, Roxy, that sounds delicious. Um, do you have a to-go mug?"

"No, you can either bring the mug back or keep it for a keepsake. Most people in town have their own mugs that they bring in daily." Her face softens, and she pats my hand where it wraps around the warm cup. "Do not let that man feed you bullshit about how this town is a call back to a simpler time. He's a stupid, old stick-in-the-mud who refuses to let the town progress." By the end of her sentence, she's leaning around me to shout the words out the door.

"Miss Ammer." Burt stands exactly a foot outside the door, his hands folded behind his back. "I have a wonderful idea. Why don't we take a walk down to the fountain in the town square, and I'll fill you in on the founding of the town. Get some *fresh* air."

Roxy's face turns red, but she keeps her lips pressed tightly together. I don't want to insult this woman. She's been incredibly nice and seems like someone I would like to sit down and talk with more.

Mayor Burt, however...

"Nope." Roxy unties her apron and flings it at her son as he walks out from what I think is the kitchen with a chocolate chip cookie in his mouth. He just barely manages to catch the apron and keep the confection from falling. "I am not letting you tell this sweet child about my family history. I'm coming, too. Knox, man the counter."

The mayor backs up quickly as Roxy storms out the door with me on her tail.

"Good luck," Knox calls. He looks entirely too sexy tying the apron around his much larger frame and making himself at home behind the counter. "You're going to need it."

* * *

For the first two blocks, my companions are mostly silent. I feel like I'm being paraded down Main Street to be put in the stockade with the way Roxy and Burt are glaring straight ahead on either side of me.

"Miss Ammer, may I call you June?" Burt barely pauses before barreling on despite Roxanne's huff of annoyance. "June, I would love to pick your brain about how we can make our charming little town more attractive to visitors."

I open my mouth to ask a follow-up question when Roxanne pipes up, "How about lifting the ancient dry laws? Letting people have a beer with their dinner would go a long way to bringing people into town."

"Our town has been alcohol-free for over a hundred years." Burt glares across me at Roxanne then turns to me. "A fact I would think families find comforting when looking for a nice place to stay."

"Family-friendly destinations aren't exactly my specialty, but I'm not sure I agree—"

Roxanne stops in her tracks, hands planted on hips and shooting daggers from her eyes at the town's mayor. "Ha! See! I told you. Your damn family has been keeping this town in the Dark Ages for far too long."

"That is not what she said. If you wouldn't interrupt, lovely June here might be able to finish a single thought."

They both look at me expectantly. "Um, well, breweries and distilleries are certainly a plus when someone is looking for a vacation. I wouldn't say it's the only thing that draws visitors."

"Don't feel like you need to appease this old fool, June. The man's had a stick up his ass since the day he was born. It's genetic."

Before Burt can respond, I continue the journey to the town square. "Let's keep up the pace, don't want to lose the light."

Burt jogs after me. "But it's only ten in the a.m."

"Yup, that mid-morning light is great for landscapes." Doing my best to not spill even a drop of the delicious coffee I've been sipping, I pick up the pace to try and hurry along the two old curmudgeons.

I try to make mental notes of all the places I want to visit once I ditch my so-called tour guides. A shop window with glinting gold and silver jewelry calls to me. The pieces are like nothing I've ever seen before: buttons and watch gears twist together with thin wire, and I desperately want to spend some time discovering how the trinkets are made. His Trash, Her

Treasure. *That's an odd name for a jewelry store.* No doubt I'll remember that.

Down a side street, I spot a woman with a fresh perm strolling out of a building holding a leash attached to a freshly groomed golden doodle who can barely contain its excitement. That must be the infamous Mutts and Cuts. I wonder if I can borrow someone's dog and get matching blowouts.

Finally, we came to the town square. We didn't drive through this part of the town when I arrived yesterday afternoon, and I'm glad I am getting to experience it on foot. A huge fountain sits in the middle of a sprawling square, green lawn. Four roads make up the borders of the park. Wide sidewalks lead to the fountain from each street corner. At each of the four corners are streetlights controlling the non-existent traffic. When a car does pull up to one of the intersections, it pauses, regardless of what color the stoplight is. Then, the driver looks around and keeps going, even if the light is red.

I love this freaking town.

The three of us stop at the corner, a pedestrian signal lit up with a red hand indicating it isn't safe to walk despite there not being a car in sight.

"Oh, for the love of goddess." Roxy crosses her arms and taps her foot on the pavement.

"You cross that street before it turns, and I will write you a citation myself, Roxy Halsted." Burt stands ramrod straight on the right of me while the obviously irritated Roxy stands to the left.

"You don't have the authority."

Thankfully, the walk signal starts blinking at that moment, and the two pick up their speed walk once again. I trail behind, taking pictures of the beautiful park on my phone as I do. Towering trees are just beginning to drop their leaves, lending pops of red and yellow to the idyllic scene. If it weren't for the most aggravating people on the face of the planet bickering in the background, it would be absolutely perfect.

Phone cameras can do pretty wonderful things these days, but I will definitely need to come back with my real camera later.

As I draw closer, the fountain calls my attention. The ornate scrollwork and sculptures stand in stark contrast to the small, old-fashioned town. It is made of shining marble with a bronze statue of a couple embracing in the middle. The woman wears a bonnet and a long, simple dress. The man is in a military uniform I don't recognize from the many battlefields I've toured over the years. How bronze can capture the unabashed adoration pouring from both the figures is beyond me. A sharp, almost twisting pain twinges behind my sternum. What must it be to love like that?

Before tears can creep their way out of my eyes for literally no reason, I turn my attention to the water trickling from the spouts at their feet, almost like a spring bubbling up from the ground rather than a grand display of water streams.

"June, meet my great, great, great, great grandparents and the founders of Amoresville, Maurice and Christine Louis." Roxy's annoyance seems to slip away as she looks at her ancestors. "Come here, look at the plaque."

She leads me over to a bronze plate on the side of the fountain wall. *In memory of the love this town was founded upon. - 1978.*

"My grandfather had that plaque placed in honor of our bicentennial." Roxy brushes some of the leaves off the fountain wall and sits, twisting around to look up at the statue. "In 1778, Christine's family was living just outside what is now Philadelphia. The Revolutionary War was in full swing. My ancestors were Quakers, so they were peaceful people."

Off to the side, Burt scoffs and mumbles something under his breath, but we ignore him.

"The war was taking a toll on their community, but they did what they could to survive and help their neighbors."

I quickly switch the camera app on my phone to video and press record.

"Christine was just seventeen when her father started letting her come to the market to sell the furniture pieces he painstakingly created. It only took a few hours that first day for Maurice to spot the young beauty." Roxy looks up lovingly at the statue versions of the couple.

"He was a young French soldier who was shipped here to fight against the British Empire. He'd been injured at the battle of Monmouth and was just finishing his recovery in Philadelphia. He struck up a conversation with her father about a rocking chair he couldn't afford and had no need for, all for the chance to steal a closer glance at the shy woman standing quietly at the back of their stand. Every weekend for a month, Christine joined her father at the market, and every weekend, Maurice came just to see her. Finally, her father began to notice the French soldier and his fascination with Christine. He obviously did not approve."

A sigh filled with longing and love slips from Roxy. This story is obviously very dear to her heart. Even Burt manages to stay quiet and listen to the tale.

"Once he noticed, Christine's father decided she would no longer come to market. You see in the Quaker religion, not only did your parents need to approve a marriage, but the whole community. Back then marrying outside your religion meant your family would disown you and you would be banished from the church.

"Christine knew this would be the last chance she ever had to speak with the striking soldier. So, she took it.

"When her father was distracted by the prospect of a large sale, Christine approached Maurice. They snuck down an alley and Maurice confessed he couldn't stop thinking about her. He dreamed of her face each night at the encampment." Roxy turns back to face me, patting the low ledge beside her. Reverently, I sit where she indicates, cradling the now cold mug in one hand while steadying my phone in the other to try and keep the frame from shaking too much. "Christine had never spoken to a man outside her family before that day. Her whole body shook with the excitement of being so near someone so unlike anyone she had met before."

I bat away the thought that I know how she felt. I am not an innocent Quaker girl, and Knox is certainly not a French soldier.

"He asked her to meet him that night. To run off and get married. She only uttered one word. *Yes.* It was the only word she'd ever spoken to a man other than her father, and yet it sealed her fate."

A chill ripples over my skin, both from the crisp, early fall day and Roxy's magical words.

"They arranged to meet a mile from her home in the dead of night. Christine was terrified. Going anywhere unaccompanied was unheard of for a young woman in her faith, let alone in the middle of the night. But according to her journals, the power of his love gave her courage beyond measure. She stumbled through the woods in complete darkness, only the moon and stars lighting her way. The moment they found each other wandering the forest, Maurice gathered her in his arms, holding her tight against his chest. Pressing her head against him, she heard his heartbeat and knew it was the right decision."

Roxy's eyes track back to the statue, a sheen of tears coating her eyes, though she isn't letting them fall. "They traveled all night and the next day to Harrisburg with nothing but the clothes on their backs, a few coins Maurice had saved, and an old horse he stole from the French troops. The next day, they managed to find passage on a boat sailing upriver on the Susquehanna. The boat's captain married them on the first night of their journey to the unsettled parts of northern Pennsylvania. A week after that, they consummated their love among the wildflowers that used to grow on this very spot. They settled here, and over the years, more people came. Christine named the town after her French love, and the rest is, quite literally, history."

Staring up at embracing lovers, I'm struck by the beauty of both the sculpture and the story. But more than anything, I can't believe this town built a fucking statue on the spot where the town's settlers first boned. *I fucking love this town.*

Chapter 10

Knox

I'm not going to do it.

The laptop's bright screen glares at me from across the cafe as I make a vanilla Earl Gray tea for Mrs. Winchester. She takes the cup and retreats to the bookshelves in the room next door. She will most likely spend the rest of the afternoon reading an incredibly smutty book and then put it back on the shelf without paying for it. Then, she'll go to church on Sunday and pray for her sins. But she'll be back again next week.

The pull of something you shouldn't be doing suddenly doesn't seem like a problem only other people have. Before the old bat walked in the door, I was about to cyber-stalk my houseguest.

It's research. I should know who's sleeping under my roof, right?

Good enough for me. I stomp back over to the table and finish typing her name into the search bar. The first result is an Instagram page. That's the one with pictures, right? Social media isn't really my thing.

Inside my chest, my heart races almost as fast as when I saw June about to get attacked by Cugo. Which is insane. Honestly, it's not like I'm looking up porn in the middle of my mother's cafe. I am looking at a public profile of a public person. This is her profession. I'm allowed to look.

Before I agonize over it anymore, I click the link, and immediately my screen is filled with beautifully curated images of June, her van, Daisy, and the places they've visited. Every image has this vintage look, like the photos fading in our family albums. I'm not so out of touch that I don't know she uses a filter on the pictures, but the look matches her for some reason. Is this how she sees the world?

I want to see more.

When I click on a photo of June sitting on the bed in her van, the back doors flung wide open, and a view of the ocean behind her, I'm blocked by a pop-up telling me to create an account or sign in.

It's not even a question. I've gotten a taste, and I need the whole damn meal now. Impatiently, I fill in the required information to make my very first social media account with absolutely zero plan to do anything with it and get back to June's photos.

There is no denying she's stunning. A bad driver? A little annoying? Absolutely, but also beautiful beyond words. I inspect each photo as if I'll be able to learn her secrets. The reason why I can't stop thinking about her. Why does it feel like I've been waiting for her even though we only met yesterday? Why I've already forgiven her for the dent in my winter fund when she killed Gertie?

For the first time in years, something or someone other than the farm has gripped my attention. One night in my house, and already I can't stop thinking about her. I'm no stranger to relationships. Besides Lesley, there was my high school girlfriend, who once swore she loved small-town life and would never leave—until she was accepted to a school across the country and left without a second glance.

If those women couldn't picture a small life with a small-time farmer, there is no way someone like June, who has the literal world at her feet, could ever settle her roots here.

Before I know it, Mrs. Winchester is scurrying out of the cafe, her face red and her eyes firmly locked on the ground. I've been scrolling through June's Instagram feed for over an hour. Seven years' worth of photos. The ones from before she got Daisy are fascinating. She's a different person in those: Younger, wilder, more restless. Each post is from a new country, a different resort.

A clothing-optional resort.

My scrolling stops on a photo taken of June in a pool. Her hands are braced on the pool's edge holding her out of the water just enough to see she has no bathing suit on. The water covers her ass, and her back is to the camera, so really, I can't see anything other than her bare back. But it's enough. Hell, it's too much. I will never be able to forget the smooth, soft expanse of her skin bathed in the tropical sunlight. The way her waist flares out into round hips, the slight hint of side boob on one side. Tilting my head, I half expect my angle to change so I can see just a little more.

There are more photos. Her sitting in a beach chair with a huge floppy hat shading her face and bare shoulders. Beauty shots of the ocean, sunsets, and the inside of her room. In the description, she tells her readers to check out her blog for full details on her trip to Temptation Resorts.

The bell over the door rings, and I slam the lid on the laptop shut. My mother and June stroll in, laughing about something and acting like they're best friends. Burt is nowhere in sight.

"Hi, darling, how were things?" Mom shuffles behind the counter and grabs two glasses, filling them with water and handing one to June.

"Good." It's all I can say.

I can't take my eyes off June. Can't shake the idea of this bubbly, stubborn woman at a nude resort. It makes me want to break things. Because other men got to see her, and I didn't. As Mom would say, the thought is patriarchal, misogynistic crap. But that doesn't stop me from wanting to track down each person who saw her on that beach and gouge their eyes out.

"Knox, you were underselling this town." June sits across from me at the table, sipping the water my mom brings her. "There are so many hidden gems here. The little bakery down the block only sells miniature desserts. *MiniBun.* The jeweler that hand makes all the pieces from reclaimed wiring. This is like an artisan's dream." She reaches across and places her hand on my forearm. "And your family's story." She puts that same hand over her heart now. "I mean, it is just so swoon-worthy."

"Oh, speaking of swoon-worthy, June, go check out the book selection. Pick out any book to take back with you. Goddess knows my son isn't much of a conversationalist, so you'll need the entertainment."

Ma has barely gotten the words out before June springs from her chair and speed walks into the next room. Every single book in the inventory is a romance novel, and they are organized by spice rating as determined by Mom. Needless to say, I don't wander to that part of the shop often.

"You like her." Mom looks at me with that no-nonsense stare that got me to break down and confess when I stole a pack of cigarettes as a teenager.

I avoid her gaze because that look might still work on me. "I don't know what you're talking about. And keep it down."

"I know that look. I saw that look on your father's face every single time he looked at me." She smiles wistfully. "That look is memorialized in our town square. Don't bother denying it. I've always been able to read you like a book."

On reflex, my eyes roll toward the ceiling. "I've known her for a total of twenty-four hours. I don't know her well enough to say I like her. I just know I don't want her behind the wheel of my truck or near my pumpkins."

"You don't need to know a person for very long to know they are meant to be in your life." Mom leans back against the counter, crossing her arms. "Look at your father and me. He was moving me into the house within a week of our first date. Look at your ancestors. Stolen looks over a furniture stand were all they needed."

Mom and Dad were the exception. They were marigolds and tomatoes. They helped each other grow and thrive, each adding something to the relationship that the other lacked. "Even if I did, which I'm not saying I do, what does it matter? She's leaving as soon as that van of hers is fixed up. The most I could ever have with a woman like that is a fling, and I don't do that." She deserves more than that.

Before Mom can press the point any further, June comes bounding back into the room, three books clutched to her chest, a smile spread across her face. "It has been so long since I read an actual, physical book. Space is so limited in the van I just have a few favorites, but mostly I use e-reader."

Mom takes the books from her hands and flips through them. "Ohhh, these are some good choices."

"How much do I owe you?" June pulls out a small wallet from her back pocket that only holds a couple of cards and some cash. It's the first time I've noticed she doesn't carry around a big bag with her like most of the women I know. Hell, I think my wallet has more than that in it.

Immediately, Mom waves her hand and dismisses the idea, handing the books back. "Everyone in this town treats this place like the library since stupid old Burt won't let the actual library have a romance section. I'm not going to start charging for these books now."

The two argue back and forth for a while before June pulls a crisp twenty from the little wallet and shoves it into the tip jar sitting on the counter. The whole interaction has me fighting a smile. Not many people stand up to Mom, not even me.

"If you insist on giving me money, at least let me recommend a little something to go along with those books." Mom practically sprints behind the register and disappears.

June and I exchange curious glances and trail after the matriarch of my family. She is on all fours, reaching down into a hole beneath the cash register, one of the floorboards pushed to the side.

"For that particular series, I would recommend some of these big blue dildos." She piles the aforementioned dildos in front of us, and I stare in horror. June obviously tries to hold back a laugh. "Or, if you are more of a clitoral stimulation girl, I have a few of the Womanizers left."

Burt threatened to shut the cafe down if she continued to dole out the vibrators to her customers, but she obviously didn't listen. "Mom, I thought you stopped selling those!"

"Oh, I have for the most part, but I have some loyal customers that I still keep some supplies for." Roxy looks up at June. "Which one would you like, dear?"

The idea of June bringing a vibrator obtained from my mother back to my house is confusing my body and brain. June using a sex toy in the room next to me? Hot. Knowing she got that vibrator from my mother? Revolting.

"Honestly, Roxy, thank you for the thought, but I'm good." June finally lets a nervous giggle loose and is distinctly avoiding my eyes. "I'm, um, covered on that front."

Does she already have toys at my house? That thought is not nearly as confusing and just downright arousing.

"Okay, Knox," June says. "Can you take me to check on Daisy? This is the longest I've gone without seeing her in years." June walks right past Mom as she shoves the contraband back into the floorboards, grabs my arm, and pulls me toward the door.

Quickly, I break free from her grasp, not able to handle her skin on mine at the moment, and backtrack to pick up my laptop and shove it into the cruddy old book bag it lives in ninety-nine percent of the time.

We're out the door and halfway down the sidewalk when the cafe door swings back open, Mom holding the twenty above her head. "You aren't paying for coffee the rest of the time you're here, young lady."

"She's serious about that, you know." We make it to the truck and I pull open her door, holding it for her as she steps into the passenger seat. "She'll wrestle you to the ground before taking any more money from you."

I stand in the open door of my truck, leaning in far too close to this strange woman. Why did I open the truck door for her? It was instinct. Natural.

"You know, she's spry enough. I don't doubt she would." June looks up at me from her seat. Her cheeks are dimpled with a wide smile, her eyes bright from a day of exploring this town I've been in my entire life and find rather boring.

As natural as opening the door for her was just a few moments ago, looking away from her now is just as unnatural. June is so unlike anything else I've ever seen, so different from anyone I know. I just want to see what she does next.

With effort, I force my eyes away, looking down the street where we'll be driving. When I look back, June is still gazing at me. "Thank you for bringing me into town today. I know carting around a tourist all day probably isn't what you wanted to do with your time."

"I'll live." I close the door, making sure not to slam it too hard.

What the hell is happening to me?

Chapter 11

June

A heavy weight drops to the pit of my stomach.

The sky behind the rundown garage is just starting to turn a pink-orange as the sun makes its way toward the horizon. It would almost be picturesque if my poor Daisy weren't sitting in the middle of the scene looking like two tons of crap.

Simone managed to get most of the pumpkin guts off the van's exterior with only minimal damage to the paint job, thank god. That part of the project had been a labor of love. I stenciled those damn flowers on there for days. A few touch-ups might be therapeutic, though.

The tire that had blown is now gone, and that side jacked up. The solar panels are down, probably stored in the garage somewhere, and hopefully getting ready to reinstall. There are still bits of pumpkin sticking out from the air vents in the front. I guess I should be happy this model holds the engine in the trunk. Otherwise, this would have been a much bigger problem.

I hold back the tears that burn behind my eyes. Crying over my van is silly. She'll get fixed and run just fine. If I could figure out how to get the pile of crap that had been sitting in a storage unit for decades going with nothing more than YouTube, a lot of cursing and bruises, and the entirety of my savings account, I have no doubt an actual mechanic can bring her back from this.

Running my fingers along the smooth exterior, the tears win. A dull thud behind me lets me know Knox has broken his promise to stay in the car.

"Simone's really good at fixing cars. You don't have to worry." His tone isn't nearly as rough as it had been yesterday. Or hell, this morning. I guess a crying girl will make any guy go soft.

I turn away, trying to discreetly wipe away the tears that refuse to stop now that they've gotten going. Apparently, I'm not fooling my host, though, because he gently puts one hand on my shoulder and squeezes.

"She'll have it running better than when it first rolled off the assembly line, I promise." His voice is barely above a whisper. The low timber makes something clench inside me. Why does his attempt at reassuring me make me cry even harder?

The need to turn around and bury my face in his chest is overwhelming. To let the past twenty-four hours, or if I'm being honest, the last few months, wash out of me with my tears. To just stand there and let this big mountain of a man hold me as I collapse is such a tempting thought.

But that isn't what I do. Isn't who I am.

I don't let my emotions get the better of me. I don't rely on other people. I pick up, and I keep moving. That is who I am. It's who I've had to be my entire life with two parents who didn't know the first thing about comforting or reassuring their daughter. Instead, I was left to figure out my own problems.

So instead, I nod, take a deep breath, and say, "I know." And I move on. "I'm hungry, how about you?"

There's a tension in the air like Knox isn't sure what to say next. I don't blame him; I'm not making any sense. Crying over a sixty-year-old van one minute and declaring my need for food the next.

"Yeah, I guess I could eat."

Emotions shoved back in all their respective boxes, I turn around and give Knox a watery smile. "I assume since you live on a farm, you have food there?"

"I got food."

"Perfect. Let's go eat your food." Without another glance back, I march toward his truck.

* * *

As we pull up to the house, I search the area for evil-in-goose-form and am relieved to find he's nowhere in sight. Even without any trace of the demon, it doesn't escape my notice that Knox sticks right by my side on our way into the house. He's like some big bodyguard, but the only harm he's protecting me from is of the avian variety.

Daisy has been the only home I've had for so long. Walking into a house at the end of the day is altogether strange. But not unwelcome.

My stomach grumbles as we walk in the door. I've had nothing but pastries to eat all day, which is a wonderful way to spend a day, but not very practical. I need actual food. "Show me what you got, farmer."

Knox smiles uncomfortably and crosses to the fridge. I get the feeling he doesn't get guests very often. He pulls open the door and bends down to peer at the neatly stacked shelves filled with food. I take the opportunity to appreciate his ass in those jeans.

"I've got some leftover lasagna from family dinner. I meal prepped Shepard's Pie for the week. Or I could break out one of my jars of chili from the pantry. Thaw some burgers." He cranes his neck around from his perusal of the contents of his fridge.

My gaze snaps up to the ceiling, and I hope to god he didn't just catch me checking out his butt.

"What sounds good to you?" Is that a little amusement I hear in his voice?

"I'll go for the Shepard's Pie." In an effort to act totally normal, I hop up on the kitchen island counter, which seems to startle Knox. "Sorry, does this bother you?"

He shakes his head and pulls two glass storage containers with individual portions of Shepard's Pie inside. "Just not used to having anyone but me here." Plates appear from one of the cabinets, and Knox dishes up a portion on each. "You already know Mom, Delia, and Orion have dinner here once a month, but that's about it. We're all busy."

Thinking about this big house with no one but Knox roaming around sends a wave of sadness crashing over me. This place is meant to have kids running around everywhere.

"That reminds me, do you know if your brother is a content creator on TikTok?" Knox turns to me with one eyebrow raised and, if I'm not mistaken, a sudden air of annoyance. "Once I got reception back this morning, I went on TikTok and one of the first videos was one of this guy who cuts down trees out in the woods and makes them into furniture. He never shows his face, it's always hidden in some weird way, but I swear it could be your brother. This guy is crazy popular, he puts my follower count to shame."

"Orion? On TikTok?" Knox lets out an uncharacteristic laugh, bracing his hand on the counter for a moment to steady himself. "He's even more remote and technologically ignorant than I am. It couldn't possibly be him."

"Maybe I'm wrong. I mean there *is* probably more than one long-haired redhead in the world."

After putting the plates in the microwave and pressing start, Knox turns to look at me with a skeptical but amused smile. "I promise, he's practically a hermit. No way he's out there putting himself on the internet. Can I see one of these videos?"

"Sure, if you had internet here like a normal person, you could. But I've got zero reception." I hold up my phone with zero bars as proof.

Knox rolls his eyes but gives me a glare that isn't nearly as sharp as it had been yesterday. Maybe I'm growing on the guy.

"If it is him, I'd give him so much shit for being a fucking influencer." Knox shakes his head firmly. "No way, can't be him."

"And what exactly is wrong with being an influencer?" I pull up one eyebrow, ready to take him down a peg or two if he tries to slander my profession.

"Moving on." The microwave dings, and Knox pulls out our plates. But instead of taking them to the dining table, he places mine on the counter next to me, then leans back on the island behind him so we're facing each other. "What about you? Any siblings?"

I shake my head, picking up the plate and blowing across the top of the food. "Only child. Parents didn't want more. Hell, they didn't want one." I don't know why I say that. I don't talk about my family to many people. There are only a few friends I've trusted with my story, and to be honest, I've lost touch with most of them. My nomadic lifestyle makes it hard to keep up with people who have settled down.

Now it's my turn to deflect and change topics. "So, how many of the ingredients in this are from your own farm?"

Knox shrugs, looking down at his plate. "Most of them. The mushrooms are from a couple at the farmer's market specializing in fungi. The tomato sauce and herbs are all from my gardens that I preserve to use after growing season. The family and I all go in on a cow each year and split the meat, so that is local, too. Everything I use, I try to get from other farmers. Got to support my peers and all that. They do the same for me."

"That's awesome. I can't cook. As you witnessed yesterday. I either burn everything, or it comes out raw. Good thing I mostly eat out on other people's dime or make sandwiches in the van."

A line forms between Knox's eyebrows as he contemplates that bit of information. He looks like he's trying to piece together a particularly complicated puzzle. "How'd you get into what you do?"

"Well, I was going to college for marketing and communications. I got an internship with a little advertising firm in Philly and started a blog for them. Ran all their social media. I had a knack for it, so I started my own channel. At first, I just posted about restaurants and little hidden gems in the city. Then, I kept it up when I went on trips. Before I knew it, I had a following. Destinations started contacting me and asking me to visit them. Once I hit a million followers on Instagram, I quit the job and started doing this full-time."

Now I shrug. I really did just fall into this work. "I used to do more international stuff, but when the pandemic hit, I was grounded. I needed something to keep me busy when I couldn't travel, so I started working on Daisy. She belonged to my grandpa." I fight the hitch in my voice at the thought of the only adult who ever showed any interest in me.

Up until I was ten, Grandpa was my babysitter and confidant. Then Alzheimer's robbed me of the only friend I had in the world by taking his memories. Five years later, it took his life, too. Refusing to let those memories pull me back to the weeping mess I had been at the garage, I continue with my very abbreviated story. "Then things opened back up, and I started going on road trips. That's when I really got my audience. I've got over three million followers now."

"Do you miss the more exotic stuff?"

People have asked me this a lot, and I always give them the same answer. Sometimes, but I love discovering things in my own backyard. But the truth is more complicated. And for some reason, I want to give this man the truth.

"Not at all. I was tired of the constant airports and currency changes. International travel is freaking stressful, even when most of the arrangements are covered by travel agencies or companies that are paying you to be there. I never had a stable place where I felt at home."

I blow on my food some more, even though it's probably perfectly cooled at this point, gathering my thoughts as I do.

"The first time I slept in Daisy, even though it was still parked in my mom's garage, I felt like I had found my home. I know it doesn't make sense to most people, but that van is the most consistent thing I've ever had in my life."

That line between his eyebrows deepens even more. I get the feeling he wants to ask more questions and dig deeper. But I've let him get far enough for one night.

"Where can I find a fork? Or do I have to eat with my fingers?"

"Between your thighs." His eyes grow large, and suddenly Knox is choking on his own tongue. "I mean, they are in the drawer under your legs."

Laughing, I hop off the counter and pull open the first drawer. Everything is neatly in its given place. Forks, knives, and spoons lined up like little soldiers. To the right of the organized cutlery is a stack of neatly folded cloth napkins. He's such a grown-up. I keep my van fairly neat, but most things were just thrown into cabinets and drawers to be rifled through later. I grab a fork for each of us then hop back up on the counter.

"Want something to drink?" he asks.

"Just water would be great. Got to rehydrate after all the walking I did today."

He nods in response and grabs two glasses of water, bringing them over to our setup on the counters.

The house is silent, with nothing but the sound of animals rustling outside and the breeze hitting the windows.

"Okay, Knox Halsted, let's see if that lasagna last night was just a fluke or if you really are a good cook." The first bite explodes with flavor in my mouth. Garlic, herbs, fresh garden veggies, rich meat, and just a hint of wine. It is amazing. I've eaten in literally the best restaurants in the world, but this reheated Shepherd's Pie rivals them all. "Oh my god." I'm not even embarrassed to be speaking with my mouth full. I moan and take another bite. "Dis is so good," I mumble around the second bite.

A low growl reverberates across the narrow space separating us, and my first thought is that the killer goose has somehow gotten into the house. But when my eyes fly open, all I see is Knox staring at me from where he leans against the island, his fork halfway between his plate and his lips. His gaze is so intense it causes a sudden heat to burn in my lower belly.

That look is all hunger, and not for Shepherd's Pie.

"Sorry," I mumble.

He shakes his head and finally takes a bite. "Glad you like it."

We sit eating our food in a strange, loaded silence. I want to ask more about the farm, and I know he wants to ask more about me, but now there is something else in the air besides curiosity. It was there this morning in the truck too.

Want.

I'll admit I've had my share of trysts while on the road. But it has definitely been a while, and the real estate between my legs is letting me know exactly how long it has been.

Knox shovels the rest of his food into his mouth, his eyes firmly planted on the plate, refusing to look at me again. With the last bite, he takes his plate to the sink.

"I gotta go lock up the animals."

Before I can say a word, he's out the door, leaving me alone in his house with a half-eaten plate of food and a million questions.

Chapter 12

Knox

Getting a hard-on because my house guest likes my food is teenage boy shit. I've been fighting the suddenly overeager monster in my pants all evening. But when that moan slipped from June, I couldn't fight anymore. The fact that it was something I provided her that produced that noise? Forget it.

I can't remember ever before eating a meal while my dick fought to get out of my pants. Not a single girlfriend or date has ever elicited that strong a response. But June has an effect on me I can't explain. The only solution was to escape.

The animals have been taken care of, but I can't go back inside yet. I need to give her enough time to finish her dinner, wash up, and get to her room for the night. If I walk in there right now, she'll still be sitting at the table, or worse, she'll be in the shower. In either case, I'm not sure I'll be able to control myself.

Instead, I pace up and down the middle aisle of the barn. I will my still half-hard cock to calm the fuck down. I move around some feed sacks to try and tire myself out. But all I see is June with her eyes closed and blatant bliss on her face.

This is insane. I can't let this woman chase me out of my own house just because she's dangerously curvy and annoyingly likable. Locking up the barn, I hear Cugo in the distance, chasing off a fox from the hen house. Poor fox.

With determination, I stomp across the driveway and into the house. No stopping in the kitchen to take off my boots. House rules be damned. I just need to get to my room without running into my guest.

Thankfully, I make it all the way upstairs and behind my door without seeing or hearing June. Her door was closed, and the hall had the telltale humidity that let me know she did indeed take a shower. The scent of whatever soap she uses hangs in the air, and I'm tempted to leave my bedroom door open so it can waft in behind me.

Safely ensconced in the last safe place in my house, I sit on the edge of the bed, breathing like I just ran a marathon, not walking upstairs.

This is insane.

I have to find her another place to stay. From the looks of her damn van, it still has a few days until it's habitable. In the morning, I'll have to call Rose at the B&B and see if they can make room around the wedding guests. It's either that or doing something I will most likely regret—not because touching June would be a hardship—but because it would be all too easy to make a habit. When she leaves, a certainty I can't deny, I'll be left with a desire nothing else can fill.

Plan in place, I shuck off my boots and stow them in the closet, then strip off my clothes, depositing them in the hamper on my way to the master bathroom. A splash of cold water on my face should help get rid of the boner still taking up far too much room in my jeans. Much to my dismay, it doesn't.

The images I looked at earlier push their way to the front of my mind, making my feeble attempts to suppress the heavy erection futile. For the first time in my life, I regret not taking on the extra cost of internet in the house. If I had just sucked it up and let the fucking phone company run the necessary wires out here, it would be so damn easy to look up her Instagram and jack off to the photo of her from the adult resort.

I wouldn't. No matter how tempting it would be. That would be a step too far in the direction of being a creep.

My dick does need some fucking room to breathe, though. Quickly, I undo the button on my jeans, and the zipper practically undoes itself with the pressure of my dick against it. I'm normally a sleep-in-the-nude type of guy. I don't have to worry about anyone else being offended by my state of undress. Except now I do. I suppose breaking out the one pair of pajama pants I own for the foreseeable future isn't that big a deal.

A rustling noise on the other side of the wall grabs my attention away from my debate about what to sleep in. Is June still awake? Then, a different noise. Something I can't place.

A whine?

No.

A whimper. A frustrated, needy whimper, barely audible through the thick walls of my old farmhouse.

My feet freeze to the floor, my breath stalling in my lungs, trying to determine if what I heard was real or wishful thinking.

There it is again. Something is wrong. Maybe the same something I've been wrestling with all night.

I tell myself to stay the fuck away, but like everything when it comes to that woman, I can't resist. With one tug, I pull my pants back over my dick but don't bother zipping up. I just need to make sure I'm not hallucinating. Then I'll take the world's coldest shower, jerk off, and get the hell to bed.

Before I know it, my goddamn ear is pressed to the wall separating my room from June's. Another whimper. Almost a cry. *Please, please.* Who is she pleading with? A creak of springs as she shifts on her bed. *Knox.* My name, whispered so low that I might be wishing it into the air. But it is quickly followed by a gasp.

All men have a breaking point. June trying to get herself off on the other side of the wall and using my name to do it is mine. Two strides have me out my bedroom door, and two more bring me to hers. The door is cracked. Did she leave it slightly open, hoping this would happen? Hoping I would lose control and come to her? If so, she has no idea what she's just unleashed.

It doesn't take much effort to push the door open and find my ruin and salvation stretched out on the bed, a blanket tossed aside. She's in a T-shirt and panties. One hand shoved beneath the thin cotton, frantically rubbing, and the other hand up her shirt, kneading at one of her breasts. None of it is visible to me. I don't see anything that would be considered indecent by the old biddies in town. But it doesn't fucking matter.

She doesn't stop when I enter the room. Her eyes grow big, and her mouth pops open in shock, but she doesn't fucking stop. A book lays open beside her on the bed.

"I'm sorry," she pants, her fingers pausing at their work. "I'm so sorry. The book is so hot. And the truck earlier. And just your eyes on me at dinner." She whimpers again and shuts her eyes, her thighs press together, her panties lifting and falling as fingers rub what lies beneath. "I left all my toys in the van because I was embarrassed to bring them here, and I can't get myself off without them." She sucks in a breath. "And I just need to come. I'm sorry." She starts to pull her hands away, seeming to realize that she's still going. "I'm sorry."

Her eyes drift down my shirtless torso. I look down at myself, wondering what she thinks of her first real glimpse of my body. I'm not exactly ripped, not in that defined way you see on movie stars and models. Or my fucking brother. I'm built for work. For purpose. Not to be looked at. But she's looking. The room is silent except for her panting breaths.

"Knox," she whispers, and my control officially snaps.

"Don't move." My voice is rough, like I've been swallowing rocks.

Her hands freeze—one halfway out of her panties—the other lying on her soft belly.

I take a step farther into the room, and June sucks in a deep breath. "If you want me to leave, you tell me right now, June. Otherwise, I'm coming into this room and rendering those toys you think you need useless."

"Please, yes, please help me." She's so fucking desperate. For me. For my touch. Nothing I have done as a man has ever brought me that much fucking pride as being needed by this woman.

There is no hesitation now. I'm at her side in an instant, pulling her panties down her thick, lush thighs. "You want me to stop, you just say the word. I'll stop."

"Don't stop." The words say one thing, but her hands covering her pussy say another. "But I haven't shaved in a really long time."

The deep laugh escaping my throat is more in disbelief than out of amusement. "You think I give a fuck you have hair on your cunt?"

Her hips buck slightly, and her legs rub together. June likes dirty talk. Noted.

"Move your hands and show me what I've been thinking about since you fell out of that damn van and into my arms." How has it only been a day? It seems like so much longer and only an instant at the same time.

Once again, she does as I ask. A patch of dark hair covers her pussy. I can see how wet she is despite still standing over her.

"Fucking beautiful." I drag one finger slowly up the inside of her thigh from the knee to just below her pussy. Reflexively, her legs spread wider.

"Tell me what you like. What you need."

June blushes. It takes me by surprise. She's so fucking confident and carries herself with such ease I don't expect her to be shy now.

"Your fingers. I need your fingers inside me. I can never get the right angle with mine."

The bed dips slightly as I climb on, one knee between her open legs and the other on the outside. With the lightest touch I can muster, I stroke over the wet lips of her pussy, getting her used to my touch. Building her back up after my interruption.

"That book does this to you, June? Words on paper get you so fucking wet there's going to be a wet spot left after we're done?"

She nods, biting her lip, her hips pulsing slightly beneath my hand.

I press my middle finger between her puffy lips, brushing over her opening and up to graze her clit. She gasps, her hands clutching at the sheets. I've barely touched her, and she's ready to skitter off into the universe. But I'm not letting her go that easy. This might be my only chance at touching her, so I'm taking my fucking time.

"Spread your legs wider, Trouble."

The way her body responds to my commands instantly is a fucking head trip. The responsibility of my position weighs heavy in my mind, and I swear that I'll get her off and leave her better than I found her.

Once her legs are spread wide, I lay down between them, breathing in the scent of her pussy.

"You don't have to do that. I don't need that, I promise." She's embarrassed to have my face up close and personal with her pussy. What kind of idiots has she been with before?

"Yeah, well, I do. I need it." I spread her open with my fingers and lick her with one long swipe, giving her clit a flick with the tip of my tongue at the top. Her fingers grip the sheets even tighter, and she moans long and hard. "Sounds like you do need it."

"Holy shit, do that again."

Turns out, I'm pretty damn good at taking orders myself. I close my eyes and savor the taste of her arousal, letting it fill my every sense. Taste, sight, smell, touch, sound, I'm completely wrapped up in June. It all mixes together in an intoxicating concoction that has me rutting against the mattress.

When I open my eyes again, they are met with June gazing down at me through a haze, watching as I devour her pussy. Her hands have moved from clutching the sheet to clutching her tits over her shirt. Regretfully I come up for air just long enough to growl, "Show me those tits, Trouble. Don't hold back on me now."

Clumsily, she shoves her T-shirt up under her chin, revealing her chest. They're big and soft with dusty rose-tipped nipples that I desperately want to suck and bite. But I have a mission, and I can't get distracted.

"Show me how you like them touched, June. I want to watch you play with your tits while I eat this greedy cunt."

"Holy shit, how can you talk like that?"

I don't answer her, instead returning my mouth to her pussy. But now I keep my eyes on her, watching as she squeezes her breasts with hands splayed over the pale flesh. Her fingers work down to the tips of her breasts, pinching and rolling her nipples before pulling away and starting the move back over.

Her back arches, her thighs squeeze slightly around my head, and she moans. Not the frustrated moan from before, but a building crescendo of pleasure. Now that she's warmed up, I slide one finger into her sopping-wet hole. She is so fucking hot and soft, I could live in this place, this moment, forever. Her head snaps back, and a scream wrenches from her throat.

There's one.

I flick her clit with my stiffened tongue and add another finger to her cunt. I keep my movements precise and consistent, letting her body lead me. The pads of my fingertips brush a spot inside her that makes her whole body jerk. I experimentally rub that spot, and her hands fly off her tits and instead fist in my hair.

Surprised eyes look down her body to find mine. I rub the spot with just a little more pressure, and she clamps down once again, her grip on my hair tightening as her whole body contracts. Her knees press together, trapping my head between her thighs. Her body undulates, humping my face as I switch to sucking on her sensitive clit while keeping everything else the same, and she screams, pulling my face tighter to her core.

The moment her hold on my hair starts to loosen, I take everything up a notch, fucking her sweet pussy with my fingers, sucking and flicking her clit. Her body twists and squeezes and flails. She can't control her movements any more than I control my desire to get this woman off until she passes out.

Her screams intensify until I start to wonder if my nearest neighbor three miles away may actually hear her.

June whimpers and tugs to get me closer and turns to push me away. I stop everything but stay where I am, waiting to see what she needs.

"No more, holy shit. No more, or I won't be able to walk tomorrow." The words spit out between harsh pants.

"That's a problem?" I give her clit a gentle lick, testing whether or not she's really done. Her body jerks and she gives a plaintive moan somewhere between protest and interest.

"Seriously, I can't take any more." Her head rolls back and forth on the pillow, a few strands of blue sticking to the sweat on her forehead.

Not one to doubt what a woman says when she's had enough, I gently remove my fingers from her body. She looks like a debauched angel with her pale skin flushed and her hair everywhere.

Sitting up on my knees, I realize my jeans worked their way down to mid-thigh during the commotion. June's eyes grow wide, and she makes a weak attempt to sit up. "Let me help with that." She nods to my dick, cum glistening on the angry head.

Equal parts of my brain scream *fuck yes* and *hell no* at the same exact time. There is nothing I want more than for June to wrap her hands or lips around my cock at this moment. But the saner part of me knows that if I let this go further, I will find myself with an addiction to this woman.

"June, getting you off was so hot I came all over the foot of your bed. You don't need to worry about me."

She looks at my cock with one eyebrow arched in amusement. "I don't think he's gotten the message yet."

No fuck. The idiot isn't getting any softer, and I have a feeling despite the sticky mess I made of her sheets, he's going to be mad at me all night long. "He'll figure it out."

Standing, I try to tuck myself back in my jeans, trying not to hiss at the pain, as June pulls her T-shirt back over her chest, yawns, and curls onto her side facing me.

"Thanks." She smiles sleepily, her eyelids already halfway closed.

I don't want to leave. I want to rip off her shirt and my pants, crawl in behind her and spoon her until she falls asleep, then stay there all night.

Which is exactly how I know it's time to go.

Chapter 13

June

For the second morning in a row, I wake to the sounds of a rooster crowing in the yard. Only the novelty has worn off a bit after one of the deepest sleeps I've ever experienced. My limbs and eyes feel heavy, and nearly every muscle protests as I stretch out against the soft mattress.

My movement kicks up the scent of Knox, and flashes of the working over he gave my body last night pummel my brain.

Holy shit.

I can't believe we did that. I've never been that horny in my life and totally incapable of doing anything about it. I'm a self-sufficient, modern woman who has a well-stocked toy collection. A book gets me hot. I take care of it. But between the tension that had been brewing between Knox and me all day and that damn romance novel, I was driven to a need I wasn't aware existed. God, I practically begged him to be my sex toy.

Not that Knox seemed to mind all that much.

I didn't even get to touch him. As wonderful and earth-shattering as the night before had been, it really is a damn shame that I didn't get to hold that rather impressive dick in my hand. Or feel his body press mine down into the mattress. Or kiss him.

Enough obsessing.

I have got to get some content on my pages today or the algorithms are going to punish me for not feeding them. Social media outlets are like hungry monsters. If you don't give them regular sacrifices, they stick you in a dungeon for an unknown amount of time. I depend on my views to help generate brand deals and offers from destinations. It is my entire career, so taking two unplanned days off with no backup posts waiting in the wings is tantamount to career suicide.

The minute my feet touch the floor, a hard hiss escapes through my lips. Yeah, definitely a little sore today. I gather my things, take a nice long, hot shower, and head to the kitchen, ready for what is most likely going to be a very awkward morning after.

Once again, there are a pot of coffee and pastries waiting. How early does this man get up that he already ran out and got muffins, made it back, made coffee, and is probably out on the farm somewhere doing work?

Picking out the muffin with the most crumble topping, I realize they are warm. "Are these freshly baked?" I cross to the oven and put my hand on the door. It's warm. Drying next to the sink are a mixing bowl and a muffin tin.

This man cannot be real. Knox did not eat me out until I saw stars last night, and then woke up early to make fresh blueberry muffins this morning. Tearing off a chunk of the muffin, I pop it into my mouth and almost lose my balance.

They are fucking amazing.

I cross to the fridge, knowing some butter will only make them better. Perched just inside on the top shelf is a brand-new bottle of creamer, which looks like it's from a local farm. It's even in a glass bottle. I grab that and the butter and get to work, doctoring up both the muffin and a fresh cup of coffee.

The muffin doesn't make it more than a few seconds because I scarf it down so fast. With coffee in hand, I tentatively step outside, keeping a sharp eye out for a killer goose or killer sex-machine.

Neither is anywhere to be seen.

I slip my bare feet into the same pair of muck boots next to the door, this time also picking up a broom leaning against the porch wall in case I need to defend myself.

Twenty minutes later, I finally find Knox at the furthest reaches of the property. I must be hallucinating, though. His arms are stretched wide around another giant pumpkin. Is he hugging it? As I draw closer, I realize not only is he embracing his giant pumpkin, he's talking to it.

"Just a little bit more, Smashley. You are doing really fine." He's practically crooning to a humongous gourd.

"If you needed more, you could have just come woken me up instead of harassing an innocent pumpkin."

"Stop right there!"

I freeze in my tracks, heart slamming in my chest, and ready the broom in my hands. "What? Is it the goose? Is he around here?"

Knox rolls his eyes and fidgets with a piece of string in his hands. "No, I just don't want you any closer to Smashley."

With a huff, I lower my weapon. "Seriously, though, why are you hugging the pumpkin? Still hard up after last night? I could have helped with that. I wanted to."

Knox turns bright red from ears to nose and refuses to look me in the eye. "I wasn't hugging her. I was measuring her." He holds up not a string but a very long flexible measuring tape. He pulls a notepad and a stubby pencil from his back pocket and scribbles something inside. "Not bad, girl." He pats the pumpkin on what I am assuming is the rump.

"How big is she?" Yes, even I am referring to the pumpkin by its gender now.

"Closing in on two thousand pounds, I'm pretty sure."

"Holy shit."

He tucks the things in his hand into his back pocket and begins pulling a flowery sheet over the pumpkin. Knox nods, picks up some tools, and cuts vines next to his feet. "Doubt she'll break any records other than my own, but I'm hoping to get her over twenty-one hundred pounds before I need to haul her out to get weighed." He stomps over a few feet and tosses the vines into the tree line nearby.

With his back turned, I inch a little closer to the infamous Smashley. The top of the pumpkin comes nearly to my chest, and I almost feel dainty standing next to her. She is in no way perfectly round. She's got stretch marks and bulges and looks as if she's had a huge meal and just plopped herself down in the grass to digest.

"Been there, girl," I whisper. I gently run my fingers over the yellowish-orange flesh, fascinated by the textures.

Knox comes sprinting back over, actual fear present in his eyes. "Hey, I just said stay back."

"Okay, I get it. I ran into your pumpkin and made it explode. I have apologized a dozen times." I flatten my palm against her cool skin, surprised at how sturdy she feels under my touch. "Besides, I don't have a vehicle with me right now. I doubt I could do much damage to the girl."

Knox shuts his mouth and takes a deep breath. "Just look before you step. You crush a vine at this point, and it could be a disaster."

"Weren't you just snipping some of the vines?"

"Yeah, the dead ones and the ones trying to sprout more flowers. I want all the energy to go toward Smashley, not trying to grow more pumpkins."

I nod as if this makes perfect sense, and I agree with his assessment. "I've never been in charge of another living thing. What person gets to twenty-six years old and has never even had a plant?"

"One that has a busy life traveling the world, I imagine."

Right at this moment, standing in a field that Knox has made come to life with his bare hands, my life seems very trivial. What do I have to show for the last six years? Didn't finish college. Shitty relationship with my parents. No close friends to speak of. My van is stuck in a parking lot across town. Everything I own can be packed up into three duffel bags and a couple of boxes. Three million strangers like my pretty pictures and videos. That's it.

An idea that has been growing bigger in the back of my head for the past few months grows a little more. What if I wrote more than just social media and blog posts? What if I wrote a book?

I brush the thought aside just like every other time. Just because I can write a couple hundred words about some of the most beautiful places on Earth does not mean I can write a whole-ass book.

"Speaking of travels, I have to go back into town to get some pictures. I also managed to get an appointment at the Mutts and Cuts. They are even going to let me borrow a dog." I step away from Smashley, suddenly a little nervous that I might do some damage to the life that Knox has nurtured from nothing but dirt and sweat. "Think I could take the truck, or you still don't trust me?"

Knox looks at me warily. "Still think you're a shit driver. That's the only truck I've got. But you're in luck. I still need to get my order from the Nail and Bail since I ended up at the cafe all day yesterday."

"Seriously? After what I let you do to my body last night, and you won't even let me drive your truck?" Does that make sense? No, probably not. But still, come on.

"Just trying to get on my good side last night then, were you?"

"No, if I wanted to get on your good side, I would have blown you."

Knox stops dead in his tracks and looks at me with more than a little anger in his eyes. "No darling, if that mouth had come anywhere near my cock, you would have seen the very opposite of my good side. You would have seen a very bad side of me."

You will not get flustered by this sexy man and his dirty mouth. Stay the course, girl.

"I'm going to call over to the B&B to see if they can make room for you. It will be easier for you to explore, and we can avoid another—" He looks me up and down, and I really wish I could develop some sort of superpower to read minds. "—incident like last night."

Incident? Really? His eating my pussy like a man starved until I nearly passed out was an incident.

"Oh, it wasn't that big a deal," I say. "You helped me with a couple of orgasms, and we both went to bed. No need to make a fuss."

His eyes darken even more, and I will not look away. "Then we both agree. It would be best for you not to be here tonight."

"Yup, in total agreement."

"Great."

He stomps off toward the house, and I'm left next to the giant pumpkin, still holding a broom in one hand and a quickly cooling mug of coffee in the other. I should be happy to stay at a nice B&B, but the thought of leaving this farm makes me irrationally sad.

* * *

After one incredibly awkward car ride where I sat pressed against the door with my arms crossed like a petulant teenager and Knox gripping the steering wheel like it might fall off at any moment, we finally made it back to town. All my bags are in the back of the truck, so I can move them to the B&B once Knox works his magic with them.

Knox heaves my camera bag from the back of the truck and hands it to me. "I'll meet you at the Nail and Bail in four hours. That should be enough time for you to do your stuff, right?"

"Yup." My whole body is tense from the aggravation I feel toward this man. I highly doubt they have a massage therapist in this town. Probably goes against those decency laws I keep hearing about.

Not wanting to be around him anymore, I turn from Knox and start walking with no real destination in mind. I just need to move. Once I make it around the corner, I take my camera out and start snapping pictures, appreciating the chance to get out of my head and look at things from a different view.

Amoresville is so freaking cute. Every porch is decorated for the fall with pumpkins, hay bales, and cornstalks. I pass by the school where kids run around in the playground, the coats their parents probably insisted they wear today discarded in a pile by the gate.

I find a tiny store on the next block that specializes in antique pens. The owner shows me her favorites and lets me take a video of how she cleans the ones she finds at estate sales. Apparently, her business is mostly online, but she enjoys having a shop. I buy a gorgeous fountain pen for fifty dollars with fantasies of writing in a notebook overlooking a beautiful view.

The view, I imagine, is most definitely not one of the mountains from Knox's front porch.

I grab a thick BLT sandwich from a local deli, make my way to Founder's Park, and sit beside the fountain, eating my lunch. I watch a young couple come running up from the other side of the park, hand-in-hand, with huge smiles on their faces. They stop in front of the fountain, throw in coins, and share a passionate kiss.

Roxy told me all about the local lore and that if you follow this routine, your love will last forever. She and her husband did it on their second date, and they were together forty years before he passed away.

The couple's kiss goes on long enough that I have time to grab my camera and snap a couple of pictures. I already know I'll do a series of posts on the fountain and the mythology surrounding it. I might even write an article about it and submit it to a few magazines I've worked with in the past. It would be a great Valentine's Day story.

The couple scampers away again, giggling as they go, probably off to make out somewhere.

Not going to think about Knox and his mouth on me last night.

My sandwich finished, I ball up the wrapper and stuff it in my bookbag to throw away later. There is just enough time to get some drone footage from here and then walk back for my appointment at the salon.

Then I'll move into my room at the B&B and be done with the grumpy farmer that I've been trying to push from my mind all day.

Chapter 14

Knox

"You slept with her." Mom doesn't miss a beat. The moment she looked at me, those words just blurted from her mouth.

"I didn't."

She squints at me, studying me for a long moment. "Maybe not, but something definitely happened. You have the look of a man who has known a woman's body recently."

"I'm not talking about this with you." I walk behind the counter and grab a mug, filling it with the one pot of drip coffee Mom has for us boring folks who don't partake in her concoctions. "I need to call down to Rose at the B&B. June staying with me just isn't working out."

"Hmmm." Mom continues to stare at me as I pull out my phone and dial. "Doubt they'll be able to help. I heard Lou Anne's in-laws are doubled in the rooms as it is. Not like Rose is running a full-scale hotel. She only has six suites."

"Well, maybe they can triple up. I just need that woman out of my house." A sour feeling churns in my gut at the thought of not having her around. Not seeing her clomp out into the field looking for me with my dad's old shitkickers on her feet. Not being able to hear her softly breathing through the walls of the old house. But that's why she needs to go. It's only been two nights, and not only have I started liking having her around, I know we'll repeat the events of last night.

After a few rings, Rose picks up at what sounds like a very busy B&B. "Rose Manor Inn, how may I help you? No, son, don't touch that teapot! It's an antique!"

"Rose?" There is some jostling in the background, then the distinct sound of a door closing, and the noise dies down a little. "Rose, are you there?"

"Knox Halsted, is that you? Why on earth are you calling me?" Rose is a staple in Amoresville. Every married couple in the town has stayed at her place at some point. I supply her B&B with produce during the growing seasons and help out in her gardens since she has a black thumb.

"Well, I wanted to see about getting a room for tonight for a, um, friend. I guess." There is a muffled crash, and Rose lets out an uncharacteristic swear.

"Oh, Knox, you need to get off the farm more often. I've got a house full of ungrateful—I mean guests as it is. Every room is full with someone sleeping on a cot to boot." Rose mumbles something under her breath about Lou Ann never having very good taste in men that I don't quite catch. "Trust me, no one wants to be here tonight."

"Rose, please. I'll give you the best of the harvest next spring. Free."

"I would if I could, Knox, but short of putting someone in the cellar, the inn is full."

I think about having June stay in Rose's damp basement for a second, but even I'm not that mean. "Okay, thanks anyhow, Rose."

I pinch my eyes shut and think. But it's hard to think when you can feel your mother's eyes watching you from across the room.

"Is having her in your house really so bad?"

No. "Yes. Have you heard from Simone? Maybe she can pick up the pace on fixing the van? Just enough so June can stay in it?"

Mom narrows her eyes at me, a look I know all too well from my childhood misadventures. "Knox Christopher Halsted, you are not going to make that woman sleep in a broken-down van in the parking lot of a mechanic just because you are out of your comfort zone. That is not the son I raised."

Shame washes over me because she's right. I can't do that. And I won't let her stay in that fleabag motel down the road, either. "Is Chuck still squatting in the apartment upstairs?"

"Yup," Mom says as she busies herself, wiping down the tables, picking up mugs, and bringing them back to the bin to wash. "You know how Ruth is. It could be weeks before she lets him come back."

Goddamn, this town and its weird little dramas. "Well, I guess I still have a house guest, then."

A bright smile lifts Mom's cheeks, but she turns her back to me to try and hide it. "Guess you do."

* * *

One thing about living in a small town in the middle of nowhere: we don't have a lot of big box stores around. For big projects, I might make the hour-and-a-half trek to the nearest Home Depot or Lowes, but otherwise, I do all my shopping for the farm at the Nail and Bail. Sam took over the shop from his dad before him, and when he married his wife, Paula, she opened the Mutts and Cuts right next door.

I peek in the large front window of the salon, trying to get a glimpse of June, but she's nowhere to be seen. The heavy door to Nail and Bail squeaks as I push it open, grabbing a flatbed cart to get the chicken feed I'll need to get the girls through the next few weeks.

Sam comes out from the backroom with a toddler in his arms and my brother at his side. "Knox, how's it going, man? It's a rare day I get my two favorite Halsteds in the store."

"Two? Since when am I sharing Favorite Halstead?" Orion flicks Sam's ear, who then elbows my brother in the side.

We all went to high school together, though Sam and Orion were two years behind me. When Orion left for the Marines, Sam and I hung out some. He helped out on the farm a lot after

Dad got sick and I took things over. He's a good guy and I feel bad we don't get to hang out much now that life has gotten in the way.

Sam looks nothing like he did back then. Balding with a big belly, thanks to his wife's cooking, has replaced the skinny kid who tried to start a chess club his sophomore year.

"I'm good, Sam. And ignore my brother, we all know who your favorite Halsted is."

"Roxy." We all say in unison.

Sam and Paula are epic caffeine addicts thanks to their wild bunch of kids. "Which one is this?" I nod at the toddler in his arms. I swear, Sam and Paula have a new kid every time I come in. I think they are up to four now.

"This is Maggie-Moo." The chubby-cheeked girl waves at me and shyly hides her face in her father's neck. I get a pang of something in my chest. I always thought I'd have kids by now. But it never worked out for me. "Her grandma is helping out in the salon today since we have a big-time writer visiting, so Maggie is helping Daddy in the shop."

"I don't know how big-time she is." Is June that big a deal? Some strangers on the internet follow her, but that doesn't make her a celebrity. Right? "She was just telling me about some other guy that reminds her of this idiot." I nod to Orion. "Said the guy has millions of followers. Way more than she has."

Orion seems to go still for just a second, long enough to catch my attention, but moves on before I can pick apart his reaction. "Oh man, has someone finally found my doppelganger? If there are two men this hot out in the world the rest of your schmucks are all screwed."

Sam and I roll our eyes and ignore my brother.

"Well, she's a bigger deal than anyone else that has ever come through this town, anyway." Sam looks over at the mound of supplies I've started forming and jots down each item in his ledger book with the hand that isn't currently holding a child. He still does everything by hand just like his parents and grandparents before him. "If we could even get a couple of people stopping in here a month on their way to the state parks or Penn State, it would certainly help a lot of us in the town. It isn't getting cheaper to live these days."

Yeah, no fuck. I never expected to get rich being a small-time farmer, but there have been some lean years when I had to get side jobs to help make ends meet. But that's fine. I'll work a million jobs if it means I can keep the family farm running even another year.

Thankfully, what started out as a weird experiment, growing giant pumpkins just to see if I could and to entertain Dad, turned into a half-decent side revenue. I know June thinks the whole thing is weird. Maybe it is. But the first year I won money for one of my entries, then the additional cash that came from selling the seeds, helped things get just a little more comfortable in my bank account.

"Speaking of things not getting cheaper." Sam taps his pencil against my page in the ledger. A lead weight sinks to the bottom of my stomach because I know what's coming. "I'm happy to keep extending you a line of credit because we're neighbors, if only in spirit and not actual property lines. And you always bring it even, I know that. But, well, Paula and I are expecting another one of these little monsters—" Sam tickles under his daughter's chin, and she giggles and does the same back to him. "—so I might need you to bring this line a little shorter soon."

"Congratulations, man. I hadn't heard." I do my best to give him a real smile, but the truth is, I don't have the cash on hand to bring us even right now. It sucks having to tell someone you respect that you can't make things good. It's even more embarrassing when your kid brother is standing there to witness it. He has the grace to look down at his feet and avoid eye contact. "I understand. Family comes first. I can get today's order, no problem. But I'll need another month to pay off the rest. I was counting on this weekend's state fair out west to get me by until I can take Smashley for a chance at the big money. That plan fell through, though. The Great Pumpkin Weigh-Off is still in three weeks. I will definitely have all your money then."

One of the ancient floorboards creaks in another part of the shop, and I turn to see June looking at us with round eyes and a brand-new haircut that somehow makes her even more beautiful.

How much did she hear?

"Well, don't you look radiant, young lady?" Sam gives June a wink, followed by Orion letting out an appreciative whistle. I'm not a violent person, but I suddenly want to reach across and give my friend and my brother a quick punch to the face.

Sam is an incredibly happily married man who literally can't stop knocking his wife up. I should not get jealous that he paid June a compliment. My brother, on the other hand, him I can take down if I need to.

"My wife sure does know what she's doing."

June directs her attention at Sam and gives him a sweet smile that would have the unknowing believe she is all innocent. I know better.

June pats her hair. "She really does. It has been ages since I got a cut. I feel like an entirely new woman."

"Knox, have you met the town's special guest? This is June Ammer." Sam is apparently the only person in town who doesn't know June is staying out at the farm. He's never been one for town gossip.

"Yeah, we've met."

June closes the few feet separating her from the sales desk and leans one hip against it. "Haven't you heard, Sam? I killed Knox's pumpkin, and now he's forcing me to marry him to compensate for it." June shifts her attention to me, her eyes twinkling with mischief. "Or was it that I killed your donkey, and you held me hostage in the storm cellar until I broke free? No, wait, I'm a dancer out at the club, and Knox took one look at me, dragged me off the stage, and chained me to his bed."

Okay, that last one piques my interest.

Sam shakes his head, openly amused at the ridiculous rumor mill in this town. "I had not heard that. How much of that is truth?"

"His pumpkin and I might have had a run-in that resulted in my van and home being rendered incapacitated. Knox was kind enough to let me stay with him a few nights since there weren't any other options." June's smile seems to fade a notch. "But with any luck I'll be moving to the B&B tonight. Right, Knox?"

"Actually, the B&B is full to the brim. Rose said she doesn't even have a broom closet for you to bunk in."

"Hey, if you are sick of this guy, you can come stay with me," Orion butts in. "I've got two extra rooms up at my cabin with your name on them."

Sam holds up a hand, stopping all conversation. "Wait, which pumpkin? Not Smashley, right?"

"Seriously, does the whole town really know your pumpkins' names?"

Sam scoffs, disbelieving that June doubts my damn pumpkins' fame. "Of course. The girls have been a topic of conversation around town since Knox started trying to grow the giant beauties seven years ago."

I hoist an eyebrow. "I think you underestimate how little there is to talk about in a town like Amoresville, June." Honestly, I wish the people in this town would find some new hobbies.

"Don't worry, Sam. It was Gertie, not Smashley," Orion supplies.

"Oh, thank goodness." Sam's hand goes to his chest, and little Maggie pats him on the back. "Well, let's get you all checked out,

Knox." He takes the baby from his hip and hands her across the counter to June. "Can you hold her, honey? Just for a minute."

June looks dumbstruck at the small child. "Uh, are you sure?"

In response, Maggie holds her arms out to the strange woman and giggles. As if in slow motion, June takes the child from her dad and holds her at arm's length for a moment before pulling her in to rest against her. They stare at each other for a moment until June suddenly crosses her eyes and sticks her tongue out the side of her mouth, making Maggie giggle even harder.

The whole time, Sam just keeps on writing down all my purchases and typing the prices into his decades-old calculator. "All right, Knox, that'll be five hundred."

June's eyes swing away from Maggie toward me as I pull out my checkbook and start scrawling out the number.

She snorts. "Whoa, a checkbook. I can't remember the last time I used one of those."

Maggie puts both her hands on June's cheeks and pulls her attention back to where the toddler thinks it should be. On her. June melts a little, screwing her face into yet another weird expression that sends Maggie into a fit of laughter.

My chest tightens. I am completely incapable of taking my eyes away from the two girls as they goof off.

"Want help getting that in the truck, man?" Orion knocks my attention away, and I'm grateful. I do not need another reason to be fascinated with this woman.

If only my goddamn heart would get the message.

"Thanks, man." I wheel out the cart and we start hefting the heavy bags of feed into the back of the truck.

"Listen man, let me pay off your tab." Orion says the words without looking at me, keeping his focus on the task at hand.

"No."

"Don't be an idiot. I've got the money, just let me help out." This is a sore sport with us. Orion gets a decent amount of disability from the Marines and makes a good income from his furniture business. He's always trying to shove his money down my throat.

"Dad left the farm to me, I can handle it."

Orion shakes his head as he shoves a bag of clover seed to the back of the truck. "I know he left it to you, as he should have. I have no interest in the farm. I do have an interest in making sure you don't lose our family farm because you're a stubborn ass."

"I'm not going to lose the farm." Rage at even the idea that my little brother thinks he needs to save me or the farm sends blood rushing to my head. "Drop it, Orion. Just because you got to miss out on Dad's entire decline doesn't mean you can buy your way out of the guilt now."

"What did you just say?" My brother turns to me, fists balled at his side. Orion had been in the Marines for a little over a year and a half when Dad got sick. No one truly blames him for not being here during those years, but he still holds a lot of guilt for only making it home a few weeks at a time.

Shame that I'm using that against him does nothing to cool the anger burning through my body.

"You heard me." Somehow we are toe to toe, and I feel the sudden need to let go of some frustration. To blow off some steam.

"Hey, everything okay out here?" June interrupts the stare down between Orion and I. Maggie is still wrapped in June's arms and Sam follows them both out the door, concern on his face.

"Fine." Orion backs down, turning to nod at June. "Nice seeing you again. My offer stands if you get sick of this asshole."

I take a step in his direction, ready to let the punch I've been holding back fly.

"I don't see that happening. Thanks though." June brushes him off and places one hand on my arm. It's a subtle gesture, but Orion doesn't miss it. He nods once more and leaves.

Chapter 15

June

I knew Knox wasn't rich, but I had no idea it could be that bad.

The look on his face when he realized I may have overheard the discussion with Sam was unlike anything I'd seen since meeting him. I've seen him annoyed, angry, horny, and amused. Mostly annoyed, though. But that expression was a hundred percent shame. And it's my fault.

At least partly. I killed Gertie. He was planning on the prize money to pay off his bill at the store. But now he can't because the remains of that pumpkin are painted all over my van.

And, like all things, shit runs downhill. Because I killed Knox's pumpkin, he can't pay Sam. Sam, whose whole family waited on me hand and foot while I got a new haircut and their neighbor's dog got her nails painted next to me. The sweet little girl I've been making faces at for the past twenty minutes while the guys loaded the truck up with supplies belongs to that family.

Will all of their lives be harder because I wasn't paying close enough attention to the road and was maybe driving a little too fast?

"Thanks, Sam." Knox does one of those man nods to his friend. "I'll be by in a few weeks." They exchange some secret man look that must mean they don't want to talk about money in front of the little lady.

Sam holds his arms out to Maggie, and she practically dives into them. "I'll take this little munchkin back."

This was the first time I had held a child. Ever. It wasn't bad. There was no crying or pooping or snot. It was even kind of nice. Fun.

Father and daughter walk back into the hardware store, leaving Knox and me standing awkwardly on the sidewalk. "Do you want to talk about what that was with your brother?"

"Not really." He closes up the tailgate and turns back to me. He takes a deep breath, obviously trying to calm himself down. "Just family stuff, no big deal."

It is an obvious lie, but I let him get away with it. I'm not exactly forthcoming when it comes to my family drama either.

"I like the hair." Knox's rough voice is like one of those thick wool sweaters I bought in Ireland and only wear on the coldest of days. It's a little scratchy, not exactly pretty, but so warm and comfortable that I don't mind the flaws. "Shorter, right?"

"Yeah, Paula took about three inches off. It needed it, too."

"You got rid of the blue." He reaches out and flips over some of the strands like he's searching for the color.

"They were extensions. Long past due for them to come out too."

"I don't know what any of that means."

He drops his hand, but I wish he would touch me someplace else now. Overhearing that conversation has left me adrift. I'm looking at Knox differently.

"It means they weren't real. I had them sewn in months ago and they were growing out. I might come back and have Paula do the real thing before I leave. She's really good at what she does, and I liked having colorful hair."

Knox nods. "It suited you."

Is that good?

Another tense silence passes where neither of us knows exactly what to say.

"Why didn't you take another pumpkin to the fair?" I ask.

Knox tilts his head and looks at me in confusion. "What are you talking about?"

"When I killed Gertie, why didn't you take one of the other ones? You still have two more out in the field, right?" I grip the straps of my bookbag, heavy with all the camera equipment I've been hauling around today. "You could have picked one of them and taken them to the fair this weekend. Why didn't you?"

"Well, Smashley is set to go to the big show. The fair this weekend isn't worth wasting her on." Knox looks down the street. "I'm not sure Lucy would make the drive. I don't think her rind is as thick as Gertie's, even though Lucy is bigger. Gertie was the safe choice."

"Yeah, but you could still take Lucy, right?" What is today? Thursday? They couldn't possibly do the prizes at a state fair until the weekend. "The fair isn't over. You could pick Lucy and take her still."

"June, we don't need to talk about this." Knox swings his gaze back to me, and I see he's shuttered any emotions I might have seen there earlier.

"Sure we do. It's my fault you couldn't go to that fair. My fault you didn't get prize money, and my fault you can't pay Sam."

The red beard covering Knox's jaw doesn't hide the way he's grinding his teeth together. "There is no guarantee I would have won any money. You can stop worrying. Sam will get paid. I always pay."

He's offended. Obviously, I mean, what man likes to be called out on owing his friends money?

"But you could try with Lucy. If she makes it and wins, you could pay him next week. Then you'd be back on track, right?"

Knox turns on his heel and stomps over to the truck, climbing in without another word. I only hesitate for a second, but then I'm climbing up into the passenger seat next to him, not willing to give up on trying to make things right.

"I'm right," I say. "You still could take Lucy."

He turns the truck on and starts down the road, ignoring me. As if that has ever stopped me.

"Knox, tell me I'm right."

"Technically, the weigh-in isn't until Saturday. But even if I got Lucy prepped and loaded in time, there is still no guarantee she'd make it. The Western PA State Fair is just outside Pittsburgh. It's a five-hour drive if I take the turnpike, closer to seven if I avoid the major highways. If I'm right and she has weak walls, one pothole and she could have a crack and be disqualified. Plus, there's the matter of my unexpected house guest."

I can't be another reason this man isn't able to go to that damn fair and get his damn money. "So, I'll go with you. It'll be a great story for my blog. *City girl goes country at the state fair.* I'll post about all the delicious, unhealthy food and the cute animals. People will eat it up." Especially if I can manage to get Knox in some of the pictures. My following is 90 percent female, after all.

"You don't want to go to a stupid agricultural fair in western Pennsylvania, June. Stop it. We're done talking about this."

This man may have eaten my pussy within an inch of my life last night, but he really doesn't know anything about me if he thinks I am going to listen when a man tells me to be quiet. "I'm from Pittsburgh. Did you know that?" Of course he doesn't. Despite our activities last night, he barely knows me. "I actually have some things I need to take care of out there if you don't mind swinging by on our way back."

As soon as the words are out of my mouth, I wish I could stuff them back in like I did all those treats in the salon. I'm not ready to deal with any of the shit waiting for me in Pittsburgh.

But if I have to deal with my demons to make things right with this man I feel responsible for, then that is what I have to do.

Knox glances over for a moment, barely even taking his eyes off the road. "I thought you were from Philly."

"Both. I was born in Pittsburgh. My parents divorced when I was a baby. When I was eight, my mom moved to Philly, and then one weekend a month from then until my eighteenth birthday, I got on a train by myself to Pittsburgh for my dad's weekends. I'm a bicoastal Pennsylvanian." I clamp my mouth shut, willing myself not to bore Knox with my entire life story. What is it about him that makes me want to spill all the secrets I've held close to the vest my entire life?

"Okay, so what's this business you have to take care of then?"

"Family stuff."

I don't want to talk about this. Not with Knox. Not with Mom, who has either given up or can't get through due to the lack of reception in this town. My relationship with my mother might be lackluster, but the one with my father was practically nonexistent.

"I'll make you a deal. You tell me what you need to do in Pittsburgh, and I'll let you come with me to the fair. Tit for tat."

"I believe you already saw my tit. And my tat." I glare out the window, considering his so-called deal. The truth is, I do kinda want to see what the big deal is with these pumpkins. Knox is out in that garden every day. I've seen him jotting in notebooks, taking measurements, and even talking to the giant vegetables. Or fruit, pumpkins are fruit, right?

And maybe a small part of me does want to tell someone about Dad. About what I've been avoiding for six months. Someone who isn't so wrapped up in the whole fucked-up story of my childhood.

"Deal." I take a deep breath, then I close my eyes and let all the shit I've been avoiding pour out like water from a facet. "My dad died six months ago. Massive coronary in the middle of a board meeting for the college he was president of. He left a bunch of assets to me, including his house. I haven't stepped foot inside that house since I was eighteen. I want to sell it, but in order to do that, I have to go meet with his lawyer and sign a bunch of paperwork. I've been putting it off. Mom thinks I should go see the place one more time. For closure. I've been putting off making a decision about any of it, and while I do, it just sits there empty in one of the most affluent neighborhoods of Pittsburgh."

The words are finally out, and I realize my eyes are still squeezed shut so tightly, my forehead aches a little. I open them to find we are sitting in a field; a few feet away is a giant pumpkin I now know to be Lucy. I turn to face Knox, and he looks at me with not pity but understanding.

"That's rough. Welcome to the dead dad's club. It's a shitty club to be in." Knox turns off the ignition, and we sit in silence for a moment, staring out at the field. "I got two rules on road trips."

"Driver picks the music. Shotgun shuts his cake hole?"

Knox gives me a confused look. "What?"

"It's a line from a show. *Supernatural*? Never seen it?"

"No."

"Never mind then." I slouch down in my seat a little, embarrassed both by the random pop culture reference and everything I just told him.

"No stupid car games. No...I spy. No alphabet game. None of that. And I'm the only one behind the wheel. Can you live with those?"

"Yeah, I can live with those." Why does his not making a big deal over my confession make me like him even more? This man is anything but likable.

"Okay. I got to give Lucy another look and clean her up for tomorrow. You might want to go get some rest. We have to leave pretty damn early in the morning." He hops out of the truck, walks over to Lucy, and pats her, his lips moving, whispering something to her. Seriously, being jealous of a giant gourd is not normal.

Five hours in the car with a man that looks and smells like Knox. What have I gotten myself into?

* * *

What does one pack for a trip that includes a state fair and a meeting with a lawyer?

I barely slept at all, not giving Fred the rooster the chance to rouse me this morning. Instead, I sat in bed all night, packing and repacking the same bag at least ten times.

Last night, I listened as Knox finally climbed the stairs around midnight, paused outside my door for the briefest of moments, and then went to his room, took a shower, and went to sleep.

I wished he had come into my room. Thought about going to his room more than once. But held back each time.

Sometime around two, I dozed off for a while, then woke again at four to the sound of Knox tiptoeing past my room.

Instead of going back to sleep, I pull on a pair of leggings under my customary big sleep shirt and make my way downstairs after him.

Nothing could prepare me for seeing Knox in the dim kitchen scooping coffee grounds into the coffeemaker while shirtless. A pair of jeans sits low on his hips. The slightly round, hard belly that I desperately want to scratch my nails down and his thick, barrel chest have my mouth watering.

"Morning," I say.

His head jerks up, and he spills the grounds all over the floor, cursing a brilliant streak as he does. "What the hell are you doing up already?"

I slide onto one of the bar stools on the island, a little delighted that I managed to take him by surprise. "Couldn't sleep."

He gives me an assessing look, taking my measure like he does those pumpkins. "Understandable. Sorry, I got a shirt around here somewhere." He looks around for the shirt and spots it hanging on the back of the chair next to me.

I pick it up and throw it on the opposite side of the room, as far away from him as possible. "Oops."

Knox shakes his head, an uncharacteristic smile curling his lips as he resumes his work.

"Here I thought there were secret coffee elves that appeared every morning. But nope, just a grumpy, shirtless farmer. I could get used to this."

His ears turn red, a sign I've embarrassed him. "Is it too early for breakfast? I usually have eggs and fruit."

"Sounds perfect." I watch in silence as he pulls a wire basket of eggs from the fridge. The shells are all different colors and absolutely beautiful. "What makes the shells different colors?"

"Different breeds of hen." He picks up a light bluish-green egg. "These are Easter Eggers." He cracks the egg into a bowl and picks up a reddish-brown egg with speckles. "Welsummer." Into the bowl it goes. Next, he grabs a bright white one. "Silkie, though honestly, I got these more because the chickens look cool, not the eggs."

"Do your chickens have names?" I wonder if he talks to them like he talks to his gourds.

Knox whips the eggs together in the bowl a little more aggressively than may be necessary. "Yes."

"You know them all on sight, by heart?"

He sighs. "Yes."

"Do they have a theme like the pumpkins?"

He crosses to the stove, turns on the heat, and puts a heavy-looking pan on top. "Yes."

"I can keep asking the questions, or you could offer up the information."

"Books. The chickens are all named after book characters. Mom started it when I was a kid, and I kept the tradition going."

That makes me smile. His family is something I never realized I had been missing out on. I knew there were families out there that were happier and closer than mine. Hell, the bar for family happiness is so low compared to my family. I know that most families are closer than my parents and me. But the way this family passes down traditions like the farm and chicken names is something I never thought about existing in the world. That families are something to hold close, not run from, is a revelation I honestly never considered. Don't all kids grow up desperate to get away from their parents and make their own way? Apparently not.

"Do you have a favorite chicken?"

"Obviously. Anna is my favorite. After Anna Karenina. She's a Silkie and has great plumage, and she likes me to carry her around during early morning chores." The pan is apparently hot enough now. Knox pours in the eggs and they sizzle on contact. "You can meet her after breakfast."

I get to meet his favorite chicken. I shouldn't be so absolutely tickled by the idea, but I am. "Can I collect eggs? Do you do any milking? I know you don't have cows, but what about the goats? Do you milk them?"

"Nope, the goats are just pets. Rescues mostly from other farms. I just let them live their best lives out in the field and don't bother trying to make an income off them." He grabs some apples from the counter and plops them in front of me with a knife and cutting board. "I assume you can figure out how to cut an apple without killing yourself this time?"

I give him a face that I hope expresses the idiocy of that question. I may not be a farmer and chef, but I'm not completely useless. "Of course."

He leaves me to the small chore and pulls more ingredients from the fridge. But I'm so focused on my task and making sure I don't accidentally cut a finger off that I don't pay much attention to what he's doing. Gradually, the air around us becomes deliciously scented. Butter, herbs, onions, and other ingredients I would never be able to identify in a million years.

"Do you like cheese on your eggs?"

"Of course."

Considering the tension that has been simmering between us for the past few days, the ease of this morning is surprising. I've never lived with anyone but my parents and a few college roommates. But we never did things like cook together or chat over coffee as the sun rose. It's nice. It's something that, if I'm not careful, I could start to crave.

And I'm leaving. As soon as Daisy is ready, I am going to finish my drive to the Grand Canyon of Pennsylvania, stay there for a few days, then figure out my next stop. I haven't thought that far ahead yet. The past few months have all been about keeping moving. It's getting to be my slow season, and I need to figure out if I'm going to make my way south, chase the warmth for the winter, or maybe pick up and start traveling overseas again. It's been years since I got on an airplane. Maybe it's time.

For some reason, none of that sounds appealing to me. I'm pretty sure the reason is sitting down next to me, shirtless, with two plates stacked with the most delicious breakfast I've ever seen.

Chapter 16

Knox

This morning was nice. Amazing even.

Sure, in routine, it was the same as many mornings on the farm. Same breakfast and same coffee. Same chores. But June was with me, and that just seemed to lift everything up to a higher level. She seems so delighted by everything on the farm. Her eyes lit up every time she found another egg under a hen. As if she was a kid on Easter morning and not a lady narrowly avoiding getting pecked by chickens.

I introduced her to all the ladies, and she carried Anna around while I got Lucy loaded onto the trailer Simone brought over last night since mine was mangled in the accident. It was actually hard to get June to put the old hen down so we could leave. Eventually, I convinced her Anna would be fine here without us and would still be perfectly happy in her arms when we got back.

We're slowly making our way to the turnpike, trying to avoid as many potholes as possible to get our cargo to the fair.

I haven't even minded all the questions.

"How did you get into the giant pumpkin circuit?"

June has her bare feet up on the dashboard, her legs covered in a tight pair of black leggings, and a thick sweater that falls just below her butt. She's completely covered, with the exception of her toes, but given how much I have to concentrate to keep my dick under control, you would think she sat naked next to me.

"It started as a curiosity thing. I always saw them at the big agricultural fairs we would visit as a family. Mom used to show her chickens back in the day, and it was a yearly tradition even after she stopped. I always wondered what it took to make these ginormous pumpkins grow. So, one year, I started talking to some other farmers, doing research at the library, that sort of thing. When Dad got sick, he couldn't do as much around the farm. It killed him not being able to work his own land. The pumpkins became a way for him to help out. The first few years we kept the patches closer to the house where his chair could be manhandled over the field. Some of my best memories are of use out there pouring over growth rates and soil amendments."

The corners of my mouth slip up into an unintentional smile. Thinking about those days isn't something I do often. The years between the discovery of the glioblastoma and the hemorrhage that eventually took his life might have been some of the hardest years of my life, but I wouldn't trade those last days with Dad for anything. "Dad loved seeing how big they got almost overnight. He was the one who named them all that first year, only they were all Meryl Streep characters. Dinner nights are Mom's thing, but Dad's were movie nights." I haven't talked about Pop like this in a long time. Now that I am, I can't seem to stop. "You think our dinners are chaotic. You should have seen movie night. Everyone fighting over what to watch and who got to hold the popcorn." The smile melts off my face.

"Then as the tumor made him sicker, as he lost more and more of who he was, growing the pumpkins gave me something to focus on other than his surgeries and the increasingly grim news from the doctors. Mom took care of Pop, Delia took care of Mom, I took care of the farm. Orion was deployed and only made it home a few weeks before Pop died."

I glance over at my passenger and am a little startled to see her looking at me with misty eyes. "Your family sounds incredible. I'm sorry about your dad."

"Thanks. He was a good man. I'm sorry about yours, too."

She shrugs and looks away. "I'm not sure if mine was a good man or not. He worked. He gave me a check for every birthday and Christmas until I was eighteen. When I was too young to stay home by myself, he made sure there was someone to watch me when he was going to be working on his weekends. That was the extent of our relationship."

"Are you closer to your mom?"

"Not especially. I don't think they ever had any intention of having kids, but things happen, and they ended up with me."

June leans her head back against the headrest, staring at the ceiling of the truck.

"When I was born, Dad expected Mom to put her career on hold to be the primary parent. She was an ambitious woman and said no. They divorced when I was two, and that's when my nomad lifestyle began, shuffling back and forth from house to house. Then Mom got transferred to Philly and I rode the train back and forth across the state twice a month. I'm more comfortable being in transit than in a home."

"I'm sorry they put that on you. That's not fair. You didn't ask for any of that."

June nods. "When I was thirteen, my parents got their weekends mixed up, and I ended up on a train to Pittsburgh with no one at the station to pick me up. I figured out how to get a taxi to Dad's house and discovered he was gone at a conference for the weekend. I stayed by myself the whole time, got myself back on the train on Sunday, and never told either of them about it." I keep my eyes on the road, afraid that looking at June now might crack something deep inside me I'm not willing to explore. But I hear a low, sardonic chuckle before she continues. "You're the first person I've ever told."

I never thought heartbreak was a real thing, but that story has my chest tightening. I'm not a parent, yet I can't help but wonder how someone could treat their child like that. How could someone forget to care for their child? I realize it happens every day in far worse ways than what June went through, but it just doesn't compute in my head.

"I think I'm going to read for a bit." June pulls the book from her bag and dives in.

I wish there was something I could say that would take away the pain of her past. The strain in her words, her body shifting restlessly next to me. June might try and write off her childhood as no big deal, but I've spent enough time around my mom and sister to know that she was fighting back tears. I desperately wish I was the kind of man who knows exactly what to say at the exact right time to make everything better.

But I'm not, so instead, I turn the music up a little to cover the silence as she disappears behind the cover of a book.

* * *

"Wow, this is huge!" June gapes out the window at the fairgrounds filled with people, food trucks, exhibits, and rides.

We kept the rest of the drive to the Western PA State Fair mostly light, only chatting about surface-level shit, not going deeper than favorite movies, books, and foods. Now that we've arrived at our destination, June can't stop gawking at the bustle around us.

It takes a while, but we eventually make it to the produce hall, where the official weigh-in and judging for all the contests takes place. I'm not surprised to see we are the last ones to arrive. Everyone watches as we get into our spot, and the forklift comes over to put Lucy in her spot.

The entire time she's held aloft by the straps, I hold my breath. But miraculously, she has made it in one piece, with no scratches or cracks. She's tougher than I thought she was.

June walks around, taking pictures of the whole process, the surroundings, and the other entries. She switches between a big, professional-looking camera and her phone. She talks to people with a huge smile on her face. One I'm starting to learn is her work smile. It is open and engaging and draws people in, but it doesn't have the magnitude of her real smile. It reaches her eyes, but there is still a wall between herself and these strangers.

Eventually, she makes her way back to me. "I want a picture of you with Lucy. Stand next to her."

I roll my eyes but do as she asks. She snaps a few pictures, and a man from nearby taps her shoulder. "Get in there with your husband, and I'll take one of both of you."

I go to correct him, and June cuts me off. "Thanks so much!" She hands him her phone, shows him what button to hit, and jogs over to me.

I'm dumbstruck when she picks up my arm and slings it over her shoulder, her own arms circling my waist. "Smile for the camera, dear." She gazes up at me with those big, brown eyes and a twinkle of mischief.

"Yes, Trouble." We both look at the camera, and the man takes a couple of photos and then hands it back to June. "We still have a couple hours until weigh-in results and awards. Want to wander around?"

"Desperately. I'm starving. I want to try everything. And I want to play those games where you try to win stuffed animals."

"You think those are good? Wait until you see the pig races."

Her eyes grow even bigger, and June grips my hand, dragging me out of the huge building where Lucy waits to get weighed.

I've been to this fair every year since I was a kid, so I know the layout by heart, but June insists on getting a map to make sure we don't get lost before the weigh-in. Our first stop is the corndog stand, where she gets a huge, foot-long corndog that I can't watch her eat without getting ideas I should not be having when families are around. I get the deep-fried mushrooms and she steals one from my plate, which I find I don't actually mind.

Once our food is gone, she drags me to the exhibit hall, where we look at all the show animals. I have to convince her there's no room for a rabbit in her van, and she has to convince me there's no room for chickens in the truck on the way home.

Through it all, she snaps pictures of the people and sights. She teaches me how to take photos of her that highlight her best angles for Instagram. Being here with her is like seeing it all for the first time again. Even better, it's like magic.

With stuffed animals won at the bottle toss in hand, we make our way back to the produce hall, ready to get Lucy weighed.

"You look nervous," I say.

She truly does. June is fidgeting with her hair, rocking back and forth on her feet as they hoist Lucy from the floor with a tractor and take her to the scale. The weights are all kept secret until the winner is announced. Then, they'll be posted on a scoreboard over the judge's stand, along with winners for prizes such as prettiest, best color, and roundest.

"I *am* nervous," she says. "You put so much work into this."

I know she's thinking about the money aspect, too, and I hate that she knows the farm is very much balancing on razor's edge margins.

"Looking around, I'm guessing we're going to be in third or fourth, depending on how thick her walls are."

"Really, I thought we would be closer to first. She's definitely the tallest."

"You'd be surprised how deceptive these things can be. If a pumpkin has thick walls, it will weigh more, even if it looks smaller from the outside."

"So, what you're saying is it is bigger on the inside." She looks at me with an expectant, amused expression that I don't quite understand.

"I mean, I guess, yeah."

"Have you never watched any TV? Dr. Who? THE TARDIS?"

"Does the Weather Channel count?"

"I swear, before I leave town, I am sitting you down and making you binge-watch something."

The comment is casual. She doesn't mean anything by it, but it hits me hard all the same. For a while there, spending an easy afternoon with her at the fair, I let myself forget that this was nothing more than a pitstop for her. I don't like how casually she talks about leaving. It's an inevitability, but I'm getting used to having her around. Thinking about the day she packs up that stupid van and heads to her next destination makes my stomach twist into a great big knot.

I should know better. She's not the first woman to pick up and leave when I want her to stay. But she'll be the last.

Our attention is called back to the scale as they slowly lower Lucy onto the platform. June grabs my hand and squeezes when the ropes fall away. I watch the judges closely, checking for any slight facial expression shift.

"Did that guy just raise his eyebrow?" June asks.

She's right. The judge on the left lifted an eyebrow. What does that mean?

"Is that good?" she prods.

"I have no idea."

Thanks to our late arrival, we were the last ones to get weighed in, so we don't have to hold our breaths for much longer. They strap Lucy back up and bring her to her spot next to June and me.

Moments later, a man in a dark blue suit that barely fits over his gut takes the microphone and taps it to ensure it's on. "Well, ladies and gentlemen, thank you for coming out. The dedication you show to growing these beautiful pumpkins is truly amazing." The man picks up the clipboard with the results and clears his throat.

"This was a close competition. Our winner is exactly two and a half pounds heavier than the runner-up. And has broken our state fair record for giant pumpkin. At nineteen-hundred and eighteen pounds, our winner is the Halsted Farm from Amoresville, Pennsylvania."

June screams next to me, jumping up and down and hugging me while the crowd around us claps and cheers. I couldn't have heard right. Lucy wasn't supposed to weigh that much. Her walls are weak. I had decided not to bring her. But June. *June* convinced me I should. And she fucking won.

"Holy shit." I turn just in time to catch June as she launches herself into my arms with a smile so wide on her face that I can't help but return it.

Before I know I'm doing it, my lips find hers. I kiss her hard, and June responds by wrapping her legs around my waist. We're laughing and kissing and totally wrapped around each other.

It isn't until the judge stops next to me with a giant blue ribbon in his hand that I realize everyone is watching us make out over a giant pumpkin.

Reluctantly, I put June back on her own feet and shake the judge's hand. He hands me an envelope with what I know will be a check for eight thousand dollars. It's not the biggest prize money as far as these things go, but it is more than I expected to be walking away with today.

As soon as the judge walks away, we're surrounded by people. I've known some of these growers for years, and they are all patting me on the back and offering congratulations. We talk soil amendments and weather. I even make a few pre-sales for seeds from Lucy.

The whole time, June is sitting on the tailgate of my truck, tapping away on her phone and doing god knows what. By the time everything wraps up, it's dark outside, and the air has turned crisp. All I can think about is that kiss and when I can get my hands on June again.

Chapter 17

June

Watching the realization dawn on Knox that he won is definitely one of the top five best things I have ever witnessed. That kiss was number one.

Knox fumbles with the hotel room key, nearly dropping it before he manages to get it in the slot and swing the door open wide. Me kissing his neck while wrapped around his torso probably didn't make the attempt any easier. The minute we got back in the truck, we were all over each other. I thought maybe all the talk of soil samples and rain would have dampened his enthusiasm. But no. Apparently, winning is big on Knox's aphrodisiac list.

The moment we're through the door, he's spinning us around, pressing me against the wall as his mouth finds mine, then his foot kicks the door closed behind us.

My whole body is on fire. I thought this man's lips worked miracles between my legs, but holy shit, the way he kisses is on another plane. The perfect combination of rough and sweet. He grips my ponytail in his fist, holding me still as his tongue dives into my mouth, tasting me and groaning with pleasure at what he finds.

I grind down on the hard ridge trapped behind his zipper. I've never been so thankful for the thin material of leggings in my life because I can feel each slide of him against my clit. I whimper, and he growls in return.

"I got no goddamn reason when it comes to you."

I don't know what he means by that, but I'm worked up enough that I don't care, either. He turns us once again, breaking our kiss just long enough to locate the bed and make his way there. He kneels on the mattress, crawling us both up to the pillows.

"Take your shirt off," I gasp against his lips.

He doesn't hesitate. Just sits back, grips it by the collar behind his neck, and pulls it over his head. Why is that move so fucking sexy?

I fumble with my own sweater, getting it off in a far less sexy manner. But the minute my head is free, Knox is back on me, our skin pressed together as he devours my mouth. I didn't get to touch him much the other night, so I take advantage now. I run my fingers down his back, scratching my nails against his skin on the way back up. That gets me a bite to the lip that sends a zing straight between my legs.

Knox peppers open-mouth kisses down along my neck, his hands circling beneath my back.

"Such a fucking shame I didn't get to worship these beauties the first time." He flicks open the clasp of my bra; quite the achievement, considering it takes five hook-and-eyes to keep my girls contained. "I will not make the same mistake again." He pulls the bra free and tosses it somewhere over his shoulder.

I expect him to attack them with the same passionate enthusiasm as before. Instead, he kneels between my spread thighs and gazes at them in reverence.

"They're just tits, Knox, they really aren't that big a deal."

"How fucking wrong you are. These are works of art." He presses them together, licking the line of cleavage he creates. "They deserve to be studied. Praised." He sucks one nipple into his mouth, swirling his tongue around the tip until I'm gasping. He closes his teeth around it, biting until I hiss.

He moves to the other one, sucking, licking, biting, playing with the first between his fingertips the whole time. Alternating back and forth, giving both breasts equal attention. Learning what makes me moan and what makes me gasp. It's like he's taking mental notes on how to grow an orgasm best.

"Every single piece of you deserves to be worshipped in the filthiest ways."

I wrap my legs around his waist, trying to get friction against the needy part of me that is pulsing so hard it might be medically considered a second heartbeat. Getting the hint, he pushes his hips down, pinning me to the bed and stroking his covered cock between my legs in long, slow drags.

Rearing back onto his knees, Knox grips the waist of my leggings and pulls them down in one smooth motion so I lay naked beneath him. "Do you know how beautiful you are? I could look at you like this, flushed and panting beneath me, for an eternity."

Something flashes through his eyes, a momentary flicker of some emotion I don't understand. Before I can think about it anymore, it's gone, and his fingers are there, spreading me wide open and making rational thoughts flee from my mind. "Need my mouth on you again."

He grips my hips, dragging my pussy up to meet his mouth so that I am resting on my shoulders and my hips are in the air. My legs drape over his shoulders, and I'm left at his mercy, someplace I am all too happy to be. The first drag of his tongue against my sensitive flesh has me whimpering, a sound that seems to be his undoing because he doesn't waste time. He bands one arm around my waist and flicks his tongue against my clit, then hooks one finger into my wet pussy, fucking me with fast, shallow strokes.

Just when I think it is too much, he adds another finger, and I know that there may not be a *too much* when it comes to this man. He sucks my clit into his mouth, fucking me with his fingers, and I'm screaming the house down with an orgasm that comes on so fast I feel lightheaded from the rush.

Just as the climax starts to ebb away, Knox picks up the pace, swiping his fingers against the spot he found that first night that not even I knew existed. I grip onto the sheets, hoping they will tether me to this Earth as Knox does his best to send me to outer space.

"Knox, it's too much. Oh my god." His hand snakes down my body, gripping one breast and pinching the nipple until another screaming orgasm comes flying from my body.

He mumbles, "Never be enough," before diving back in, adding a third finger that somehow forces me to accept that he's right. It will never be enough.

He twists and grinds his fingers into me, working every angle until I'm swearing and writhing in his arms.

"I need you inside me, Knox. Please." I love that he's dedicated to the craft of making me come, but I don't want to miss another opportunity to give him as much as he puts out.

Instead of responding, Knox sucks my clit into his mouth, giving me rhythmic waves of pleasure that have my focus slipping. But I fight back from that edge, determined to show him what this means to me.

"I'm serious." Jesus, why does he have to be so good at this? "I need you, Knox. Need you filling me."

"Can't," he mumbles against my skin.

I push his head back with a palm to his forehead. "Why not?"

He hesitates, considering his answer. I get the feeling Knox likes to believe he's this impenetrable force of a man, but I can see his thoughts and emotions play out across his face like a movie projected on a screen. "No condoms."

Not a lie. But not the whole truth. "Shit, I don't have any either."

"We don't need them. I can make you come in ways you had no idea were possible." He pulls me back toward him, but I somehow manage to crabwalk back up the bed.

"I don't doubt that. But I don't want this to be a one-way street. I want to touch you. To give you pleasure." I lean back against the headboard, still catching my breath from the interrupted orgasm. Knox's eyes track up and down my body, taking in every detail.

I'm not a skinny girl, not by any stretch of the imagination. I have stretch marks and rolls and imperfections aplenty. And not one of them means a goddamn thing to Knox. He's looking at me like I am the most gorgeous thing he's ever seen.

And he still has his goddamn jeans on. This man has been face-planted in my pussy on two separate occasions now, and I can't even get a finger on his cock. What the fuck?

"Bringing you pleasure gives me pleasure." Knox's gaze falls to the space between my legs as I let them fall open ever so slightly.

"You don't think I'm the same? I'm not some pillow princess who likes to sit back and be a passive participant." I run my fingers up the inside of my thigh since it's obvious I have his attention. "You may not know this yet, but I'm good with my hands." I slide my finger between my very wet lower lips, sliding it over the sensitive bundle of nerves Knox has become very intimately familiar with. "Not bad with my mouth either." I remove my finger from my pussy and draw it up slowly to my mouth, sucking the juices from it while I look Knox dead in the eye.

"Motherfucker. What are you doing to me, Trouble?"

"Nothing. Yet. Want me to?"

"More than you can possibly know." He swallows hard, his prominent Adam's apple bobbing up and down. "But if I let go with you, I'm not sure I can hold back. I'm not sure I'll recover."

"I can handle it." I spread my legs farther apart. "You want any more of this? Of my pleasure. I want you naked, and I want to be able to do the things to you that I've been fantasizing about since you caught me falling out of my van."

Idly, I play with my nipples, not shying away from the heated stare he gives me in return.

"Or you can sit there and watch as I take care of things myself. With no help from you." I may not have known him for long, but I know he won't touch me again until I say he can. I'm not sure I've ever trusted a man to follow through on that in my life.

"I knew you were trouble." Knox stands from the bed, making quick work of his jeans. The moment he stands back up to his full height, I get my first real look at the man in all his glory. He's the very definition of thick. Thick chest, thick arms, thick thighs that practically beg to be straddled. Everything about him is made for work on the farm. "Okay, Trouble, have your way."

Oh, I plan to.

Knox crawls back onto the bed, but instead of attacking me as I expect, he lays flat on his back beside me, his cock pointing straight up at the ceiling like a divining rod. "Climb on, June."

What? "But we don't have condoms."

Knox chuckles. "You aren't gonna be riding my cock, Trouble. My face. You thought just because you got to play your way meant I wasn't going to get my favorite treat, too?"

Holy shit. And he thinks *I'm* trouble? I'm not exactly inexperienced, but I've never done this. "Are you sure? I don't want to hurt you."

He smirks. "I've never been so sure of anything in my life. Now get that pussy where it belongs before I lose my patience and put you there myself."

Curiosity wins, and I clumsily position myself hovering over Knox's mouth, my own face getting up close and personal with what might be the most impressive dick I have ever seen.

I've barely settled myself when Knox hooks his arms around my hips and pulls me down until I am fully seated on his mouth. And then he gets to work. His tongue is everywhere. Licking the insides of my thighs, flicking my clit, piercing into my painfully needy cunt.

A loud thwack fills the room at the same time as a sting spreads hot over my ass. "You talked a good game about wanting to give as good as you got, but look at you know. Struck dumb with one lick of my tongue. Get that smart mouth moving, Trouble."

That arrogant son of a bitch. I'll show him who's all talk. I grip his thick cock in one hand and angle it up toward my mouth. At the same time, he starts in on my pussy again. Experimentally, I dart my tongue out to lick around the fat head of his cock. His taste explodes in my mouth, salty and smooth. Earthy. He's fucking delicious, and I want him filling me in every way. But this is what I get for now, and I plan to make the most of it.

His own ministrations between my thighs stutter from their rhythm when I draw more of his length into my mouth, stroking the base of his cock with my hand.

So, he isn't completely immune.

He pierces a finger into my dripping pussy, and I pull my mouth up his shaft, sucking my cheeks around his girth as I go. I drop back down, making another inch of progress to get him all the way to the back of my throat.

A groan vibrates through his chest and feminine pride I've never felt before slips through my veins. Bringing this man to the brink is going to be the most addictive drug I've ever known. I can tell already.

I pull his cock from my mouth and lay it flat against his belly, licking a long line down the vein that stands in stark relief on the underside. His hips pump up off the mattress once, and that uncharacteristic loss of control has me grinding against his face in reward. My mouth meets his balls, and I suck one into my lips, letting it audibly pop out as I release it.

"Fucking hell, woman." He slaps my ass in return, but I'm honestly not sure if it is a punishment or a reward. I'll take it as either.

With a smirk he can't see, I return my attention back to his cock, this time taking it in as far as I can and then forcing it to go just a little bit farther until I gag and retreat.

Knox must realize he's losing the game of chasing the orgasm because he takes a deep breath and gets back to treating my pussy like it is his favorite meal. He puts his palms on the inside of my thighs, prying my legs open wider and fucking me with his tongue. The sensation is so amazing I accidentally let his cock fall from my mouth as I pant against his hip, trying my best not to come yet. I want to stay present. Want to show this man he doesn't know who he is messing with.

With effort, I ignore my own orgasm, barreling down on me fast, and plunge his cock back into my mouth, working it up and down with wet sloppy sucks.

I get another slap to my ass and scream around his cock, but this time I refuse to let him go. I cup his balls in one hand, weaving my fingers around them in gentle patterns while bracing myself on the bed with the other hand. In a rhythm now, I bob up and down on his length. Every muscle in his body begins to tense beneath me, and I know he's getting close. Either that, or I really am suffocating him. The man is so fucking stubborn I don't think he would stop even if he was about to expire from lack of oxygen.

He plunges two fingers deep into my pussy, brushing the rough pads of his fingertips against the spot inside me that has stars exploding behind my eyelids.

I can't hold it back anymore. Can't fight the rising tide of pleasure threatening to crash over me and pull me under. But if I'm going down, so is Knox. I cup his balls in my palm and press two fingers against the sensitive spot just behind them. At the same time, he begins fucking me hard with his fingers, sucking my clit with deep pulls.

I detonate. Giving up the fight against my orgasm, I let it wash over me in waves of ecstasy. Each new surge of pleasure runs into the next, and I can't tell if this is all one long orgasm or a series of them.

Determined to give just as good as I got, I suck Knox's cock to the back of my throat and swallow, trying to take him as far down in my throat as physically possible. Tears leak from the corners of my eyes, but I breathe through my nose the best I can. I'm rewarded by a deep rumbling moan around my pulsing clit. Warmth coats my mouth as Knox releases his own orgasm into my mouth, which I eagerly drink down. It all becomes too much, and I let him fall from my mouth, still spilling his release and probably getting it absolutely everywhere.

I can't muster the energy to care, though.

My entire existence has been reduced to atoms crashing against each other. Oxygen rushes in and out of my lungs in a torrent. Blood surging through my veins. Aftershocks rip through me, my muscles twitching. I am nothing but a sensation. Something as common as logic has raced out the door to be lost somewhere else out in the real world. Inside this shitty motel room, I give into the bliss of being with this man. I allow him to gather me in his arms, positioning me until I'm curled on my side with my back to his chest.

The excitement of the day, the incredible orgasms, it all presses down on me as my eyes slip shut. In that hazy space right before sleep takes over, a thought drifts through my mind that I would shut down at any other time.

Why do Knox's arms feel more like home than any place I have ever been before?

Chapter 18

Knox

Last night should not have happened. True, I said that after the first time and only managed to keep my hands off June for two days. But last night has to be the last time. I can't keep touching June, or worse, sleeping with her curled against my side and expect to make it out of her short stay in Amoresville with my heart intact.

But even as I say the words to myself over and over again, I'm also looking for another reason to touch her.

I can't even blame it entirely on the adrenaline of taking home first place. No, it had been building all day. Each time she grabbed my hand or arm to pull me in the direction of something else she wanted to see or do weakened my defenses until they were all but decimated.

"Do you want to grab something to eat?" I ask.

All morning, she's been quiet as a mouse. At first, I thought it was because of what happened between us the night before, but I'd be an idiot to miss her getting more anxious with every mile we drove toward Pittsburgh.

She's nervous, and I have no idea how to make her feel better. Emotional maturity has never been one of my strong suits. Just ask my ex-girlfriends and my sister.

"No thanks." She keeps staring out the window.

Cars pass us on the way into the city with confused expressions on the drivers' faces. Not every day you see a pickup hauling a giant pumpkin in Pittsburgh.

The only reason she's doing this is because she wanted me to come to the fair. And she was right. Now, she's going to put herself through something traumatic because of me. The thought makes me want to punch a hole through the dashboard.

"If you aren't ready to do this, you don't have to," I say. "We can keep driving. Go back to the farm. I'll cook you dinner."

Finally, she turns to me. "No. My mom was right. I need to stop running from this." She reaches across the seat and picks up my hand from where it rests on my thigh. "But I'm glad you're here with me."

I'm supposed to make her feel better, but with that one gesture, June has made me feel like the most important person in the world. She doesn't let a lot of people into her life. Even without her telling me, she obviously doesn't have many friends. Hell, her best friend is a van still stalled in a garage five hours away.

The rest of the ride is spent in uneasy silence, with us hand in hand. The GPS takes us down busy streets until we hit a section of the city called Squirrel Hill. There are huge historic homes with wide expanses of pristine lawns lining each side of the narrow, winding streets.

I fucking hate perfect green lawns. Such a waste of good planting space. Grass is a useless crop.

I never thought about whether or not June was rich. But pulling up to the grand stone house, it's obvious she grew up wanting nothing except her parents' love.

I pull into the driveway and shift into the park. We both sit staring at the huge, cold-looking house. "Dad was the president of the university. He loved that school more than anything. Took a lot of pride in what it meant to run a huge university that turned out brilliant young minds. I think he was insulted when I decided to go to a college in Philly." She might be talking to me, but she couldn't sound further away.

Behind us, another car pulls in. An older woman makes quick work of parking her expensive car and making her way toward us. Reluctantly, June climbs down from the truck. She didn't ask me to come in per se, but there is no way I'm letting her go into the house of bad memories without armor.

"Miss Ammer, it's so nice to finally meet you." The woman holds out her hand, and June takes it with a weak smile.

The two couldn't be more different. Where June is soft sunshine, this woman is hard efficiency. Exactly three pumps of their hands and the woman drops the handshake and pulls out a pile of papers. "I have the listing all ready to go. I don't expect it will last long on the market. Properties in this section of Pittsburgh have been highly sought after."

Christ, money signs are practically spinning in the woman's eyes. She didn't even offer her condolences at the loss of June's father.

The realtor turns on her pointy high heels and sashays to the front door. Instead of a key, she inputs a code on the high-tech-looking lock, and the door swings open. Her heels clack against the marble floors as she retreats into the house.

June and I stand on the stoop, staring after her without moving. "Take as long as you need." I lace my fingers with hers, giving them a soft squeeze.

Her shoulders rise and fall dramatically as she takes in a slow, deep breath. "I can do this." Spine steeled, she steps into the house, her head swiveling left and right, taking it all in.

I don't know exactly how long it's been since she stood in this very place, but I know it's been a long time.

"It's exactly the same." She runs her fingers along the intricate railing of the stairway leading to the second floor. Someone must be coming to clean the place because there isn't a speck of dust.

I look around for signs of the life that was lived here. Family pictures. A sweater draped across a chair. Papers left in a stack, waiting to be sorted. But there's nothing. The furniture looks as if it has never been touched. The walls are bare except for framed degrees and a few generic-looking pieces of art.

I can't imagine a child living here. I can barely imagine a human living here.

The realtor bustles in. "We have an auction company coming in to price and list the furniture and more impressive pieces of art. There are a few pieces the university would like returned to their collection. My assistant boxed up anything that looked like it might be sentimental and they are on the table."

I glance in the direction she points and notice two small banker's boxes with the lids neatly resting on top. A whole life, and that is all the evidence. I don't think I've ever seen a sadder sight. It took months for Mom and me to go through all of Dad's crap. Only now, those drawers full of stamps and silly notes don't seem like crap as much as evidence of a life well lived.

"Thank you. I will take a look." June nods, tries to muster a professional smile, but fails and continues to look around the house she grew up in for a portion of her childhood.

"So now the only thing is to sign a few documents, and then I will let you know when we have an offer."

June hesitates. I glance over to see if I can figure out what's going on in that complicated head of hers, but she just looks lost.

I turn to the realtor and she seems to notice me for the first time since arriving. "Excuse me, I didn't catch your name."

"Oh, yes, of course, I am Maxima Seilly." She doesn't bother holding her hand out for me to shake. She knows the only person here who holds the power to grant her a big paycheck is June. Plus, she probably thinks my hands are dirty.

"Maxima, can we have a minute to look around?"

She looks at June and nods slowly. "Of course. I'm so sorry. I should have guessed this would be difficult. I'll just make a few phone calls out on the patio."

As soon as the realtor leaves the room, June's entire body seems to deflate. That straight spine curving in exhaustion. "It is so weird being here after all these years. I keep expecting to hear Dad's voice on a call in his office."

"Felt the same way after my pop passed. I could swear I heard him laughing every time I closed my eyes."

"I'm not sure I ever heard my dad laugh." She turns to look at me with profound sadness. "Not a real laugh anyway. Just that fake chuckle he gave his colleagues when they told lame jokes over scotch at fundraising dinners."

With my hand still in hers, she turns, and I follow her through to the front hall again. "The only time he really paid attention to me was when he pranced me out for those events. Had to keep up the appearance of an upstanding family man even if he didn't really care much about having a family. But we had a silent agreement that if I went to the dinners, sat quietly, and gave polite responses to anyone that spoke to me, he'd leave me alone the rest of my visit to read."

We make it to the bottom of the stairs and climb to the second floor. "I spent most of my time here in my bedroom." We make it to the first door at the top of the stairs, and June takes another steadying breath before pushing into the room.

It's not what I was expecting. The room is painted white, but the bedspread, pillows, and curtains are all a bright, buttery yellow that I know teenage June probably picked out. There are a few signs of the girl she was, stuffed animals and books on shelves. But not a single trophy, no pictures of friends, nothing that says a life was actually lived here. It looks more like a guestroom than some place a teenage girl used to live.

"He didn't change a thing." She looks around the room and picks up a stuffed otter sitting in the middle of the bed. "It's like he never came in here. I wonder if it was out of sentimentality or apathy."

I think she knows the answer to that question.

June hugs the otter to her chest and turns back to me. "Okay, I'm ready."

I walk her back downstairs, and as June and the realtor begin signing each page of a very thick stack of documents, I head outside to give them some privacy.

But the quiet street I left behind just an hour or so ago now has about a dozen kids and parents loitering around the trailer of my truck, all looking at Lucy.

"Hey, sir, is this your truck?" A man in track pants and a bright white T-shirt waves at me from the street.

"Yeah. Is it blocking the sidewalk?" I don't want to piss off the neighbors, even if we are leaving as soon as June is done inside.

"No, actually. Do you mind if I take a picture with my kid next to the pumpkin? It would be great for our Hanukkah cards." He nods to one of the kids, who's wearing a pair of jeans and a flannel, gawking at the pumpkin.

"Yeah, no problem."

I pop the tailgate down on the trailer and help the kid up to stand next to Lucy. The dad snaps several photos from different angles before I offer to take a couple of them together.

By the time they are done, a small line is forming with families from the neighborhood, all asking to take photos with my nearly two-thousand-pound pumpkin. A few try to slip me twenty-dollar bills like I'm a maître d' at a fancy restaurant.

I don't know how many families I've taken pictures of when June reappears from the house. She looks tired but brightens when she sees the small commotion we've made in the sleepy neighborhood.

"Who knew you were this popular?" June laughs as an adorable little girl in a blue dress hugs my leg before running off.

"Not me, the pumpkin. I guess city folks don't see pumpkins this big very often."

"No, they certainly don't." Lucy looks at the last two kids, who are trying to hug Lucy and touch their fingers together, and cocks her head to one side. "Have you ever thought about opening the farm up to the public? Letting people come out and see the animals and the pumpkins?"

"Nah. Nobody wants to come to a farm for fun. Farms are for work."

"You'd be surprised. Agritourism is actually a huge thing these days. People like to know where their food comes from and how it's made. And baby animals are always a draw."

I have to laugh because she is absolutely pulling this out of her ass. "You just made that word up, agritourism."

The last of the looky-loos wander off, and I close up the trailer again, covering Lucy in the tarp for the trip back home. "Ready to get on the road?"

June looks back up at the house and nods. "Yeah, I'm ready. Let's go home."

Damn if I don't love the way that sounds.

Chapter 19

June

Fred's call wakes me once again, quickly followed by Knox telling him to shut the hell up or he'll find himself at the bottom of the freezer at the local food pantry. I smile and roll over in the bed, appreciating the sun pouring into the window.

I should go out exploring more today, but the road trip and seeing my father's home for the first and last time in years has left me drained. Maybe I will just hang around the farm and see if I can help with some chores. Do some writing. Edit some photos.

Another trip to town will be necessary so I can post all the content I've been gathering, but maybe I can have Roxy come out and grab me so I don't have to bum a ride from my host again.

Just like each morning since I've been here, I find coffee ready to go in the kitchen, and this time, a stack of pancakes with fruit and fresh whipped cream in the fridge.

If farming doesn't work out for Knox, he really should think about opening a bed-and-breakfast.

Next to the food and coffee is a little Post-it note that says, "Wi-Fi Network: BigBumpkin Password: ILikeBigGourd$."

He got internet?

I grab my coffee and make my way outside, where Knox is unloading Lucy from her adventures.

"You got internet? For me?" The words come out like an accusation.

"No. It was long past time I got it out here." He doesn't give me a glance. He just keeps up his work of unhooking Lucy from the complicated-looking hoist he's rigged up.

"Bullshit. Would you have even thought about it if I hadn't been here?"

He doesn't answer.

"You had internet installed while we were gone, so I would be able to do work from the house."

Why do I sound like I'm mad? I'm not. I'm confused. My presence here has seemed like an inconvenience. Yet he went out of his way to try and make my life easier when I will probably only be here a few more days.

Knox shrugs. "It's not that big a deal."

But it is. Maybe it's the residual emotions from being at Dad's house yesterday, or maybe it's just nice having someone take my needs into consideration, but suddenly, I can't stop from launching myself at Knox.

Our bodies collide, Knox stumbling back a couple steps before finding his footing. I wrap my arms around his neck in a hug so tight I might actually be restricting his oxygen intake.

"Thank you." The words come out softer than I intended. A thick whisper that almost sticks in my throat.

After a moment, Knox's arms close around my waist, and he holds me tight against him. "You're welcome." The words sound as if he has to struggle to get them out, and I'm not sure if it is because of my chokehold on his neck or because he is having as strange an emotional reaction as I am.

We are two fiercely independent people who rely on no one but ourselves. I don't know any other way to be.

My earliest memories are of being left behind by my parents in the care of strangers or to fend for myself. I had no choice but to take care of myself. Being back in the house yesterday made all those lonely feelings rush back. Such a stark difference from the warmth and comfort I felt in Knox's arms at the hotel and now in the middle of a farmyard. Logically, I know not every family is like mine.

All I have to do is see Knox with his mom to realize they are nothing like my family. The way he holds me so close to his chest.... I've never been held like this in my life. Hugs weren't something that happened in my family. The most affection I can remember was a stiff pat on the shoulder when I achieved something outstanding that they couldn't ignore.

After a moment, Knox slowly releases me to the ground, laying a soft kiss on my forehead before letting me go and turning back to his work. Despite feeling his warmth and affection deep in my bones, I also sense there is something holding him back from letting himself go.

I debate wrestling him to the ground and fucking him right here in the field—delving deeper into this enigma of a man. But that probably wouldn't be comfortable, both because of the pokey straw covering the ground and my complete lack of experience with emotions.

Instead, I make my way back to the house, excited to take his brand-new Wi-Fi for a spin by posting all the photos from the state fair.

An idea has been percolating in the back of my mind since walking out of my dad's house yesterday to find a crowd of families taking pictures with Knox's prize-winning pumpkin. A way I can help Knox and this farm, a farm I find myself falling more in love with each day.

I set up my computer at the kitchen table, signing into the Wi-Fi with a smile curling the edges of my mouth. I sign out of my Instagram and start putting in the information for a brand-new account. One for the farm. As far as I know, the farm has only had one name, the Halsted Farm, but this account needs something snappier. Something that will be memorable. Pumpkin To Talk About Farm? Hotties and Harvests?

I look around the space, taking in the many framed photos with Knox and his family prominently featured. Everyone is so happy, smiling, making faces. One of his sister flipping off the camera mid-leap into a wide, blue lake makes me laugh. I don't know how I accidentally ended up in this place, but it is one of the happiest accidents of all time.

Happy Accidents Farm. *That's it.*

I make the profile picture a photo of Knox kneeling next to Smashley in the field, the sun at the perfect angle to light his face as he checks some perceived blemish on her rind. The first post is one of the photos I took of Knox and Lucy at the state fair. I do a little research on what hashtags work best for agritourism accounts and start scheduling posts for the next few days.

Once the new account has some content posted, I'll share a post from my account detailing my visit, which should net him some views and, hopefully, follows. I have a feeling my mostly female fanbase is going to love the quiet, grumpy farmer.

Before I leave, I'll hand over the account to Knox, and maybe give him a lesson in running it without me. A hollow space grows in my chest, making it hard to breathe as I think about leaving this place.

There is always a little sadness when I leave a town. That small desire to stay in a magical destination forever. But the magic would wear off eventually. Rubbed out by the daily grind of re-sponsibilities and boredom. The only way to avoid the eventual disappointment is to keep moving. To the next town, the next view, the next group of people showing me the attractions. It is better that way. Better than letting people down or allowing them to let me down.

Or at least that is what I keep telling myself.

After hours of working, a small snack break is definitely in order. Thankfully, there's a bowl of watermelon in the fridge that caught my attention, and I grab it and head out to get some fresh air on the porch. Knox is nowhere in sight, and I resist the urge to look for him. He has work to do, and I need to stop angling for more time with him.

Instead, I sit on the stoop and scroll through all the missed notifications that have been popping up on my phone since connecting it to Wi-Fi. More calls from my mom that I ignore. A few text messages, too. I've had enough parent drama for a little while, so I leave them unread with only a slight twinge of guilt.

Just as I start responding to comments on some of the posts from my last trip, a distinct feeling of being watched washes over me. I glance up from my phone and freeze, hand halfway to my mouth with another morsel of fruit.

Cugo.

I haven't seen the evil goose since the day he attacked me in the driveway. But there he is, ten feet away, staring at me with those beady black eyes. A quick glance around the porch proves fruitless for a weapon.

His eyes shift down to the bowl next to me, still half full of watermelon. Maybe I can throw him a piece and make a run for it?

Just as I am lobbing a piece in his direction, I have a terrifying thought. Is watermelon toxic for Satan-sent geese? I don't like the stupid bird, but I also don't want to be the reason for his demise.

Cugo gobbles up the small piece of fruit, and I quickly type *watermelon toxic for geese?* into Google. Thankfully, the answer pops up quickly. "The high water content in watermelon makes it the perfect treat for your geese, especially in the summer, as it helps to prevent dehydration."

"Huh, so this is your special treat, you little demon."

Cugo squawks at me, and I throw him another piece. It lands a few inches in front of him, and he scuttles forward, picking apart the chunk with surprisingly delicate little nibbles until it is all gone.

Popping a piece into my mouth, I get why Cugo is so enamored. The watermelon is sweet and cold and practically melts in my mouth. The next piece goes to my uneasy enemy-turned-ally.

Once again, I throw it just a little short, and he scrambles closer to snatch it up. Now he's only five feet away, and I do my best not to show fear.

Can birds sense fear?

One for me. Another for Cugo. We continue like that until the bowl is almost gone, and the bird that tried to peck my eyes out just a few days ago is slurping watermelon from my fingers. "You aren't such a bad guy." The words come out low and soothing. Like I'm taming a bear, not a goose. "Just need a little sweetness."

Tentatively, I reach out one hand, stroking the feathers on his head with one finger. They are slick and softer than I expected.

"I knew you were an adventurer, but I didn't take you for an extreme adrenaline junky." The low voice I've started hearing in my dirtiest of dreams floats over from the end of the porch.

Cugo swings his head that way, and I swear to god he growls at Knox before looking back at me expectantly. I give him another piece of watermelon and another pet. "Maybe he was picking up the grumpy, testosterone vibes from this place. He just needed a woman's touch."

Knox grunts and stomps toward us, keeping a close eye on my new friend. The next time I go to grab a piece of watermelon, I come up with nothing but wet fingertips from the layer of juice left over at the bottom.

"Sorry, buddy. Treat time is over." Cugo honks at me in what I think is a not entirely unfriendly manner and waddles away, leaving behind a frown on Knox's handsome face and a giant smile on my own.

He shakes his head. "I can't believe you wasted the last watermelon from the garden on that little demon."

Out of nowhere, I blow a raspberry at him and then immediately collapse into giggles. "You're just jealous your pet goose likes me better."

"He's not my pet."

"Whatever you need to tell yourself."

A ring breaks the silence, and it takes a full minute for me to realize it's a phone inside. "You have a phone?"

"Of course I have a phone. A landline for emergencies and for Mom to call."

Okay, I guess that makes sense.

Knox clomps into the house and cuts off the next ring when he answers. "Hey, Ma, what's up?"

Eavesdropping is incredibly rude. Does that mean I try not to listen? Nope. In fact, I lean back on my hands to try and get just a little closer while still maintaining an aloof position.

"What do you mean she has a delivery?" Knox's voice gets louder, and I turn to see him standing in the open doorway. "Did you have something delivered to the cafe?"

"No."

Why would I have something delivered to a place I've only been to a few days? If I need to order something from Amazon, I have it delivered to the closest locker. All my other mail either goes to Mom's house, where it sits until she eventually either throws it away or I swing by to pick it up when I am nearby.

"Okay, Mom, we'll head that way now." Knox returns and hangs up the phone before emerging with a confused look on his face. "She says we need to come to the cafe."

A sense of dread settles over me, and I am suddenly very nervous about going to the cafe that has been my favorite part of the small town.

Chapter 20

Knox

Mom isn't usually one for mystery or surprises. She lays everything out on the table for all to see, take it, or leave, which is why I'm confused about why she won't tell me what is waiting for June at the cafe.

June doesn't seem concerned, though. Maybe she is still riding the high of befriending that stupid goose. I'm definitely not jealous that she was cooing and petting a giant, surly bird. She just has this way about her that wears everyone down until they are her best friend. I don't want to be her best friend, so there is no reason to be jealous.

Apparently, lying to yourself is really easy.

Pulling up to the cafe, everything looks normal. The same people mill about the neighborhood with mugs of concoctions from Romancing The Bean. June is busy looking at something on her phone as we climb the stairs to the cafe. My hand goes to the small of her back to make sure she doesn't accidentally trip since she isn't looking where she's going.

Just as always, the bell over the door rings, announcing our entrance. But Mom isn't standing at her post behind the counter. Instead, she's sitting at one of the small cafe tables with a woman I don't recognize.

The woman is tall and slim, with a severe gray bob. She's wearing a black cardigan set and black pants. As soon as we walk in, the woman stands with a nervous smile on her face. Something about her is familiar even though I'm positive I've never seen her before.

"Hi, Junie," the woman says hesitantly.

June's head snaps up from her phone, her eyes wide and her mouth gaping open in shock. "Mom?"

The woman steps forward and gives her daughter a peck on each cheek. "You're looking well. Not at all the state I thought I would find you."

Silence fills the cafe June is obviously too stunned to speak.

My mom steps forward tentatively, trying to break the tension seeping into the room. "I was just telling your mother that our reception out here is famously awful, so that is probably why she hasn't heard from you in a few days."

"I had all these images of you murdered in the woods, so when I saw the cafe tagged in one of your Instagram posts, I figured I would just drive up and check on you." The woman that I can now see has a resemblance to June turns back to my mom and gives her a shaky smile. "I've been watching too many true crime shows, obviously."

An unhinged laugh bursts from June's mouth. "You were worried about me, so you drove nearly four hours to check on me at a random cafe I tagged in a post?" June rubs her hands over her face, shaking her head. "Who are you?" The words come out louder than we expect, and June's mother flinches a little at the outburst. "You can't be the same woman who put me on a train at twelve without checking to make sure my dad would be on the other side of the trip to pick me up. Certainly not the woman who missed every graduation, school event, or award ceremony because there was a crisis at the office. I've been traveling solo for nearly a decade, and you have never once wondered if a serial killer would pick me up off the streets."

"June, I am your mother as I have always been." The older version of June straightens her shoulders and lifts her chin in defiance, a move I've become very familiar with over the past few days since it is the exact same move June pulls when she's ready to head into a verbal battle with me. "Of course, I have always worried about your safety."

June turns and paces the length of the cafe. "Oh my gosh, that is such bullshit!"

In the other room, Mrs. Robinson peeks her head out from around the corner, eyes wide with delight at the quickly developing drama right in our sleepy little town.

"You cared about what the Fed was going to do with interest rates or markets crashing—you never cared about whether your daughter was home on time or getting good grades. You paid nannies and tutors to care about those things. You hoisted me off onto your dad every chance you could until you put him into a home to wither and die when he was too much of a bother." June is working up a nice head of steam, her face turning red as she rants. "But now that you don't have a job to occupy you all of a sudden, your fully grown daughter is some big concern in your life?"

"June, you are making a scene. Perhaps we could go back to your hotel room and talk about this."

"Oh, I'm sorry. Am I embarrassing you?" June's voice rises to another decibel that I honestly find impressive. "I know how you hate to be inconvenienced by people having emotions." She stops in front of her mother, her eyes a little wild and her breath coming in harsh pants. "And I don't have a hotel room. I've been staying on the very remote farm of a strange man. And guess what? All my limbs are still attached."

To prove her statement, June waves her arms above her head.

The woman's eyes swing my way with curiosity.

I wave. "Hi, I'm the stranger. Knox Halsted, Roxy's son."

The woman glances down at my outstretched hand and takes it in a firm handshake. "Meredith Ammer. It's nice to meet you." Meredith turns back to her daughter, disapproval plain on her face despite what I think is some Botox going on. "Why on earth aren't you staying in a hotel?"

"The B&B is all booked up," I offer.

"And the closest motel would most likely result in a staph infection just from touching the doorknob," my mother kicks in her own two cents.

"And because I am a grown-ass woman who can make her own decisions," June throws in.

"Well, you certainly aren't acting like a grown woman. You are acting like a petulant teenager." Meredith is starting to lose her cool.

From the corner of my eye, Mrs. Robinson pulls out her shitty little flip phone and holds it up, obviously recording the exchange to show the rest of the ladies at bingo this Sunday.

"How would you know? You never dealt with a teenager a day in your life." June's eyes take on a suspiciously glassy haze. "I stayed out of the way and took care of myself once you and Dad stopped paying for the nannies to deal with me. You have made it more than clear over the years that I am not worth your, Dad's, or anyone's time and attention."

Her words nearly knock the breath out of me. Is that what she thinks? That making space for her is a burden on people? I've never been tempted to hit a woman before, but I can't deny the surge of rage that I have to wrestle down in my stomach before it bubbles up and attacks this Meredith woman.

Giving June a place in my life has been all too easy. Like a puzzle piece sliding into the rough edges around it to make a whole picture come into focus. Doing things for her, like coffee every morning and ordering fucking internet, has been a privilege this week. Not a burden I have lapped up every chance to do something for my house guest, despite knowing each gesture would mean the moment she inevitably leaves will be all that much more painful.

From the corner of my eye, I track my mom as she spots Mrs. Robinson as well and gracefully makes her way over to the old busybody, escorting her out the door as June and Meredith's standoff continues. Mom takes the phone from her neighbor and fiddles with it, hopefully deleting the video. Once Mrs. Robinson is outside, Mom flips the neon open sign off and turns to our guests.

"Ladies, obviously, there is a lot of pent-up history and emotion here that needs to be addressed." She sweeps behind the counter and starts brewing two cups of tea. Hopefully, it's her special calming tea with just a hint of CBD oil that she hides from Mayor Burt. "Why don't we have some tea and take a couple of deep breaths?" She demonstrates this by pulling a slow drag of air through her nose and letting it go through her lips.

June crosses her arms over her stomach and comes to stand beside me. "This is ridiculous. I cannot believe you drove all the way here for no reason."

I foolishly hope it's because she is looking for my support and have to force my arm not to go around her back.

June huffs. "You should just turn back around and go back to Philadelphia. I am obviously fine here."

Meredith smooths her hands down the front of her wrinkle-free pants. "Well, yes, I suppose you are fine." She glances at what I am guessing is a very expensive wristwatch.

"It is much too late to drive home tonight," my mom speaks up, always the voice of reason. "Meredith. I happen to have an extra bedroom upstairs. You could stay there for the night, and we can decide what to do tomorrow morning."

I narrow my eyes at Mom because I could have sworn that the apartment upstairs was currently occupied by the porn-watching Chuck. "I thought you had a renter?"

She smiles at me indulgently. "Oh, Ruth took Chuck back last night. He moved his things out this morning."

"No," June says firmly. "She can't stay here. I have work to do, and I'm sure she has something to do at the country club or some class to take back home." June glares at her mother—a look I would have been smacked upside the head for if I gave it to my own mom.

"Actually, my schedule is completely clear." Meredith turns to my mom. "I would very much appreciate a place to stay since you say the motel in town is not acceptable. I'll go get my overnight bag from the car."

"Knox, will you take me home, please?" It is the second time June has referred to my house as home, and I like it a little too much.

"Sure."

I honestly have no clue what to do to help June right now. Should I try to get her to talk to her mom? I can't imagine not having a relationship with my own mother. But our families are very different. From what I've heard, I'm not sure Meredith deserves another chance from her daughter. With my hand on her lower back, I direct June to the door and down the sidewalk to my truck.

Simultaneously, Simone is hopping out of her own tow truck. "Oh, hey, June, Knox, how's it going?"

June grunts and gets in the passenger side of my truck.

"Everything okay?" Simone looks in at June with concern. "Is she mad that the van isn't ready yet?"

"No, let's just say there is some family stuff going on that she's dealing with. But since you mention it, how is Daisy coming along?"

Simone shifts back and forth on her feet, her eyes darting up to my mother on the porch. "Um, nope. Having trouble sourcing some parts."

Why are all the women in this town lying to me? Something is going on, and I have a feeling my mother is the culprit behind most of it.

Chapter 21

June

Back at Knox's house, I hole myself in my room with my laptop. Did I act like a brat when I saw my mom? Yes, absolutely. Embarrassment has kept me hidden away since the day before. Knox must think I am a complete headcase.

He's not wrong.

But Meredith showing up out of nowhere has completely thrown me for a loop. The woman never even showed up to the many school events, soccer games, or even to take pictures of me and my prom date when I was in high school. Why does she suddenly want to play the protective mom now? Does it have something to do with Dad's death?

I don't know. And I'm tired of thinking about it.

Instead, I've been throwing myself into writing. Only it's not the normal blog posts or spec articles. It's something else entirely. During my travels, I've come across hundreds of characters and thousands of stories. For the past twenty-four hours, they've been pouring out of me into a beautiful notebook I bought at the state fair. I've always wanted to document the people and places I've come across over the years, but a book seemed so far out there. Pretty pictures and simple words were more my speed.

Until now.

My hand cramps once again and I stop to shake it out, massaging the muscles that aren't used to writing by hand. But this is how the words are coming out, so I'll keep it up until they stop. I have a loose framework in my head. Small towns and the people who built them. Not necessarily a travel book, but not a history book either. Some weird hybrid of nonfiction and fiction that will probably never go anywhere, but it feels good to tell these stories, even if it will only ever be for myself.

And it is an excellent avoidance tactic.

To his credit, Knox has checked on me almost every hour since I stumbled down the stairs for coffee and eggs. He's made sure I stayed hydrated and fed but seems to be at a loss for what to say. That's okay. I don't need to hear from anyone that I was an idiot yesterday. I've been telling myself the same thing,

Beside me, my cell phone rings once again. I'm starting to resent Knox for getting me the magical Wi-Fi because now my mother's calls and texts have been coming through clear as day. I am just choosing to ignore them until I figure out what the hell to do about her.

Only a glance at the screen shows not my mother's name, but an unknown number from Pittsburgh. "Hello?"

"Ms. Ammer, hi! How are you?" The familiar voice of Maxima Seilly, the realtor we met with at Dad's house, surprises me.

"Oh, hi, Maxima. I'm doing fine. Did we miss something in the paperwork?" It's only been three days, the listing only just went live, so I wasn't expecting to hear back from her anytime soon.

"No, nothing like that. I wanted to let you know I am sending over three offers on your father's house. They are all extremely generous. One of the potential buyers has asked for a response within twenty-four hours." Her voice is crisp and brokers no confusion, yet I can't believe what she's saying.

"What? There are three offers already? I thought it would take months to sell." I've never bought a house, but I always thought it was this long, drawn-out process.

"Oh no, dear, this is a highly sought-after neighborhood. I am honestly surprised we don't have more offers on the table. But it is at the higher end of price points in Pittsburgh, making the pool of buyers considerably smaller."

In the background, I hear a computer mouse clicking, and I picture the glamorous realtor working efficiently on her computer while talking to me. "Now, the details are all in the email, but here are the basics. The first offer is actually from the university. They are offering fifty thousand over asking and will also waive the inspection, which should considerably speed things along if you are looking for a swift close to the sale. The second is from a real estate corporation. They will most likely use the home for short-term rentals to local doctors or other professionals. They are offering thirty thousand over asking. The third is a family. They actually came in exactly at the asking price, so I think we can safely discard that one."

Honestly, I don't especially need the money from the sale of Dad's house. I've made a good living as a travel writer, and since I have next to no living expenses, I live comfortably. I hadn't thought much about what the house would go for or what I would use the money for.

"June, are you still there, darling?"

"Yes, sorry. This is all just happening really fast. It has taken me a bit by surprise." That is a vast understatement. The room seems to be spinning, and I close my eyes tight to try and make everything just stop.

"I understand. And while I would love to tell you to take your time and think it over, as I said, there is a time limit on how long we can take to get back to the university."

"Do you know what they will use the house for?"

"I believe they said it will be the permanent housing for university presidents. As you will see in the offer, they will be naming the house in your father's honor should you accept. It will be the Ammer Presidential Residence."

Something about that doesn't feel right. I picture future generations of girls just like me forgotten in that big house, their busy parents barely noticing their presence. I have no doubt not all university presidents and bank CEOs treat their children like mine treated me, but I can't stomach the idea that the tradition of that house will be passed onto another family.

"I'll take a look at the offers and get back to you before the end of the day."

After some more pleasantries, I hang up with the realtor and click to open my email. There on top of the messages from several stores offering up their latest sales is the email from Maxima.

One by one, I go through the three offers. The amount of money these people will be paying for Dad's house is astounding. I really had no idea it could cost that much. They are all fairly straightforward until I get to the last offer, which has a letter attached to it from the potential buyers.

Dear Ms. Ammer,

The moment my husband and I saw your house, we fell instantly in love. We pictured our son playing in the backyard with the puppy he has been begging for since we moved to this city. Had visions of baking together on the weekends and hosting grand family holidays. Up to this point, we have been living in a small two-bedroom apartment, a place not conducive to puppies, while we searched for our forever home.

I have just received a position as an oncology resident at the university hospital. My husband is an engineer for an environmental firm looking to clean up the famous three rivers. Your house is in the perfect location for both our offices and is in a magnificent school district. Plus, the local synagogue is within walking distance, making it much easier for us to walk to services on the Sabbath.

We know you must be getting a lot of interest in the house. There is no doubt you have much higher offers. This is something we have run into time and again in our search for a home in a growing city like Pittsburgh. But we hope that this letter might show you that your house will not only be in good hands but loving ones that will fill the rooms with laughter and memories.

Thank you for considering our offer.

Sincerely, Scott and Joseph

Quickly closing the letter, I text Maxima back: *I'm going with offer number three. The family.*

Are you sure? She replies almost immediately. *It's the lowest offer. The university is much more money and will honor your father's legacy.*

I'm positive. I want the house to be filled with laughter. I want to give that house the life I could never have there.

Okay. I'll let the buyer's agent know.

The next few hours are a whirlwind of texts from Maxima and emails with contingencies. But by the time the sky begins darkening outside my window, a seller's agreement is drafted and in my email inbox.

A knock at my bedroom door makes me jump. "June, do you want some dinner?"

"Come on in, Knox." The door inches open, and my host tentatively pokes his head through.

"Hey, is there a notary in town?" Turning to face Knox, I nearly fall out of my chair. He's dressed in gray sweatpants and a white T-shirt. Neither of which leaves anything to the imagination. Goddamn, the man is built in all the right ways. My mouth waters at the memory of the appendage being lovingly hugged by the soft material of his pants.

Pulling my attention back to his face, I see him blushing and avoiding my eyes, probably because he just caught me unabashedly ogling him. "Yup, we have a notary, but she's not exactly in town."

"Oh, is it a long drive? Do you know how late she is open?"

"No, it's not far, and I am pretty sure she stays open twenty-four-seven. Why do you need a notary?"

"Well, I accepted an offer on the house."

Knox has the same reaction I did when Maxima called. His mouth falls open, and his eyes grow about two sizes. "Already?"

"I know, right? I thought it would take a lot longer." While I fill him in on the three offers and the one I chose, I close out the documents and give my laptop a much-needed break. "I guess the buyers have been burned a lot with people backing out of deals to go with higher offers from the real estate holding companies that are buying everything up in the city. So they've asked that I get the purchase agreement notarized to give an extra layer of intent."

"I guess that makes sense."

"Do I need to make an appointment with this notary, or what?"

"Nope." Knox looks at the ceiling and rocks back on his heels. "But we might need to swing by the bank and get some singles. The local notary just happens to also be the owner of Club Barely Over the Line."

"Wait, the strip club you were telling me about?"

"The very same."

"Shut up, a stripper and a notary. I freaking love this town."

"One more thing you should know before we head over."

Every additional tidbit of information I learn about this place is icing on the cake, so I can't wait to hear what the latest will be. "Yes?"

"Remember my sister? Delia?"

It couldn't possibly be. "Shut up."

"Yeah, the notary, the owner of the club, and Delia are all the same person." Knox leans his head back again, staring at the ceiling as if it might open at any moment, and a tractor beam from a passing spaceship might pull him up to save him from having to say that single sentence.

"Holy shit. Way to bury the lead! How on Earth did this not come up during family dinner the other night?"

"They were too focused on impressing you and embarrassing me." Knox drags his hand down over his face, suddenly looking very tired. "Besides, as proud as I am of my sister and her various ventures, remembering that she owns a strip club, and at one point did dance there as well, is not something I try to do."

Suddenly, a task that I have been dreading and avoiding is becoming possibly the best night ever. This town really is just full of surprises.

After Knox leaves, I have just one more question: What does one wear to a strip club where they are conducting professional real estate business with the sister of one's situationship? Flipping through the clothes in my bag, I settle on a pair of skinny jeans, a velvet tank top in a deep royal blue, and the one pair of heels I own, plain black things that I am sure will be put to shame by the ones worn by the dancers.

I've been to a lot of clubs in my travels, but never a strip club, and I find I'm a jumbled mix of nerves, excitement, and curiosity. I give my hair a little curl and throw on some makeup for the first time since arriving in town.

When I descend the stairs to find Knox sipping a glass of water in the kitchen, I almost stumble down the last few steps. Knox has changed into a crisp, clean pair of jeans, a white button-down shirt, and, god help me, real cowboy boots. It is the closest I've seen the man to dressed up and I suddenly want to stay right here and rip the clothes from his body.

"Do you have a sweater or something?" Knox's eyes wander my body with obvious heat. He looks just the slightest bit pissed off.

"No, it's still pretty warm out. I think I'll be okay."

"You're more than warm, June. You are hot, and I'm not sure it's a good idea to be parading in front of a bunch of pent-up horny men looking at half-naked women when you look that hot."

"I'm not sure if I should be flattered or insulted that you think I can't handle myself."

Knox rubs his hand over his face before giving his head a shake. "Fine. Let's get this over with."

He grabs his truck key from the counter and opens the front door, signaling for me to go out before him.

As I pass, I tap him on the cheek with my palm. "You look real warm too, Knox."

He just shakes his head and follows me out into the warm fall night.

Chapter 22

Knox

Club Barely Over the Line looks nothing like it did the one and only time I was here before. When Delia opened this place, I swore I would never step foot inside. My sister and naked women should not be things I associate together. But Mom dragged Orion and me out a week after they opened in a familial show of support. Nothing like a family outing to the local strip club to make things awkward. No one should have to sit through seeing their mom get a lap dance.

Delia has done a hell of a job with the club since then, that's for sure.

June's face lights up as she takes in the club. "Holy shit, this is gorgeous."

Ornate crystal chandeliers hang over nearly every table, the walls are papered in emerald green and gold geometric patterns, and velvet couches and chairs are scattered around the space in groupings. In the very center of the room is a giant square stage with a pole in each corner, as well as one in the center. At the far end of the building is a bronze bar that looks like it came straight out of a 1920s speakeasy. The whole place is classy and sexy. A far cry from the empty, dingy warehouse it had been when she got a hold of it.

Is it weird to be proud of your little sister while standing in the middle of her strip club?

It's still early in the evening, so the place isn't exactly busy. But there are a few men in the club chairs surrounding the stage, and a woman wearing boy shorts and a bikini top is performing death-defying tricks on the center pole.

June continues to gape at the club, the woman dancing drawing her attention. I cannot think about June watching another woman strip. I am a one-woman man and have never particularly had the whole two-girls fantasy, but a man is only so strong.

"Well, if it isn't my brother from the exact same mother." I've heard men describe Delia's voice as smoky, but to me, it's just annoying. It's the same voice that teased me about being a stinky boy when we were kids. She struts into view in an outfit that is somehow professional yet revealing enough that I feel like I should throw my jacket over her.

Knowing she wouldn't appreciate that gesture, a slight nod in greeting will have to do.

"Never thought I'd see you here again. How very out of character for the good town farmer." She smirks in my direction before her eyes drift over to June and light up. "And with my new favorite person, hey June." The two exchange a quick hug, then Delia holds June out at arm length, giving her a thorough look over. "You looking for a side-gig while you're in town?"

Delia tilts her head toward the stage and waggles her eyebrows. A deep growl burns up from my lungs, but thankfully the music in the club covers it.

"Ha! Definitely not." June glances back to the stage, her gaze following the woman currently taking her top off while hanging upside down from the very top of the pole. "I'm actually here for your professional services." June's face turns an uncharacteristic shade of red. I don't think I've ever seen her get embarrassed before. "Um, I mean, your notary services. Not your stripping services."

Delia smiles kindly at June. "I'm happy to provide you with any services you like."

"Jesus, Delia, do not flirt with my..." I cut myself off, not entirely sure how that sentence was going to end, considering June is technically nothing to me other than a woman staying in my house and occasionally in my bed.

Delia raises one eyebrow as the unfinished sentence hangs between the three of us.

The red deepens along June's cheeks, spreading down her neck to her chest. It's a fascinating show, calling my attention more than the half-naked woman on stage.

"Calm down, big bro. I will leave your lady friend alone." Delia leans into June's side, whispering something in her ear to make the woman I am becoming increasingly fascinated with turn an even brighter red. Delia smirks, then straightens back up and sweeps her arm toward the back of the club. "Why don't we go back to my office, and you can tell me all about your needs." Delia links her arm through June's and walks her back to a discreet door behind the bar.

I follow behind, feeling like a puppy following his master.

The office is much quieter, with only a hint of the music from the main floor coming through a speaker on her desk alongside several monitors showing every angle of the club. Delia mutes the speaker and turns off the monitors. "They can manage without me for a few minutes. How can I help you?"

She sits behind the huge wooden desk and folds her hands on top. June and I sit in matching green velvet club chairs. I have no idea what to do with my hands. Or my eyes. There are artistic black and white photographs framed on each wall of different parts of the female anatomy. Close-ups of nipples, the curve of a hip, a perky ass, and manicured feet in pointed heels.

June looks around the office, scrutinizing the photos and decorations. I decide it is best to keep my eyes on my hands folded in my lap. "So, does the whole town really come here to get contracts notarized?"

"No, usually I travel to my clients. Believe it or not, most of the fine folks that live in Amoresville don't like to be seen walking through the doors of the club." A barely concealed note of disdain laces Delia's voice.

My sister, much like the rest of my family, has a love-hate relationship with the town we call home. Our childhood on the farm was idyllic, with days spent outdoors getting dirty helping on the farm. Reading books under trees with Mom. There was no shortage of love in the house I still live in to this day.

The rest of the town was a different story. Being we are literally the oldest family in the town on my mom's side, we were often the center of all that gossip. Delia got the worst of it. A spitfire feminist like her doesn't tend to make a lot of friends. Neither did a shy guy who only wanted to talk about first frosts and soil amendments with his father. Orion was the only one of the Halsted kids to score on the popularity scale. But even he didn't come out unscathed.

All three of us siblings left town for various spans of time after high school. I went to college at Penn State and got my bachelor's in agricultural studies. Orion went straight to the Marines after graduation. Delia went to NYU for exactly one week before our father got sick. She had big dreams of acting on Broadway, dreams that got crushed when she came back to help our mother with the coffee shop and the never-ending appointments. I took care of the farm. She took care of the family. The town picked up the gossip as if we had never left.

"Well, they're missing out," June says. "Your club is gorgeous."

Delia gives June her first real smile since we walked in the doors. "Thank you. It's definitely come a long way since I bought it." Sliding open a drawer in her desk, Delia takes out a contraption that looks like a sparkly, bright pink, glorified stapler and sets it on the desk along with some pens. "So, what is it you need notarized?"

The two women chat as Delia prints out the official purchase agreement and goes over each line with June, explaining where she needs to sign and what it is exactly she's agreeing to. By the time Delia puts her official seal on the paperwork and slides it into a folder, the two are practically best friends.

The whole time, I sit silently in my chair, staring at my hands.

"You must try this mocktail my bartender has been working on." Delia rises from the desk and pulls June from hers. "I don't let the dancers drink while they're on shift because I firmly believe they need to keep their wits about them at all times. But they like to sip something fun when they're entertaining clients. It helps everyone feel at ease. Most of our customers don't even realize there isn't alcohol in the girls' drinks."

We head back into the main club, and in the hour or so since we entered, the place has picked up a little. There are now two dancers on the stage, and men occupy almost every chair lining the four sides with stacks of cash sitting before them.

A glass appears in front of June, and she takes a small sip, her eyes widening. "Oh my god, that is amazing. It makes me wish I was sitting on a beach somewhere. What is it called?"

"We're calling it the Barely Bahama-Mama." The bartender leans over the glossy counter, her breasts nearly bursting out of her tube top so I have to look away. I'm pretty sure she was a couple of classes below me in high school. Everywhere I look, someone is dancing topless or walking by in barely any clothes. Some I recognize, some are complete strangers. I settle for looking at the pristine black floor tile.

Delia elbows me in the side. "Still not a fan of strip clubs?"

"The scars from seeing Mom get a lap dance will never fade." I chance a quick glance up at Delia, who is laughing at June's wide-eyed expression and gaping mouth at my comment. "Besides, I'm not here for the show. Shouldn't get to look if I'm not paying."

"No one here minds if you look. These women are proud of their bodies and are making a very good living." She leans around me and nods to June. "Your friend certainly doesn't mind taking a look."

I follow my sister's gaze and see June has now shifted so she can see the stage and is watching the action. Two more women have appeared so that there are now four dancers, one on each corner of the stage. This is obviously a choreographed number because they are all climbing the poles simultaneously, using the same panther-like movements. Once they reach the top, the women wrap their thighs around the pole and bend backward so they aren't holding on with their hands. All at once, the music stops, and the girls drop quickly down the pole only to catch themselves just before going splat on the stage.

"Holy shit." My heart races a mile a minute. "How the hell do they do that?"

"Lots of practice." Delia cheers her employees on, and next to me, June raises her fingers to her mouth and lets out a loud whistle. "June, how much longer will you be in town?"

June shrugs. "I'm not sure. It depends on how long it takes for my van to get fixed."

"Well, if you are here this Wednesday, you should come take our pole dancing class. I just started it over the summer, and I have a few ladies from town that come out to take it every week."

I wonder who in town is taking pole dancing classes? "You do?"

Delia gives me a strange look. "Yeah, Mom comes every week. She has the flyer at the cafe. She didn't tell you?"

If there was a mental image worse than Mom getting a lap dance, it is definitely Mom on the pole.

Delia chuckles. "You know Mom supplies our coffee, right?"

I shake my head. It doesn't surprise me.

"She also gives the girls discounts at her shop, and she'll even bring books over for the back room so they have something to read between sets." The way Delia talks about our mom, you'd think she really was destined for sainthood.

"Your mom is the best." June takes another sip of her drink, and I'm starting to wonder whether it really is alcohol-free because she is looking very relaxed. "She gave me a tour of the town, and I could listen to her telling stories about its history all day. I'm definitely going to interview her for my book. Oh, and don't think I've forgotten about the lap dance story. I definitely need to hear how that happened."

Book? Is that what June's been doing up in her room for the past twenty-four hours?

June jumps up from her stool and comes to stand in front of me. "Oh, Knox, you have to get a lap dance!"

"No."

There is no way. Honestly, the whole lap dance thing seems awkward. What's the fun of having a woman right in front of you if you can't touch her? Can't make her feel good?

"Aww, you're no fun." June pouts, which is somehow sexy as hell. "This might be the only time I'm ever in a strip club. I need to see the whole experience."

"Why don't you get one, June?" Delia pipes up beside me.

"Can I do that?" June's eyes widen and she definitely looks interested.

"Of course. As long as you are respectful and follow the rules, anyone is allowed here." Delia turns to face the room. "Anyone catch your eye?"

This is torture. Why have these women teamed up to slowly kill me?

"They are all so beautiful." June keeps looking around until her eyes land on someone she must like. Fuck, why is watching her pick out someone to get a lap dance from so fucking hot?

June points. "What about her?"

I can't not look. I'm too curious to see what kind of woman June would be interested in. Fuck, anyone but Harley. I've known Delia's best friend for as long as I can remember, and she's been trouble the entire time.

Harley is tall and lean, with her hair cut close at the sides and curled into an almost Mohawk-looking pompadour that is colored a deep purple. She's wearing leather chaps, a bikini triangle top that barely covers her round breasts, and a thong. Her makeup is dramatic and dark, and her arms are covered in tattoos. She looks like she could beat the shit out of any man in this place. Definitely different from the girl that used to run around our farm in clothes a size too small that her mom got from the church closet.

"Oh this is going to be amazing." Delia signals to one of the buff security guys milling around, trying to look intimidating. "Would you please ask Harley to grace us with her presence?"

While the security guard fetches her, Delia moves our little group to one of the plush benches lining the walls. She indicates a club chair for me to sit in and then asks June to sit on a bench seat against the wall.

"Okay, here are the rules. Keep your hands on the seat beside you at all times. Do not touch the dancer unless she says you can. She gets to choose how much she keeps on or takes off. You get one full song. If you would like more time with Harley, you'll have to pay for one of the private rooms, which is two hundred dollars per half hour."

June nods, taking the instructions seriously. Just as Delia wraps up her spiel, Harley approaches, looking as if she is ready to eat June alive.

"Tonight's my lucky night. A virgin."

Fuck me. Maybe I should wait outside. I'm not sure I can take this. Harley definitely isn't my type. I like women with soft curves. But there is no denying the raw sexuality coming off her in waves.

June gives her a sweet, if not somewhat nervous, smile. "I assure you, I am not a virgin."

"But you've never had a woman dance for you. I'm right, aren't I?"

"You're right." June swallows hard and nods. She starts to move her hands from where they rest on the seat but stops and glues her palms back down to the leather.

"Harley, be gentle." Delia gives her friend a look, and some unspoken agreement passes between them. "Have fun, you two. I need to get back to work."

Just as Delia walks away, the music changes from a pop song I didn't recognize to the iconic opening of "Back In Black" by AC/DC.

An internal battle wages between my head and my dick. I shouldn't watch, but there is no way I can do anything else.

"What's your name, sweetheart?" Harley bends at the waist, lowering herself to eye level with her client, and as a result, her ass is pretty much in my face.

"June."

"Mind if I get you a little more comfortable, June?" Harley brushes a strand of hair behind June's ear, and fuck, I'm torn between wanting to tell her not to touch the woman I'm developing a slightly unhealthy obsession with and wanting to see more.

"Um, sure."

Harley grabs June by the hips and pulls them forward until June's ass is on the edge of the cushioned bench and she is half-reclining on the seat.

"That's better." Harley glances in my direction. "Enjoy the show, farm boy."

Chapter 23

June

Holy Shit.

Why did I pick this woman out of all the perfectly beautiful, amazing dancers in this club? Harley is beyond hot. She's intimidating and confident and performing the most hypnotic dance right on top of me.

Harley spreads my legs wide, straddling one of my thighs while she does graceful body rolls. Her chest is inches away from my face, her hand planted against the seat back above my head, and I can see how men would be tempted to push the lines and reach out to touch her. But I obediently keep my hands right where they are.

"He can't take his eyes off you," she whispers in my ear.

The dancer's body is all I can see, but Knox's presence across from us is impossible to miss.

"Here I am, almost naked and dancing right before him. But the man can't stop watching you. Trying to get glimpses of your face." Harley throws her other leg onto the bench so she's fully straddling me. She glides her hands down my arms, then back up to my shoulders, leaning in to whisper in my ear. "I've been watching you both since you came in. He orients himself to you. Always puts himself between you and other men. Has barely looked at any other woman here. He's in love with you."

"No, we've just messed around a couple of times. We barely know each other."

Even as I say the words, I can feel the lie. Having Harley give me a lap dance would be hot no matter what. But knowing Knox is watching me makes it even hotter. My jeans are undoubtedly soaked by now, but I don't know how much of it to blame on the woman sitting on my lap or the man not even touching me.

"Deny it all you like. But if I weren't a woman, that man would be throwing me off you and dragging you out of this place. I've known the Halsted family my whole life, have met everyone of Knox's girlfriends. He has never looked at one how he is looking at you now." Harley rolls her hips, arches her back, and bends over backward so that her hands touch the ground between my feet.

My gaze goes immediately to Knox, whose eyes are already on me. His stare burns down to my soul, setting my body and possibly my panties on fire. His fingers grip the arms of the chair as if he's trying to force himself to stay where he is. To not do exactly what the stripper said he would do if she were a man.

Harley does a complicated backward flip off my lap and lands on her feet, prowling back toward me. She's magnetic. It's impossible to keep my eyes off her, even as I want to keep witnessing Knox's reactions to the show.

With a spin, the dancer puts her back and her ass to me and performs a body roll so that she's sitting firmly in my lap, her ass cradled in the curve of my hips. As she rolls her body against mine, her hands come around behind her and pull the string keeping her top secure until it comes loose.

"Okay, that's enough." Knox is at my side, and two security guards make their way toward us, but Harley waves them off.

"I was wondering how far you'd let me go." She re-ties the top and stands to her full height. She smiles down at me, giving me a saucy wink. "I was kinda hoping we would get to make out a little before he jumped in."

With a glance around the room, I see quite a few of the other patrons are watching our little drama play out. Uncomfortable at being the center of attention, I shove my hand in my purse and fish out the entire wad of cash I brought with me, nearly two hundred dollars.

"Thanks for the dance." Well, that was lame.

Harley takes the money and folds it into the band of her tight leather chaps. "Anytime. You get bored with him, come on back, and I'll finish it for you." She turns to Knox and I don't totally love knowing that the two know each other outside of this setting. "See you at Thanksgiving dinner in a couple months."

The warmth of Knox's body overwhelms my already heated skin as he steps in close to my side. "You walking out of here with me, or do I have to throw you over my shoulder?"

"When did you turn into a caveman?" I should hate it. Feminism and dignity and all that. But my aching pussy is making it clear she very much likes his proprietary show.

"Right about the time you did that little squirm you do when you get turned on." He places his hand on my opposite hip and starts escorting me from the club.

We pass by Delia on the way out, and she gives me a smirk and a wave.

Knox's silence as we make our way to the truck is thick, wrapping around me in a cloak of uncertainty. Is he mad? Turned on? Neither?

His composure disappears as soon as we reach the truck, pressing my front up against the passenger side door with his arms caging me in. "Watching that show was the worst kind of torture. Watching you get turned on from the sidelines and not being the one to do it killed me."

The pressure building low in my belly has nowhere to go but to expand with each word he growls in my ear. I arch my back, pushing my ass back into his very hard cock. "It seems not all of you hated it."

"Make no mistake, that was hot as fucking hell. I loved it as much as I hated it." He bites my shoulder as I circle my ass against him, mimicking the moves I just learned from Harley. "Unless you want me to make you come right in this parking lot, I suggest you stop teasing me and get in the truck, Trouble."

"But what if I do want you to make me come right here? What if I can't wait until we get home?"

Knox sucks in a harsh breath. "Fucking trouble." He moves me back from the truck door and wrenches it open. I don't have a chance to climb in before he picks me up in his arms and deposits me on the seat. "Try to behave yourself for the fifteen fucking minutes it will take to drive home."

"I make no promises."

Knox growls and slams the door closed, jogging around to his side. Every time he's been behind the wheel with me in the car, he's driven like a goddamn grandma, never going more than a few miles per hour over the speed limit and making sure to signal early and often. But apparently, horny Knox is reckless Knox. The tires squeal and a distinct scent of burned rubber surrounds us as he slams on the gas, shooting us out of the parking lot onto the empty back road that leads away from the club.

The whole ride he keeps one hand on the steering wheel and one hand high on my thigh. His fingers are so close to where I want them. Where I need them, but he refuses to touch me. Even when I not so subtly move his hand between my legs, he moves it back to my thigh with a shake of his head.

Such a fucking Boy Scout.

Fine, he likes calling me Trouble so much, maybe it's time I really cause some.

Reaching over, I unsnap his jeans.

"You're trying to kill me."

"No, I'm trying to blow you."

He takes my hand and tries to put it back on my side of the seat. "You keep your ass in that seat."

"Fine. You have exactly two minutes to get someplace where we can get naked, or I am making myself come in this truck without your help." I unbutton my own jeans, pulling the zipper down slowly until the lace of my panties peeks out.

"Fucking hell." Knox takes a sharp turn, and I'm thrown off balance, my body pressing into the door. The headlights illuminate trees as they zoom by.

Another minute goes by, and I shove my hand between my jeans and panties, massaging the space between my legs with the heel of my hand.

"I haven't even touched myself yet and I'm ready, Knox. You really want it to be my fingers that get the job done?"

"You make yourself come, and I will spank that ass until it's red."

My breaths are coming faster, the pleasure building in my core. "Cute how you think that's a threat and not a reward."

Knox brakes fast enough that I slide forward slightly on the seat. His arm shoots out across my chest, pressing me gently back into the seat. What is it about that move that makes my ribs tighten along with my pussy.

He turns the wheel, and we're bumping along between the trees. I'm fairly certain whatever road we are on isn't on any map, if it even is a road.

After a few feet, Knox stops the truck and unbuckles his seatbelt. He's out before I can even catch my breath, stomping around the front of the truck, the headlights glaring across his body in the night.

The next moment, my door is flung open, and Knox reaches in to unbuckle my seatbelt. He grips my legs and swings them around to hang out the door. His movements are rough and precise. His eyes light with lust and maybe a little anger.

My jeans have already slipped down a little. He makes quick work of pulling them down my legs the rest of the way, taking my panties and my shoes with them.

"Look at this needy pussy." He slaps the offending body part with an open palm, and I gasp with shock and pleasure. The sting travels from my clit to my toes and back up. "Can't wait five fucking minutes to get what she needs."

I'm not sure if he's talking about me or my vagina, and I really don't care as long as he keeps touching me.

"Please, Knox, I need you."

"So fucking impatient." He pulls my ass to the edge of the seat, slinging my legs over his shoulders and burying his face in my pussy. The first touch of his tongue to my clit has me falling back against the center console.

Searing pleasure burns through my limbs as he works the throbbing bundle of nerves. The edge of my climax is right there, teetering just out of reach within seconds. I want to fall over that cliff and get lost in the endless sensations, but just as I'm about to explode, Knox pulls back.

"You thought it was going to be that fast? That easy?" A dark chuckle fills the truck. With a much gentler touch, Knox runs his fingers up and down my slit, barely grazing over my hyper-sensitive clit. "So wet. What was it that got you like this? Watching the women on stage? Harley grinding in your lap?"

The words won't form. I'm so fucking wound up, all I can do is whimper and try to get his fingers to touch me more directly by tilting my hips toward them.

He slaps the inside of my thigh, not close enough to my pussy to make me come, but not hard enough to hurt either. "Answer, or you'll wait longer."

The pleasure is so close I want to cry. "It was all of it. Watching them. The lap dance. But mostly, it was the way you looked at me. I liked you watching me."

Knox rewards my answer by slipping one finger deep into my pussy, pumping it in and out slowly. "I couldn't keep my eyes off you. A club full of naked women couldn't compare to the way your whole body comes to life when you're turned on."

His fingers keep working inside me at a consistent pace that keeps me hovering on the edge of bliss. Meanwhile, his other hand goes to his jeans. Finishing the job I started by pulling down his zipper and taking out his very hard cock.

I moan as he pulls his fingers from my cunt and smears my arousal around the head of his cock. And he calls me trouble? That move was so filthy but so fucking hot.

Returning his fingers to my opening, he pumps them in and out of me at the same rhythm as his other hand shuttles up and down his cock.

"Yeah, you love watching. Love being watched. That first night you didn't bother to stop when I walked in on you trying to make this pretty pussy come." He twists his fingers inside me, the new sensation making my back arch, trying to get him deeper. "Just kept right on fucking yourself, letting me watch."

His words, his fingers, and seeing him touch himself are like the holy trinity of dirty deeds. The pressure that's been building inside me tightens until it's almost painful. "Please, Knox, I need to come."

The bastard slows down.

"Somebody needs to learn to wait. Made me drive like a fucking lunatic just to get to your pussy." There is no real anger in his voice. If anything, he says the words with awe. Like he can't believe I drove him to such lengths. "Get your tits out. Let me watch you play with them."

It takes some work, but I manage to pull off my shirt and throw it in the back of the truck. I'm splayed out on his front seat, naked and needy, while he's still got all his clothes on and is in complete control.

"You like to watch, too." I prove my point by gripping my breasts, pushing them together into an obscene show of cleavage.

"I like to watch you. Feels like I watch you all the fucking time. Have to force myself out into the field so I don't just sit and stare at you walking around my house."

I twist my nipples until a sting of pleasure ripples down my body. "Knox, I want to come with you inside me." Fantasizing about his cock filling me has become an obsession.

He picks up the pace, his fingers going deeper, faster inside me, his thumb circling around my clit.

I stop playing with my breasts. I know what I want, and it's him, all of him, inside me. "I've been patient. Please, fuck me, Knox."

"No."

"Why?" I want to weep with frustration. He won't let me come. Won't fuck me.

"Because once I'm inside you, I'm never going to want to leave."

"Then don't. Please." I reach down between us, covering his hand, still pumping up and down his cock so that we are both working the length. I pull him closer, running the head of his cock up and down my slit. "You feel so fucking good, Knox. Don't you like how I feel?"

"You have no idea." He throws his head back, and his hips thrust forward, skating the entire length of his cock along my pussy. "You are going to be the end of me, woman."

Chapter 24

Knox

There's no resisting June when she's naked and begging for me to fuck her. The last shred of my willpower snaps along with my hard-fought patience.

The soft, silken slide of her outer lips around my cock is too much and not enough. "You don't know what you're getting yourself into, June. If I fuck you, there's no going back."

"I don't want to go back. Please, Knox. I can't wait much longer."

"Open the glove box."

She does as I say, and sitting there is a fresh box of condoms. There's another in my bedroom. I'm no idiot. There was no way in hell I was going to be able to resist her if we got to this point again. I could tell myself I wasn't going to fuck her all I wanted. That taking that step would make her leaving impossible instead of just hard. But I am lying to myself. Letting her go is going to be impossible, no matter what.

June rips open the box and pulls out one of the packets. With unsteady fingers, she tears it open and pulls the rubber out. Not coming while she rolls it carefully onto my cock might be one of the most impressive things I've ever done in my life.

Once she has me covered, she lines my cock up with her opening, and I thrust in, both of us gasping for air.

"Oh my god, Knox." June's hips start moving, trying to fuck me from below.

"Jesus, stay still, June, or this is not going to live up to your expectations." I'm about two seconds from losing my mind.

"I can't. You feel so good, Knox." She hooks her legs around my hips, pulling me deeper.

My hands grip the door frame, holding on for dear life as June grinds her hips up and down, rubbing her clit against the base of my dick.

"Don't you fucking come, June."

She's panting, her fingers clawing at her tits, and needy moans echoing off the mountains. "I can't help it."

No way I'm letting her come apart on my dick like this.

I gather her into my arms, and her eyes go wide as I lift her from the truck while keeping myself firmly seated inside her. She cries out as I walk us to the back of the truck and open the tailgate.

"You want to come so bad?" I sit my ass back on the truck bed and lean back so she's straddling me with her feet flat on the floor. "Ride me until you come."

My little troublemaker doesn't need any more convincing. She starts bouncing on my cock, her hands gripping my shoulders for balance. The heat of her surrounds me, tempting me to let loose. To reverse our positions and fuck her hard and rough in the back of my truck.

But this is her show now.

She leans forward, switching to her knees so she can grind down hard on my cock. I sit up, unable to resist her mouth any longer, and take it in a deep kiss, exploring her mouth with my tongue. Memorizing her taste, a mixture of the drink she had and something uniquely June.

Lacing her fingers in my hair, she directs my mouth to her neck. "Kiss me here, too."

I suck gently on her neck, grazing the delicate skin with my teeth. Her pussy clamps down hard around my cock, and a long moan slips from her mouth. "Yes, oh god, Knox, I'm going to come."

I grip her hips, helping to push her down harder with each bounce of her body until she's coming apart, wrapping her arms and legs around me. I stand, taking over as she loses her rhythm to the tidal waves of her orgasm.

Gripping her ass, I thrust up into her, letting gravity do its thing to push her down farther on my cock until she's screaming with another orgasm. Or maybe it's still the first one. I don't know. As long as she keeps coming, I'll stand here, bouncing her on my cock for as long as she needs.

A familiar tug in the base of my spine signals my impending climax. June's fingers scratch at my shoulders. The sharp pain does nothing to slow the approach of what will probably be an earth-shattering orgasm. If anything, her switch from sweet, sunny writer to the sex-crazed wild child makes it harder to hold off on my inevitable end.

"I can't take any more, Knox," she pants between moans and screams.

"You'll take as much as I give you." Big talk from a man trying his best to keep his balls in check.

"Knox, come inside me." She grinds down on my cock, gasping and writhing as her wicked movements drive her own orgasm higher.

"You trying to make me lose my mind?"

"Yes, I want to be the one that makes you lose control."

Fuck. This woman really is going to be the death of me. With a grunt, I fall to my knees, pressing June's back into the cool grass and rutting into her like an animal. I'm beyond words. Every cell in my body is focused on one goal: Fucking June into oblivion and losing myself in her.

Gripping behind her knees, I press her legs back and open, giving me full range of motion to snap my hips forward in swift, brutal thrusts. She clutches at the ground, her back arching toward me like a woman possessed. My grunts and her screams echo around us.

One last push forward, and my grip on reality slips. The power of my orgasm hits so hard that I have to squeeze my eyes shut. I fall on top of June, holding her to me as I let go inside her, wishing like hell there wasn't a piece of latex separating us so a part of me would stay inside her at least for a little while.

Once I'm depleted, I shift slightly so I don't crush June. We're both gasping despite being out in the fresh air.

A sudden giggle bursts from June next to me. "Holy shit. That was insane."

"That's putting it lightly." Silence descends around us, and I wish it weren't so goddamn dark out so I could witness what June looks like right after I've made her come six ways from Sunday.

I climb to my feet, pulling June up before lifting her up and over my shoulder. "Knox, what the hell are you doing?"

"Taking you to bed to see if round two will be even more insane."

Can't say I've ever walked across my backfield with a naked woman on my shoulder and my half-hard cock still wrapped in a condom and hanging out of my jeans. Thank god I don't have any neighbors nearby.

"Wait, this is your field?"

"Yup. That little road we came in is the same place I was coming from when you crashed into my world."

Despite my best intentions, we only make it as far as the couch before I need to take June again. But for the third round, we finally make it to my bed.

* * *

I can count the number of times Roger has woken me up on one hand. Usually, I'm up long before the animals start to rouse from their slumbers. I'm outside before the sun comes up. But when a warm, soft body is pressed against you all night, it makes it a lot harder to drag yourself from bed.

June stretches her arms out from the blankets, her ass pressing back against my rapidly expanding dick. How the hell is that thing still capable of getting hard? He got more action last night than in the last five years combined. The damn thing should be bruised and limp for the next week.

But that is the power of June.

"I appreciate the morning salute," she says, "but if you bring that thing anywhere near me, I'm going to have to karate chop you." June's sleepy voice is just about the cutest thing, and I debate testing to see how serious she is.

"You sore?" I ask.

She rolls over, snuggling her face between my beard and shoulder. "Just a little bit. But I require caffeine before anything else can happen."

This tightness in my chest has become all too familiar since June's arrival. Every time she walks by, it's like I can't catch my breath for a second. I wrap my arms around her and press her closer.

"Stay with me. Even after Daisy is done. Stay." The words are out before I can stop myself. I had no intention of asking June to give up her life and stay on my farm, but fuck if I don't want it so bad it hurts.

She freezes, her body going stiff and her breath stalling.

"Knox—" God, just her saying my name with that pitying tone is a dagger to my chest.

"There is something here, June. I felt it from the moment you fell out of your van and into my arms." I run my hand down her back, gripping her hip. "I know you feel it, too."

"We have chemistry, Knox. But chemistry doesn't make a relationship. It fizzles out until you're left with two people who resent each other. You'll resent me for wanting to travel and go places when all you want to do is stay on your farm and grow things. I'll hate you for holding me back. There is no such thing as a happy ending. Not in real life." June sits up, and a sick part of me wants to pull her back down. To trap her in my arms and hold on tightly so she doesn't slip away.

I'm not that guy, though. I wasn't before, when Lesley left town, and I'm still not. The pull to push harder, to convince June to stay, is so much stronger than it had ever been with my college girlfriend. It was easy letting her go.

"That's bullshit," I say. "We have more than chemistry. It's only been a week, and you are all I think about. In the fields. Behind the counter at the café. When I'm lying right next to you, I'm still thinking about how I can make you happy. How to be a better man so you will never want to leave. I'll loosen up, travel. I'll do whatever it takes to make you happy every day."

June's face is drained of her usually bright light. The blood has rushed from her normally rosy cheeks. There is a hardness behind her eyes I've never seen since meeting her out on that country road.

"I can't," she says resolutely.

"You can really walk away from this once your van is fixed? Just pack up and leave without a glance in the rearview mirror?"

June turns to face me, her expression shuttered from any emotion she might be feeling. "Yes. I can. A few weeks from now, these past few days will be pretty pictures on my Instagram and a few stories I try to sell to magazines. They'll be memories that I look back on fondly. It's the way I like it."

"That's sad. That's not a life. It's avoidance of a life."

Why am I pushing this so hard? I know better than anyone that when this woman puts her mind to something, she doesn't budge. I've only known her for five days, but I know she's stubborn beyond measure. The idea of not having her in the house, not driving her all over town, not waiting for her to wake up and come find me in the field, opens an empty pit in the bottom of my stomach.

The shutters that kept her eyes impassive blow open, revealing anger like I've never seen before. "Not everyone wants to stay in the same place their whole life."

I hit a nerve.

She struggles to rise to her feet, fumbling with the sheets. "Maybe a small life in a small town is enough for you, but it's not for me. This was a warm place to sleep and a convenient cock. That's all."

She spins on her heel and stalks from my room.

I fling off the blanket, lunge from the bed, and stomp into her room just as she tries to swing the door closed behind her. "That's bullshit, and you know it."

She's throwing her things back into her bags, stopping to pull a sundress I've yet to see her wear over her head, not even bothering to put on a bra or panties.

I can't stop myself from saying, "You're telling me each morning you woke up in this house, your first thought wasn't about where I was? What was I doing?"

"Yeah, so I could get you to give me a fucking ride. You were a glorified Uber." She slings the bags over her shoulders, but I block her exit from the room. "Move."

"Not until you calm down and talk to me."

That was the wrong thing to say.

June tries to duck under my arm, push past me in the doorway, but it's no use. There is no way in hell I'm letting this woman go until we talk. I reach out for her arm, to halt her from trying to escape. She rears back, pulling her arm from my grip and causing the bags slung over her shoulder to swing wildly. One connects directly with my balls. My completely unprotected, naked fucking junk. The breath rushes out of me in a huff, my lungs seizing and the contents of my stomach nearly spilling on the floor.

June gasps and mutters a tearful apology that I barely hear over the rush of the pain radiating from my crotch. But she's not sorry enough to miss her opportunity as I crumble to the floor. She steps over my prone body and rushes from the room. I make it back to my feet just as she starts down the stairs. Spots swim before my eyes as I try to stand upright.

Stumbling after her, I make it to the top of the stairs just as she runs out the door barefoot, the dress she threw on barely covering her ass thanks to the bags rucking it up.

Through the wide-open door, I see her hop into the truck that I moved into the driveway while she slept, and I curse because I left the damn keys inside. I always do. No one out here is any threat.

"June, get out of the fucking truck!" I sprint the last few steps, my balls slapping against my thighs and causing aftershocks of pain to surge through my limbs. She ignores me, revving the engine and peeling out in a spray of dust. "June!"

From the barn, Cugo comes waddling out, squawking up a storm after his new favorite person. But she's already pulling onto the street.

I watch as she speeds down the road, leaving me behind naked and terrified I'll never see her again.

Chapter 25

June

Do not cry. There is absolutely no reason to cry.

I've only been here a few days, so the streets are still mostly unfamiliar. But somehow, after pulling a few U-turns, I manage to find the garage where Daisy has been parked for nearly a week. Of course, I forgot to grab my phone off the charger before making my dramatic exit from Knox's house, so I couldn't even rely on the power of GPS to get me where I needed to be.

Daisy is nowhere in sight as I pull into the lot. I park alongside the office, careful to keep all my bits covered when I hop out of the truck. Would taking the time to pull on panties have been such a big deal?

The garage is dark, the "Closed" sign still facing out through the front door. Goddamn it. I cup my hands and press them against the glass, trying to see if Daisy is in the bay, but I can't see a damn thing through the dim light.

Maybe she's around back? I wander that way, passing half-broken-down and smashed cars waiting to be junked or fixed. Just around the corner sits my baby, sparkling in the rising sun and looking better than brand new. The solar panels are reattached to the roof, and the once-flat tire is now replaced. You can't even tell there was ever a dent in the driver's side door.

"June?" Simone's deep voice startles me, and I jump about a mile high.

The mechanic is just climbing out of her car, a low, sleek sports car of some type. She's wearing a bright orange pair of coveralls that remind me of a neon version of a prison jumpsuit. But somehow, she manages to make it work.

Simone and I have only talked a couple of times, but she's always had a quiet calm about her. Not now, though. She seems on edge, her eyes shifting back and forth from Daisy to me.

I lovingly run my hand along the flowers I painstakingly painted on the van. "When did you finish her? She looks great."

"Um—" Simone's eyes go to the ground, then back up at me. "I'm so bad at this. I told Roxy I was a shit liar."

"What do you have to lie about?"

"I finished working on Daisy three days ago." Simone has the decency to look ashamed.

This doesn't make any sense. "Why wouldn't you tell me? I could have been gone already." A little voice whispers, *But then you wouldn't have slept with Knox, and that would have been a damn shame.* I tell that little voice to jump off a cliff.

Simone kicks at a stray rock, refusing to meet my eyes.

"Roxy asked me to stall to give you and Knox more time together."

What the hell? "Where are the keys?"

Simone jogs into a back door and returns a moment later with my keys in her hand. "We just thought there was something between you and Knox. He's been happier the past week than I've ever seen him. And you seemed like you were enjoying your time with him, too. I didn't think it would hurt anything to wait a few days. Roxy is very convincing."

"This whole damn town is crazy. Do you guys try to trap women here to shack up with the townsmen often?"

Simone shoots me a weak smile, but I can't return it. "I swear, almost never."

Anger is still boiling just under the surface, I can practically feel my skin bubbling from the heat of it. I don't want to spew that all over Simone. "How much do I owe you?"

"Don't worry about it. It was mostly just scrubbing."

Normally, I would insist. This is her livelihood, after all, but given the circumstances, yeah, okay, I'll take the freebie.

With a weak goodbye, I throw the bags from Knox's truck into the van, resolving to organize everything once I get to my next stop. I do, however, take a moment to fish out a clean pair of panties and slip them on.

Settling into the driver's seat, I expect to feel like I've come home. But it's not the same. The same space closes in around me, everything seeming too small, too tight. A glance into the back doesn't help. It doesn't look like my home anymore, even though everything is pretty much the same. There's no kitchen with coffee brewing. No boots toed off by the door. No beautiful clawfoot bathtub. No crazy, guardian geese.

This is the same feeling I had walking through Dad's house just a few days ago. Like this was some place I spent time once a long time ago.

How could Knox do this? How could he make me feel so safe and comfortable on that damn farm of his? Five days is all it took for him and this town to make me question everything about my life, and it isn't fair.

A good head of steam working its way inside of me again, I turn downtown instead of toward the road that will lead me away from this place.

Romancing the Bean is busy at this time of the day. The locals come in and out, greeting each other as they go about their mornings, heading to work or school or whatever else they do in small towns. Everyone knows everyone else. They are all up in each other's business. Asking about their kids or relatives, hell, even their pets. How do places like this still exist?

I park Daisy in Knox's usual spot since it is the only one at the curb still open. It always is

The bell over the door rings as I enter, but I don't get in the back of the line. Instead, I stomp up to the counter like a petulant child. "Was Knox in on your plan to get me to hang around longer?"

Roxy stops mid-coffee pour, her eyes wide. Good, I caught the town's unofficial ringleader by surprise. A small seed of satisfaction grows in my stomach, and I nurture it with more anger.

"June? What are you talking about?" The glorified barista finishes the drink she's working on and then pulls me aside. No one in line complains. They are all too busy watching the fireworks.

"You know what I'm talking about," I hiss. "You convinced Simone to lie about the van being ready so I would stay. What else did you lie about?"

For once, Roxy has nothing to say, and it pisses me off.

"Was the B&B really booked up? Or was that a lie, too?"

"Yes, I mean no. Of course, it was full. There is a wedding this weekend."

"Right, of course, Lou Ann Reed's wedding. Sounds like a made-up name to me."

"Hey." A woman from the line crosses her arms and glares at me. Well, I guess I know who that is. "Lou Ann Reed is a real name."

"Okay, so that was true. What about the apartment upstairs being full, then conveniently free for my mom to stay there?"

Roxy looks away, smoothing the front of her apron down with both hands. "Okay, that might have been a little bit of a fib."

"Is the motel outside of town really that disgusting?"

"Yes," choruses the whole line of people waiting for coffee. I swear someone even gags.

"Okay, then tell me, was Knox in on your plan to trap me here?"

I want her to say *yes*. To give me a reason to write off the man that I know won't be easy to forget. No matter what I told him back at the house, this place, this week, isn't going to leave my heart any time soon, and I hate it.

Roxy crosses her arms over her chest, annoyance worming its way past her embarrassment at being caught in a lie. "No, of course not. He's just as stubborn as you and would have insisted you stay here."

"I don't believe you. What was the next part of your plan? Were you going to poke holes in our condoms so I got pregnant and had to stay here? Trap me with a kid just like my dad tried to trap my mom?" There is a wet plop on my hand, and I reach up, surprised to find tears pouring down my face.

"June?" The familiar voice of my mother comes from the door leading out of the kitchen, but the woman that follows it looks nothing like the one I grew up with. She's wearing a maxi skirt that obviously doesn't belong to her and a white tank top.

I'm not sure I've ever seen her so dressed down before. Even during the lockdown, she wore khakis and blouses around the house. Even her hair looks different. The normally pin-straight gray bob has a slight wave that tells me she didn't use a straight iron this morning. It's a small change, but shocking when I'm so used to seeing her one way.

"Mom? What are you wearing?"

She blushes. My mom, the woman who has stared down men in boardrooms her whole life, blushes.

"Well, um—" She looks at Roxy, who gives her a small smile back. "—Roxy was nice enough to loan me some more comfortable clothes since I left in a hurry yesterday."

My eyes dart between the two older women, unable to get the idea of the diametrically different people together. "Did you two hook up?"

Someone from the line gasps, and another patron mumbles, "This is better than *The Bachelor*."

My mom steps toward me, her hand outstretched like she wants to lead me to the back room. "June, this is not the way you behave in public. Let's talk about this in the back. Or better yet, upstairs."

On reflex, I flinch back a step.

Roxy snaps her fingers. "I have a better idea." She turns to our captive audience and points to the door. "Everyone out."

She goes behind the counter and pulls out the two huge carafes of coffee and takes them out the door. A few people shuffle out, but most stay.

"Now. Out." She grabs an armful of mugs and takes them to the porch as well. "Everyone gets free black coffee today, and if you bring your mug back tomorrow, you'll get free coffee then too."

That gets people moving, some grabbing mugs as they pass by.

Once everyone is gone, Roxy closes and locks the door, turning off the neon Open sign in the window. Her skirt flares out as she spins quickly to face me. "June, your mother and I did not *hook up.* That is ridiculous, and you should realize that. I had exactly one love in my life. As lovely as your mother is, I have no interest in making room in my heart for someone else."

Her indignation grates on my already frayed nerves. How dare she be mad at me when she's been lying to me this entire time?

"Can you really blame me? How do I know this town doesn't have some sort of population problem where every single citizen is required to lure one unsuspecting outsider in to keep the gene pool fresh? After all, the man I've been hooking up with has been conspiring with his mother to trap me on their farm. Were you feeding him hints on how to butter me up? Leaving me coffee every morning. Installing Wi-Fi at his house. Cooking meals." A sob rips from my mouth, making my words come out pained. "The sweet words and gestures certainly don't feel like the work of a small-town farmer."

With a plop, my butt hits the ground, my legs no longer seeming to have the will to hold me up. I don't even bother to take the handful of steps to the closest chair.

Mom gathers her skirt and does something I would never expect of her: she sits on the ground in front of me. "Wait, I'm missing something. What is this about a man trying to trap you? And why did you say your father trapped me?"

"Oh, come on, Mom. I've known since I was a teenager that Dad pressured you into having a baby."

"June, that is not true. Your father may not have been the warmest of men, but he also wasn't evil." She crosses her legs and leans closer. "I admit, we decided to try and get pregnant for entirely the wrong reasons. It was expected of us to have a family. People thought it was odd that we didn't have children. We sat down and had a conversation, made pro and con lists, and in the end, decided it would make sense for us to have a baby."

"So, my entire existence was a business decision." A humorless laugh huffs from my mouth. It's hard to know where you belong in the world when the people who were meant to love you unconditionally were never there for you.

"I wish I could say no, that we felt a calling to be parents. But that would be a lie. Just because the decision was an analytical one doesn't mean we didn't love you." A tear falls down Mom's cheek, and it is the first time I can recall seeing her cry.

"We didn't know how to express love. We were analytical people who saw the world through facts and figures, not colors and emotions. Suddenly, we had this tiny baby that didn't respond to logic or rules. It threw us both for a loop. Your dad was a brilliant man, but he was also a little on the old-fashioned side, and he thought I should naturally know how to be a mother. How to soothe you. Not knowing those things made me feel like a failure. I threw myself into work because I knew what to do there. The nannies and babysitters seemed to know what they were doing, and I thought as long as you were well-cared for, it didn't matter how that was accomplished. I was wrong. I realized that far, far too late."

A hiccup racks my chest, tears streaming down my face no matter how hard I try to stop them.

"The six months that we were on lockdown together were some of the happiest I've had. Even with you doing everything you could to avoid spending time with me, I was forced to take my nose away from the grindstone and look at my life. I realized that I had missed your entire life because I was stubborn and self-centered." Tentatively, she reaches out and wipes away a few of my tears. "As my therapist says, there is nothing I can do about the past. All I can do is try to fix our present so we can have a future."

"You're seeing a therapist?"

Imagining my mother lying on a couch and talking about her feelings with a stranger is no different from imagining myself staying in this town forever and growing a life with one man in one town. Impossible to fathom. Yet there is a tiny wish inside me pulsing and expanding until it takes up too much room in my chest.

She nods with a sad smile. "I have been for a few years now. Losing my job was hard. Realizing I had lost you long ago was harder. She kept telling me I couldn't force a relationship now without airing everything out, but I kept hoping. If I just kept texting and calling and kept showing my concern, you would see how much I love you. I see now she was right. There is no relationship for us unless we address the past wounds I have inflicted on you. It's why I really came here, to ask you to go to therapy with me."

How do I respond to this revelation? That everything I believed about my childhood might not be as cut and dried as it seemed. Everything up until this moment has been in black and white. They didn't love me, didn't want me, so I made myself disappear. I faded into the background while they lived their important lives. When I got older, I kept disappearing into new places and new adventures. Never formed bonds with the people around me. Relying on the love of thousands of faceless people behind a computer screen. It was easier that way. If I never let anyone in, never let them close, they couldn't leave me. They couldn't hurt me.

"I want to know my daughter." Mom's tears are coming just as fast as mine now. We both suck in choked breaths, her hands enveloping mine. "I hope it isn't too late for that."

"I don't know, Mom. I really don't."

Chapter 26

Knox

Pain radiates through my limbs, but I don't let that stop me. Three trees came down in a storm the other night, and they aren't going to chop themselves. Could I call my brother, the literal lumberjack, down from his mountain to help? Sure, but then how would I kid myself into believing I'm fine?

Sore muscles and the work that causes them are the only things allowing me to sleep the past two weeks. Twice as many days with her gone as when June had been here. Days spent in an empty house with nothing to fill it but silence. She may have only been one person and here for a mere five days, but the house doesn't feel the same without her.

Pulling the axe over my head once again, I swing it down through yet another log. I've got enough firewood to keep the house blazing hot for the whole winter and part of the following one. But I keep going. With the growing season pretty much done and the animals all cared for, it's the only chore I have left.

Cugo waddles by, shooting me an accusatory look. The damn goose has been underfoot ever since June left. Always honking and glaring at me, obviously mad at me for scaring away the only human he has ever liked.

I know the feeling. I'm mad at myself, too.

The truck sits in the driveway, returned by Mom and Simone the same day June left. They stood in my driveway, explaining the whole plan to give June and me more time together. To fall in love. It worked. I fell in love, hard and fast. The problem is June didn't.

Simone apologized for her role in the whole lie about the van needing more time, then climbed into her car, waiting for Mom and me to finish talking. But I didn't want to hear anything the woman who raised me had to say. She stuck her nose where it didn't belong and left me with a broken-hearted goose. Okay, my heart might be a little worse for wear, too.

The really sad thing is, as much as I am mad at Ma, I'm also grateful. Her meddling gave me five days with a woman I will never forget. Even with the June-sized hole in my chest, I can't bring myself to regret the short time we had together.

Eventually, Ma and I will patch things up. I just need time to lick my wounds out here by myself. Until then, she'll just have to deal with me sending her calls straight to voicemail and leaving her texts unread.

Turning to grab another log from the pile, I come up empty. I've chopped every single inch of those damn trees. "Fuck." I bury the axe in the chopping block and get to work stacking the firewood in the barn.

The crunch of tires on gravel pulls me from my single-minded chore. Guess Mom finally got fed up with the cold shoulder and came to shove her way back into my good graces. Well, she can wait a damn minute while I finish up.

Cugo starts bellowing as he waddles his way past. "For fuck's sake, calm down, stupid goose, it's just grandma."

"If Roxy is Grandma, does that make you his daddy?"

The smoky voice I've come to love is uncharacteristically shy but still makes me freeze on the spot.

"Did you forget something?" I ask, unable to face her.

I know she did. The phone sits heavy in my pocket. I've been carrying it around since she left, like some talisman that might hold me to her. It ran out of batteries after a few hours, and I didn't have the right kind of charger to give it more juice. Yet I still carry it around. My own phone sits in a drawer in the laundry room because I couldn't take the non-stop buzzing from Mom's calls and texts trying to apologize.

The last piece of firewood thunks on top of the pile when I heave it with just a little too much force. "Don't know why else you would want to come back to this. What was it?" I roll my eyes up to the ceiling, pretending I have to search for the words she threw at me when I last saw her. "Oh right, backwoods, Podunk town."

The whisper of fabric behind me lets me know she's moving, not closer though. The atmosphere in the barn has gone from cold and empty to scorching and tense in the blink of an eye. The swish of fabric around her legs indicates she's swinging back and forth on her feet, probably fidgeting, too. I can't bring myself to look at her and confirm my suspicions, though.

"Technically, I never left town." The hesitation in her voice kills me. June should be confident and self-assured, not scared. "If you had picked up any of the phone calls or looked at any of the texts from Roxy...."

I cut off her words, not willing to listen to why I should have been answering my mother's calls.

"Really? You're defending her?" Anger spurs me to turn around and finally look at her. I have to fight to keep the air in my lungs because June is a goddamn vision. Knee-high boots, leggings clinging to her legs, and a top that isn't quite long enough to be a dress but not short enough to be a T-shirt. What do they call that? A tunic or something?

I forge ahead. "From the little gossip that's made its way back here about that day, I thought you were almost as mad at her as I am. I wish the damn delivery driver would pick up that I don't like to chat."

"Heard about that, huh?" she asks.

"I'm pretty sure Frank was third or fourth down the gossip chain. The way he told it, you came in waving a knife around because my mom knocked you up."

I'd shut the door on him before he could tell me much more than that. A doubt starts to grow in the back of my mind like a seed in spring. Should I have listened a little more?

June tries to hide her smile, but I don't miss the quirk at the corners of her mouth. When it comes to her, I don't miss a single thing. "This town. These people. They are something."

"Something I thought you would have left long behind. Why are you here, June?"

The damn seed starts to germinate and put out roots, digging its damn hope into my heart. I try my best to smother it so it goes the fuck away. No matter how much I try to kill the hope, the damn thing keeps growing, its branches and leaves trying to climb up my throat, trying to get out in the form of more pleading for her to stay. She made it clear staying in this town was not part of her plan. I never begged when I was left behind before. I won't do it now.

Before she can answer, another car comes bumping down my gravel driveway.

I throw up my hands. "Why has this place all of a sudden become Grand Central Station?"

"Two people is hardly the equivalent of the world's largest train station." June's smile grows just a little bigger, and that damn hope seedling grows even more.

My mother climbs out of her car, shutting the door behind her and leaning against it. She doesn't say anything, but something passes between her and June. Some silent conversation

I am not privy to. It ends with a nod from Roxy, which is mirrored a moment later by June.

She turns back to me, her face pale and her lip quivering in a way that makes me think she could start crying at any moment. She takes a deep breath before speaking again. "Instead of me telling you why I'm here, can I show you?"

"June, what could you possibly want to show me in the town I've spent my entire life?"

Mom comes stomping toward us, wearing her usual flowy clothes, except she's got the same shitkickers she wore around the farm when she lived here. "Oh, for goddess's sake, just go with her, Knox."

She quickly places a peck on my cheek, followed by a smack to the back of my head. "Don't you ignore your mother's calls ever again."

"Yes, ma'am." The words are a reflex left over from a lifetime of showing the woman respect.

"Now, this beautiful young woman wants to show you something. Go with her before I give you a concussion." She leans in closer, her hand on my shoulder. "You might not think so right now, but I would never intentionally do something that would bring you pain. Please remember that."

I hesitate, a large part of me still trying desperately to protect my heart from the destruction June could bring down. But the stupid seedling that is more like a tree at this point wins out.

"Can I at least shower first?" I ask.

June checks her watch. "As long as you make it fast."

* * *

"Where are we going?" I demand.

Have I been sitting with my arms crossed like a pouting toddler for the past half hour? Maybe. But in truth, if I let my hands be free, they are more likely to reach for June and never let her go.

"You'll see." June steers down another back road, the van taking the bumps along these long-ignored paths better than I would expect for a fifty-plus-year-old vehicle. "I'm honestly a little surprised you haven't figured it out yet. I thought you knew this area like your own backyard."

That could possibly be because my mind hasn't stopped spinning since June showed up at my barn, and my mother practically forced me into the passenger seat of Daisy.

For the first time, I take stock of where we are. "Pine Creek Gorge?"

"Yup, also known as the Grand Canyon of Pennsylvania. It was supposed to be my next stop after a night in Amoresville." June turns onto a barely visible back road, the van bobbing and weaving with surprising agility around large trees. "But, well, you know what happened."

The air in the van grows tense, and silence descends around us. What happened was the best week of my life and apparently a big regret for June.

But if that is true, why is she here?

The woman I can't figure out swings the van around and backs it up between two trees. This is the first time I've let her drive since she crashed into my pumpkin, and it turns out she actually isn't as bad as I've made it seem. My own idiotic machismo just wanted to be in control with this woman.

"I thought you might like to get a glimpse into my life since I got to live in your world for a little while." She opens the door and disappears behind the van.

I should ask her to take me home. That spending even one more night with her will cause me that much more pain when she leaves. But the truth is, I'll take every bit of pain to spend more time with June.

Behind me, the back doors swing open, and I'm pulled by an invisible string to join June in whatever she is doing for as long as she stays.

I step out of the van, turning to follow her. But before I can take a step, the beauty of the scene stalls the breath in my lungs. I've lived in this area my entire life, but the views from these mountains never cease to amaze me. The sun is starting its slow descent to the horizon, making the canyon glow in brilliant oranges and reds as the light catches the turning leaves.

June walks into view, the vista framing her in a way that makes me wish I had a single bit of artistic ability. June, in her tight leggings, ankle boots, jacket over her tunic, and a beanie pulled down over her ears, is the personification of a cozy fall night. A strange urge to capture the scene, take a picture, paint it, sculpt it, anything that will preserve the moment erupts in my soul. The only thing I can do with my hands is coax the earth to produce food. I don't have the skills to bring this scene to life.

"Are you hungry?" June holds up a picnic basket, a shy, reluctant quality to her voice that I don't recognize.

"Sure." Truth is I'm starving, but not for food. For June's touch.

June hops up in the back of the van, and I finally make my way toward her. She's perched on the edge of the bed, her legs dangling over the backend of the open van. She pats the mattress next to her, and my mouth goes dry. The last time we were in a bed together, I scared her away. It might have only been two weeks ago, but it feels like a lifetime.

Gingerly, I climb up next to her, the basket placed between us. She pulls out a couple of sandwiches, my favorite chips, and two mason jars filled with a concoction from the cafe.

"Your mom helped me make everything. As you know, I can't cook to save my life. The past few years I've lived on gas station food, microwave meals, and free dinners provided by PR people." She hands me one of the sandwiches wrapped in the reusable beeswax wraps Mom is fond of using in her kitchen. "It's a hummus and roasted veggie sandwich. I burned the first round of veggies, but your mom and mine helped me fix it the second time around."

She says the words to the sandwich clutched between her hands in her lap, not meeting my gaze. If she would look at me, she would see how touched I am she put in this much effort for a sandwich.

For a moment, we eat in silence, looking out at the landscape stretching between mountains. "I can see the appeal of your lifestyle if this is what every meal looks like," I say.

June takes a deep breath and looks around, seeming to take in the beauty of the canyon a little more closely. "It is beautiful. But to be honest, most of my meals were eaten in the parking lots of truck stops, Targets, and Cracker Barrels." She takes another bite, chewing and swallowing slowly. "But views like this definitely made the parking lots worth it."

I hate the thought of her eating and sleeping in random parking lots. Much like family dinner night, when she told us about the dangers of her way of living, fear begins to claw at my chest. Just the concept of her alone in parking lots sends a wave of primal fear and a need to protect shivering through my bones. But she doesn't need my protection. She doesn't need anything from me.

"Why are we here, June?" The question that has been floating around in my head finally pops out.

"Can I show you something?"

"I thought this was something." I gesture out to the view before us. "But, yeah, what's one more thing?"

She puts the last few bites of her sandwich down and reaches into her pocket, pulling out her phone, which I returned on the drive here and she plugged in to charge while we traveled.

A few taps, and she hands me the device, an Instagram page filling the screen. But it isn't her profile. I've memorized every single photo she's posted, not that I'm proud to admit that piece of information. I couldn't bring myself to look at it after she left, and I never sunk so low I tried to get into her phone. The pictures on the screen now aren't of her travels. They are of my farm.

Me.

The competition where I got first place. Me tending to Smashley in the field. That damn goose that fell in love with her as much as I did. Each picture has more likes and comments than I would expect. Nothing close to the numbers I saw on her page, but still. At the top, where the profile names go, it says "Happy Accidents Farm."

"I made you an Instagram page. You have about five thousand followers so far."

I scroll through the posts as she talks, not sure how I feel about so much of my life being out there for people to see.

"They are curious about how you get the pumpkins to grow so big. They love the animals. People want to know if you will put the winning pumpkin on display for pictures. Where they can buy seeds." She huffs a little laugh. "Way too many women want to know if you are single."

"Why did you do this?" I don't understand why a small farm in northern Pennsylvania would need a social media presence or why on earth people would follow it.

"I got the idea at my dad's house. All those people asking for photos with Lucy got me thinking that people are fascinated by what you do. So, I started the page." Finally, she looks at me. "I could go into the details of why people are interested in where their food comes from these days and the attraction of a simpler lifestyle. But really, I wanted to do something for you that wasn't giving you money since that didn't turn out so well for me the first time I asked."

I nod slowly. This is her way of helping the farm. Since I was such an asshole about the money thing, I can see why she didn't ask first. "The name?" I trace those words with my eyes over and over again.

"It felt right. The accident was the only reason I found your farm. And I am so happy I did, so it was a happy accident."

How can my heart feel as if it has stopped beating and is racing all at the same time? Her words inspire hope that I refuse to give into. She left. She doesn't want this life. This is just her goodbye. A goodbye on good terms.

I hand the phone back, and she takes it slowly. "You'll have to show me how to keep this up. I don't want your work to go to waste."

"I could keep it going."

"That will be hard when you're traveling the country." I desperately want to beg her to stay. That I can make this life good for her. But I won't hold her back.

"That's the thing. I'm not going anywhere. Not without you."

Chapter 27

June

"What?" Knox demands.

It's as if he finally breaks through the wall that has been separating us since I showed up at his barn. I knew I would have to work to gain his trust again. After the way I left, I don't blame him.

But as soon as the words *I'm staying* leave my lips, life enters his eyes once again. He leans a little closer, his chest rising and falling with intense breaths.

"After I left your house, I went to confront your mom, but I ended up getting into it with mine. We fought in front of half the town. If you'd looked at your mom's texts or listened to the voicemails, you'd have seen it was actually me trying to reach out. "

"You could've come back." His words are quiet at first, but as he continues, his voice gains more confidence. "If you had walked back through my door that day, hell, the next week, it would've been like nothing happened. Like you had never left."

"That's why I couldn't come back. Because if I had come back that day, or even that next week, I wouldn't have gotten to where I am now. To where I think I could be in the future."

"I don't understand."

"Part of Frank's story was true. I did storm into the cafe and start yelling at your mom in front of half the town. I might have said something about her planning to put holes in our condoms so I would get knocked up and be forced to stay."

I do my best to keep looking at Knox, to not turn away from his intense eyes that follow each word that spills from my mouth in a rush to get the story out. "My mom came to her defense and before I knew what was happening, we were both sitting on the floor crying together. We talked, really talked, for the first time in my life."

I glance out at the setting sun, not able to make eye contact anymore. A sense of calm washes over me. This is where I belong—in these mountains with this man. Now that I'm not fighting it anymore, the certainty spreads through me like water filling the soil. "Turns out I want to talk with her more. I've spent my whole adult life insisting I didn't need a home. I just needed to keep moving and keep relying on no one but myself. But I think maybe I was just running here the whole time."

"So, you're staying?"

I nod, basking in the heat of Knox next to me. "I'm staying. So is Mom. She's selling her house in Philly and buying one of the old Victorian houses downtown. She said she wants to be where I am." I turn to Knox, fighting to hold back the tears that brim against my eyes. "Can you believe that? She's moving across the state for me."

"Yeah, I can believe that. Truth is, I might have thought about buying an old camper and hitching it to the back of the truck and following you around the country. But that seemed an awful lot like stalking, so I decided it might not be a good idea."

"I think it's time I set down some roots. Find a place that I can stay. Since I already have a job offer here, it just makes sense."

"A job? Where?"

"That first day I met the mayor, he asked me to consult on how to help the town attract more tourists. He wants me to start social media accounts for the town and maybe even research how to start a tourism bureau. I decided to take him up on his offer. Your mom even helped me negotiate my contract."

I can't help but laugh a little at the memory of Burt sitting uncomfortably as Roxy browbeat him into giving me healthcare and vacation days.

"She actually let him sit in the cafe, but he wasn't allowed to have coffee or look in any other rooms."

"Holy shit, I can't believe it." Knox's smile grows. I've never seen it overtake his face like this. "Move in with me. Sleep in my bed. Wake up to my stupid fucking rooster."

"No."

That brilliant smile falters. "Why not?"

"I want to do this right. I want us to get to know each other. I want to date." I've spent most of the last two weeks thinking about how to make this work. How to make sure Knox doesn't get hurt while I figure out my shit. "Before, I tried to convince myself it meant nothing. That we meant nothing. Now I want to get to know you when I believe this could be everything."

Knox nods, seeming to accept my words. "Where will you stay?"

"The apartment above the cafe. Mom and I have both been staying there while she gets her house on the market."

"I guess I can live with that for a little while." Knox's smile returns, his eyes growing hotter by the second. "So, you're staying. Indefinitely."

"That's the plan. I'm staying as long as you and this town will have me."

"So forever then."

"We'll see. I'm still thinking there is a fifty-fifty chance you'll get sick of me within a month." My stomach does an uneasy turn. Once I let that little fear out, it seems to double in size. I grew up feeling inferior to my parents' careers and social lives. It turns out that has caused some lasting damage that one conversation won't fix. At least that is what Mom's therapist, who is now also my therapist, says. To make this work, I'm going to need to do some major work on myself.

Looking at Knox, I know it will be worth it. This life is worth everything. I'm starting to believe I might be worthy of it, too.

"I will prove to you each day that is not true."

Finally, Knox reaches across the picnic basket and takes my hand in his, bringing it to his mouth for a sweet kiss on my palm.

"We're going to take this slow. Get to know each other." He kisses the inside of my wrist, the sensitive skin tingling with a rapid burning desire. "No living together. No nights in my bed."

His lips travel up my forearm, soft words brushing across my skin and bringing goosebumps to the surface. "No hot sex in the field."

"I never said that." My impatience gets the better of me and I push the picnic basket to the ground, barely noticing as the dessert I had so carefully prepared earlier tumbles to the ground. It's worth it when I bridge the gap between us and straddle his hips. "I mean, we can't really un-ring that bell. No point in depriving ourselves."

"What if I said no sex until you agree to move in?"

"I would take that as a personal challenge." I grind down slowly on his cock trapped beneath his jeans, using the naughty hip movements I learned in the striptease class I took at his sister's club. "As you know, I can be quite stubborn."

"So can I." Knox fists my hair in one hand, drawing us closer together. "Who do you think gives in first? My cock or your stubborn streak?"

I lean closer, bringing our mouths within kissing distance without closing that final millimeter of space separating us. "Your cock, no question."

I press my chest against his and do a full-body roll against him. He clenches his jaw, groaning as the whisper-thin fabric of my leggings does almost nothing to separate my pussy from his dick.

"Fuck, I hate it when you're right." In a flash, our positions are reversed, my back on the bed with Knox wedged between my thighs. "I can't resist you."

Urgent hands push my leggings down, revealing my legs to the cool air surrounding us until my entire lower half is exposed. "Fucking white cotton panties." His fingers caress the soaked material covering me. "These panties are such a lie. So innocent looking when you are anything but innocent."

Fabric ripping fills the van as he twists off the offending garment. Involuntarily, my back arches, and a needy moan escapes from my throat. How did I go years without a man's touch while I was on the road, but two weeks without Knox touching me feels like it has been an eternity?

"Two fucking weeks without this pussy was too long. I was never going to make it another day."

Knox shoves my jacket off, moving quickly to pull my tunic over my head next, taking my skimpy lace bralette with it. He descends on me like a man starved, his mouth everywhere in a frenzy of lust and longing. My head spins with the sensations. His mouth is on my nipple, then fingers slip between my thighs to circle my clit. In no time, I'm panting and writhing on the too-small mattress.

He grips my hips, dragging me to the edge of the mattress, planting his feet on the ground just outside the rear of the van. It's the perfect height for his mouth to be even with my pussy.

I've spent countless nights in this van pleasuring myself, but nothing compares to Knox's big hands holding me down as he feasts on me.

He licks a line up from my opening to my clit, grunting with pleasure. "Nothing like this taste. I crave it." He spreads my legs wider, thrusting his tongue into my core.

I grip the edge of the mattress over my head. Holding on for dear life as he rushes me right up to that line of pleasure.

I hold back; I don't want to go over yet. I want to savor this moment. Our reunion. We only knew each other for a week, then separated for two. This shouldn't feel like the culmination of a lifetime of love and pain. But it does. It feels like the sealing of a deal. I'm staying. Not just for him but for me, too.

He growls between my thighs. "Get out of your head, Trouble."

Knox eases one finger into my pussy, quickly following it with a second. His hands are so big and rough from working the fields. They feel amazing in the soft center of my sex. The tips of his fingers trace over that spot deep within me that has my head flying back and my legs closing in around his head.

"There you go. No more thinking. Just feeling." His mouth descends on me, sucking my clit and circling it with his tongue. An unearthly scream bursts from my mouth, echoing off the mountain around us. People camping nearby will probably think the sound came from some unknown animal and be a little frightened.

Hell, I'm scared by the sheer intensity of my orgasm bearing down on me fast and hard. I can't stay still, my arms reaching for Knox's hair, pulling him closer as I try to wriggle away at the same time. He rides each buck of my hips like a champion bull riding, never skipping a beat or changing the pressure he is exerting on my most sensitive parts.

My whole body coils into a tightly wound bundle of nerves, and then everything explodes, every nerve singing at once. My hips grind against his face, draining every second out of this orgasm I can until my body collapses back against the bed once more.

Knox crawls next to me, scooping me up in his arms and positioning the two of us so that he is sitting in the center of the bed with his legs crossed, and I settle into his lap. At some point, Knox managed to get rid of his clothes, though I honestly don't know how or when that happened.

His cock stands tall between us, the tip glistening with a bead of precum. "I don't have condoms." The regret in his voice is almost comical.

"We don't need them. I don't want them." I have never in my life felt a man inside me without a condom. Something about Knox being the first feels right. "I'm on birth control. I trust you."

"We don't have to. I'm happy to just touch you all night. Wouldn't mind if you did a little touching of your own, too."

"I mind. I want to feel you inside me." I rise up on my knees, taking his length in my hand and notching it at my entrance. "Want to feel you cum inside me." Slowly, I lower myself onto him. Knox leans back, propped up on his hands, and gazes at where we join, watching with rapt attention as each inch of him disappears inside me.

"Fuck, June, you feel incredible." He tilts his head back, squeezing his eyes shut. "I can't watch, or I swear I'm not going to last."

I grip his shoulders and give an experimental lift of my hips, pulling off his cock and sinking back down. The slide of our flesh together ignites inside me, sparking a fire that rushes through my limbs.

"You are so fucking beautiful. Riding my cock with the setting sun lighting up your face." He reaches up, pushing a strand of hair back over my shoulder as I lazily rock on his cock, getting used to the size of him in this position. "Move in with me. I want to wake up and fall asleep looking at your face and feeling your body against me."

"I already said no."

"Doesn't mean I'm gonna stop asking. Someday, that no will turn into a yes, and that will be the best day of my life."

There is no doubt in my mind that I will say yes, far sooner than I probably should. Because when it comes to Knox, I can't seem to resist. For once, the thought of being in one place and relying on one person doesn't send the same zap of fear and panic through my body. Just the opposite. It makes the pleasure building inside me grow. Letting go and falling over the edge isn't so scary when you have someone right there to catch you.

Knox pulls me in close and I wrap my legs around his waist, my arms around his back. Every inch of us pressed together until I can't tell where he stops and I start.

With his hands gripping my ass, Knox pulls me tighter against him, rocking our hips together, my clit finding the friction it so desperately needs against the base of his cock. It's not the frantic fucking I've come to expect. It's slow, luxurious, and altogether new.

My orgasm builds inside of me, expanding until it consumes every thought.

"Come with me, June." Knox grips my ass cheeks, gliding one finger between them to press at my backdoor. That illicit act finally detonates the ball of pressure gathering in my core, sending another earth-shattering orgasm through my body.

Everything is falling apart and stitching back together. The world, my soul, my heart. We grip each other almost to the point of pain while Knox finds his own release deep inside me.

The pleasure gradually ebbs away, leaving us exhausted, clinging to each other, Knox peppering sweet kisses along my neck.

Looking out the back of the van, the cool breeze drying the sweat on our bodies, the horizon stretches out for miles. Our future seems to go even further, to the ends of the earth. I can't wait to explore it all right here in Amoresville.

Epilogue 1

Knox

One Year Later

The fall air had turned from crisp to damn near frigid almost overnight. Thankfully, that isn't keeping people away from the First Annual Fall Harvest Fair in downtown Amoresville, co-hosted by Happy Accident Farms. The first of hopefully many.

There have never been this many people milling about the town square. Faces both familiar and foreign smiling from ear to ear as they take in the decorations, vendor booths, and activities that June has worked tirelessly on for the last three months.

The past year has brought many changes to not only the town, but my farm as well.

With June's help, Happy Accident Farm is no longer strug-
gling to stay operational. Between selling my giant pumpkin
seeds, the new market stand in the barn, and the pick-your-own
pumpkin and wildflower fields, the farm is in the black for the
first time since my father passed away. Granted, nearly every
dime I make at this point is being filtered back into improve-
ments and growing the business.

I never thought of the farm as a place for people to gather.
But that's what it has become. My neighbors are all too happy
to spend their hard-earned dollars on my produce and products.
They know that every dollar they spend there is going to go
back to our community in the form of me frequenting their
businesses as well. And it is all thanks to June.

As if the mere thought of her could make June appear from
thin air, her arms wrap around my waist from behind, her cheek
pressing against my back. "This is amazing!" She squeezes me
with all her strength before letting go so I can turn to look into
her gorgeous eyes.

"And all thanks to you."

Her gaze sweeps over the square. It took damn near an act of
divine intervention to get Burt to agree to shut down the four
streets surrounding the park. But June worked her magic, and
before long had the mayor thinking it was his idea, not hers.

In every corner, people are taking part in crafts, games,
demonstrations, and tastings. Nearly every business from town
is represented, and even a few from the neighboring towns. The
Nail and Bail has a table where people can buy and build bat

and bird boxes. The ladies from Cuts and Mutts are doing complicated braids for excited little girls. My mother and Delia are giving out free cups of coffee and hot chocolate. A woman I've never met before has a table selling crystals, herbs, and giving free tarot readings. Wesley, the town librarian and nephew of the mayor, joined in with a book sale and coloring spot for the kids. And those are just the ones I can see from where I'm posted at my produce stand.

Even Cugo decided to make an appearance, sneaking on the trailer as I loaded the animals for the petting zoo. He seems happy, waddling around with his chest out and honking as kids scream and run away, giggling.

"There is no way anything like this ever would have happened without you," I say. Taking her face in my hands, I lay a chaste kiss on her mouth, lingering with our lips pressed together for slightly longer than is probably appropriate considering our surroundings.

When I pull away, a dark cloud seems to settle over June, her face trying a little too hard to keep the smile plastered there. It's a look I've been seeing a little more of lately. A look that I worry means she's getting tired of the same town every day and wants to get back on the road. Truth be told, I thought I had gotten past these fears.

I've been avoiding asking her about it. Afraid of the truth. No more, though. "What's wrong?"

June looks into my eyes, her arms still wrapped around me in a side hug. "Are you ever going to ask me to move in again? You haven't asked in months."

I hold back the laugh fighting to escape. Is that what she's been worrying about? "What are you talking about? You *do* live with me."

"I do not. I still pay rent on the room over the Bean, and I still have my whole office set up there."

"Yeah, that is your office. But you live with me. You've slept at the house every night for three months. All your clothes have taken over my closet. I only have two drawers now, for god's sake. You live in *our* house." I stopped asking because it seemed settled. But I've been thinking about asking another question for months.

"I never said yes." Her brows scrunch together, and June tilts her head, thinking about it. "The last time you asked was in the car on the way home from the state fair. I said no, but I guessed I would stay a couple of nights."

"Yeah, and you never left."

June shrugs but doesn't seem appeased. I guess she wanted to say yes finally. Well, it's about time I gave her the chance to say yes to another, bigger question.

"Let's go check out the carving." I loop my arm over her shoulder, and we make our way to the fountain, where Orion is set up with his carving tools and the three giant pumpkins I grew this year. None of them were prize winners like the two I had last year, but that's okay. Holly, Sabrina, and Eliza, all named for Audrey Hepburn roles, were good pumpkins, just not quite big enough this year. Maybe I was distracted by the new life June and I have built. Or maybe the conditions just weren't right up here in the mountains this year. But I'm not quite as concerned about it.

People gather around the pumpkins as my brother carves the giant gourds with his tools. He had been reluctant to shift his furniture-making skills from oak to pumpkin, but June is pretty good at convincing people to do what she wants.

But then, so am I. After all, I convinced him to carve an intricate ring on the largest pumpkin instead of the scary jack-o'-lantern June had requested.

"What is that?" June turns her head to the left, then the right, trying to see around my brother. "It doesn't look scary. Or like a face."

I guide her around the rope separating Orion's workspace from the crowd. As we approach, my brother nods his head once and steps aside.

"Oh wow." June moves closer, her mouth falling to an O shape as she takes in the intricate artistry of Orion's carving.

Behind her, I fall to one knee, fishing the ring Mom gave me out of my pocket. It's been in our family from as far back as the founding of the town. I have another one she'll wear every day, but this is the one I want her to wear today. And on our wedding day.

The crowd behind us gasps, catching June's attention. As she spins around, she catches sight of me, ring held up, knee planted in the damp soil. Her hands fly to cover her mouth, and tears gather on the edges of her eyelids. To our right, the fountain bubbles at the feet of my ancestors in bronze form.

"June. You've been a whirlwind of color and chaos since I met you. You crashed your way into my life and my heart. Before I met you, I had no idea my world could be so full. Will you keep filling it with your beauty and sass for the rest of our lives? Will you marry me?"

A cross between a sob and a laugh bursts from her mouth as tears stream down her face. She nods, for once seeming to be struck speechless, and collapses on her knees in front of me, throwing her arms around my neck and peppering kisses on my face.

"Yes. I'll marry you." Our lips meet, keeping it relatively innocent for the spectators gathered around.

I dig into my pocket and pull out two quarters, handing her one. "I never believed in the stories that kissing by this fountain and throwing a coin in would make your love last forever. I still don't. But just in case."

June smiles and leans in for another kiss as we both flick the coins into the fountain, and the twin plops of them hitting the water make me smile against her lips.

Friends and family descend upon us and we reluctantly pull away. Meredith is there right away, looking at the ring on her daughter's finger, tears in her eyes. Since making Amoresville their permanent residence, June and Meredith have managed to forge a relationship closer to friends than mother-daughter.

Witnessing them heal old wounds and grow closer has been a privilege.

My own mother pulls me into a hug, tears streaming down her face. "You did good, honey."

I pull her in tighter, wishing like hell my Dad was here to see this moment. I know she feels the same without either of us having to voice the thought.

Delia steps up beside us, punching me in the arm, then by-passing me to hug my fiancé.

Fiancé. Damn, that sounds good.

Even Burt skulks over to offer his congratulations, Wesley beside him as they both offer handshakes to me, and hugs to June. Burt gives my Mom a wide berth, and my sister glares at both the men. Don't fuck with the Halsted women.

Slowly, everyone goes back to enjoying the festival and June cuddles into my side, looking at the ring sparkling on her finger. "I guess this means I'm moving in?"

I can't help but laugh. This woman is nothing but trouble. And I want nothing but her for as long as we both shall live.

The End

Want more June and Knox? Sign up for my newsletter to read about their wedding day! I promise I won't spam you.

About the author

Brandy Ayers has been inventing stories in one form or another since childhood. Whether telling soap-opera-level-dramatic lies to her new neighbors at the tender age of six or daydreaming about how she would definitely run into and marry Keanu Reeves (her very age-appropriate crush in eighth grade), there was always something brewing in that weird little brain. After becoming a mother, Brandy decided she needed to do something other than care for her baby and go to work. Something for herself. That something ended up being writing down her crazy stories. More than ten years and fifteen books later, she's still at it.

When Brandy isn't writing, you can find her drinking way too much coffee, making jokes that produce groans and eye rolls from her kids, and growing her hodge-podge crew of pets. Lucky enough to have found two great loves in her life, Brandy lives with her second husband and fellow author James W. Farley in southern Pennsylvania.

https://www.brandyayersauthor.com/

Facebook

TikTok: @BrandyAyersAuthor

Instagram: @BrandyAyersWrites

Newsletter

Also by Brandy Ayers

Welcome To Amoresville
Pumpkin To Talk About
Up The Wrong Tree – Coming Soon
Casting Shade – Coming Soon

Rock Hard, Love Harder Series
Protecting His Brat
Chasing His Tease
Restraining His Runaway
Taking His Diva
Not Without You – Coming February 2026

Double Virgin Collection:
Only Us
Only You
Only Me

WQUZ News Series:
Standby

Breaking

Stand Alone Books:
Piece by Piece: A Modern Retelling of Jack and the Beanstalk
Wanted: No Strings
Unwrapping Her
The O Doctor
Taking Over

Blue Line Series:
Reckless Conduct
Possession
Intoxication
Disturbing the Peace

9 781737 509905